SNOW ON MAGNOLIAS

BETTY BOLTÉ

ALSO BY BETTY BOLTÉ

Becoming Lady Washington: A Novel

Notes of Love and War

Hometown Heroines: True Stories of Bravery, Daring, and Adventure

<u>Fury Falls Inn</u>

The Haunting of Fury Falls Inn

Under Lock and Key

Desperate Reflections

Fractured Crystals

Legends of Wrath

Homecoming

<u>Secrets of Roseville</u>

Undying Love

Haunted Melody

The Touchstone of Raven Hollow

Veiled Visions of Love

Charmed Against All Odds

<u>A More Perfect Union</u>

Elizabeth's Hope

Emily's Vow

Amy's Choice

Samantha's Secret

Evelyn's Promise

SNOW ON MAGNOLIAS

Betty Bolté

Mystic Owl Publishing
Huntsville, Alabama

Mystic Owl Publishing, Huntsville, AL 35815

www.MysticOwlPublishing.com

www.bettybolte.com

Digital ISBN: 979-8-9860450-4-7

Paperback ISBN: 979-8-9860450-5-4

Cover design by Sweet 'N Spicy Designs (http://sweetnspicydesigns.com)

CHAPTER 1

I need her. I need her. I need her.

The three-word mantra matched the urgent cadence of his horse's canter down the muddy road back to the place he thought of as home. Back to his love, Magnolia Merryweather. Lia, to her family and friends. And to him. At least at one point before he'd fouled everything up.

Captain Bryce Day finally rode his jet-black stallion, named Jet, down one road after another, striving for the courage to arrive at Hopewell, the country manor of Lia's family, as soon as he could manage. Now that he'd been discharged from the cavalry, he needed to make amends. He'd been distant far too long and made the biggest misstep of his life during that time. Would Lia forgive him and give him a second chance at a future with her? Her brother's reply to his apologetic letter seemed to say he should try, which gave him a glimmer of hope.

The once-lush rolling landscape of north Alabama showed signs of the drought and destruction of the past few years of the Civil War. It didn't help that it was December so the trees stood starkly bare against the dreary gray clouds warning of rain. As he cantered slowly down the empty road, he noted where a barn had been burned. Had the livestock been confiscated or merely shot in place? Anything to keep resources from the hands of the enemy. A troubled sigh escaped his lips and he clamped his mouth shut. He had to look forward, not back.

Five years had passed since the first time he'd visited the Merryweather clan clustered on the sprawling two-hundred-acre property. He'd moved to the area without any firm plans other than to take advantage of his friend Doctor Samuel Merryweather's offer to come check out the growing city for opportunities. Back in December 1860, despite the tensions in the air, he'd been focused on following in his father's footsteps so far as finding work, and then a loving wife and raising a passel of children. But he wouldn't follow his father's lead when it came to discipline. He winced at the mere memory of a raised belt or switch. He vowed to be firm but compassionate in the discipline he doled out to his children. They'd respect him, not fear him. Unlike his own experience.

A rumble in the distance augured bad weather approaching. The temperatures had been warmer than usual, and thus rainier than customary. But after the drought of the previous two years, the rain was welcomed with open arms by everyone. Even if it meant that as the winter approached the possibility increased of freezing rain or even snow. Ah, snow. That thought brought the stirring memory of standing with sweet Lia in his arms beneath the snow-covered magnolias, sharing a kiss or two. Her beauty as rare as the snow falling on those dark green shiny leaves. He could never forget the love they shared, the hopes they'd shared. In hindsight he knew he'd been an idiot, but the war had befuddled his senses to the point of making such a grave error as to cut off their burgeoning courtship. Would she welcome him back? God, he hoped she would.

Though, he'd not argue with her if she pushed him away. He'd had enough of violence in all forms. During the war, he'd seen and done things he'd never imagined possible. Never thought he'd be called upon to burn women and children out of their homes, for one thing, whether they were enemy dwellings or not. The terror in the mothers' and children's eyes haunted his every moment. He'd done what he could within the scope of his orders to ensure they were not in whatever structure had been deemed necessary to destroy so the rebels wouldn't have use of it. But homes? He understood they were used also for headquarters and hiding places, but it hurt his tender heart to leave women and children and the elderly and infirm to fend for themselves. His only consolation came from knowing they were alive when he rode away.

Unlike the rebels he had fought with saber and pistol, and even with his knuckles at one terrifying moment when he thought his own life was about to be cut short. At that moment, Lia's beautiful face—vibrant green eyes, a smattering of freckles across the bridge of her nose, sweet lips ready for kissing, all framed by lush dark-red hair—flashed into his mind for a brief moment, but long enough to remind him of why he was fighting in the first place. To secure a safe environment in a free society to have a family and to have a life filled with promise and prosperity. He'd redoubled his efforts and knocked out the other soldier so he could get away. The sights and sounds—bloodshed and explosions—couldn't be erased from his memory as much as he longed to do so.

After the excitement of the battle ebbed away, all he really wanted was to be with Lia. But he'd stupidly cut off their correspondence while he'd been forced to lie out in the mountains hiding from the rebel posses looking for men like him, unionists who refused to enlist or be conscripted into the Confederate Army but awaited their chance to join the Union Army forces. Months had passed and he'd managed to dodge the groups of hunters in search of their human prey. Slowly it dawned on him what he had to do for the woman he loved: let her go. He'd sent word by a trusted friend to Lia to let her know he freed her from her vow to wait for him until the war ended. He didn't want her to harbor hope when he felt none as to his own survival in the brutality of the war. Then the Union Army captured Huntsville in April 1862 without a shot fired and he'd come out of hiding and joined the Union forces for the remainder of the war. A war that cost him Lia.

He turned onto the lane leading to Hopewell, hoping with all his heart she'd give him a second chance to make their future come to fruition as they'd once planned.

* * *

THE THUD of running feet echoed through the house. Rain beating on the tin roof was no match for the yells and laughter of the five young boys dashing about inside the large home, zipping in and out of the parlor and dining room. All five, ranging from ten-year-old twins down to the youngest at four, were the sons of Lia's brother and his wife. On this rainy Thanksgiving day in December 1865, they'd grown bored and thus started a game of tag. Much to everyone's dismay.

Lia lifted the steaming bowl of mashed potatoes up above her shoulders to avoid the darting figure of the laughing kid as she made her way from the kitchen. The youngest of the bunch perhaps, but he'd proven time and again to be the most determined. Or stubborn. Lia smiled to herself as she pirouetted and placed the fragrant bowl on the cloth-covered trestle table, the aromas of butter and parsley underlying that of the creamy potatoes. She'd do anything for Travis, forgive him most any transgression, too. She surveyed the table, silently applauding the creative centerpiece of pine cones and lemons and the enticing scents from the roasted wild turkey stuffed with walnuts and scallions. Her youngest sister Aster crafted the specially designed decoration for the table using her unique gifts with plants, flowers in particular. The dark-green tablecloth, the pleasing color of magnolia leaves, created the perfect background for the familiar glistening plates and silverware. Two three-branched candelabras provided gentle lighting at either end of the immense table where so many family meals had been shared. Several bowls and platters held the scanty essentials for their holiday dinner, obtained over the last few weeks with some difficulty by their mother and father. Enough to share among them but not the overly abundant feast of bygone times. But now, everything was in place and ready for the family to come together again.

"My goodness, if you don't stop running through this house, I'll…" Laura halted in the shadow of the doorway, a silver spoon raised at ear height as a silent warning to the boys to behave.

The woman scowled at her children. Her long, blonde hair was braided and wrapped into a bun on her head. Green eyes flashed as she let out a long-suffering breath. Laura had melded with the family easier than butter in cookie dough. She'd fallen for Samuel, Lia's brother, but the entire family had fallen for her too. Her quiet good nature soothed Lia's unease and helped her find a path forward when the world seemed bleak indeed. The day she'd received that heart-breaking note from the man she longed to hold her, to comfort her during the worry and horror of the war years. Lia loved Laura like one of her own blood sisters and appreciated everything she'd ever done for the family. More than she could ever put into words, truth be told.

"Oh, Mama. We're just having fun." With a burst of laughter, Michael dashed around her and out of range of the weakly threatened smack with the utensil. Blond-haired like his mother, and slender like his father, the ten-year-old was becoming a fine-looking young man.

"Yea, right!" His twin, Ian, darted around the vibrant figure of their mother as they made for the open kitchen door onto the back porch, sliding out of sight in a jiffy.

While December brought cooler weather and more moisture to the state, Alabama still enjoyed a temperate climate. The winter had started off with more rain than usual, however nobody would complain about a little rain. But on this Presidentially declared holi-day, one her family always celebrated unlike many of their neighbors, Laura insisted the boys stay presentable in their good clothes, such as they were, until after the family gathered for dinner. The result of boys being dressed up on a rainy day was they were stuck inside and their active little bodies craved something to do. Lia didn't blame them. She understood. She'd rather be out at the stable working with her horses despite the rain drumming on the roof.

Her thoughts strayed to a previous winter day when she'd been delighted to awaken to find a rare snowfall on the ground. She'd taken advantage of the unexpected opportunity to hitch up a pair of horses to the sleigh to teach them how to pull it. They'd taken a while to adjust to the difference from wheels to runners but were soon on their way. It had been a cold, windy day but her companion had kept her warm. His kind eyes, boisterous laugh, and gentle caress… Whoa. No. She couldn't allow herself to even think about him ever again. He'd told her he didn't want her to wait for him, so she'd moved on. Broken heart and all.

"You boys stop running about like jackrabbits on fire!" Samuel bellowed, his light-brown hair swishing about his shoulders. "We're about ready to eat our Thanksgiving dinner and you're acting like imbeciles." He shook his head and rammed his fists onto his narrow hips. "Now wash up and sit down."

The younger boys calmed immediately and, hanging their heads, scurried to the kitchen to do as told. They trickled out of the dining room, but Lia couldn't find it in her heart to be upset with them. She wiped her hands on the apron tied at her waist as she arched a brow at her brother.

"Sam, you didn't have to yell at them. Did you?" Lia eased around the large table set for twelve.

"Somebody had to stop the chaos. That will at least give us one thing to be thankful for on this special day." Samuel gripped the back of the chair at the head of the table, pulling it out and settling onto its cane-bottom seat.

Aster sauntered into the room, her curly brown hair pulled back with combs to fall down her back. Her youngest sister's pink-and-green-striped muslin dress fit her perfectly, not only the style and color but the cut. All thanks to their other sister Rose's special talents with fabric and stitching of clothing of any kind. Give Rose a few yards of material and she'd whip something beautiful together in no time. Not a talent Lia had despite her mother's efforts to instruct her on the basics. Both her sisters were very close and they shared many things in common as a result. Even their worldview and hopes for a peaceful and loving future ahead, although Lia's didn't include a man. She'd prefer to work with horses.

Lia's talents lay with animals, horses in particular. During the recent war, she'd cautiously and secretly developed a strong and docile saddlehorse breed. She'd crossed a Morgan stallion with Quarter Horse mares, which gave her some sturdy and willing horses. She'd managed to keep them largely out of sight and thus out of the hands of either the Rebel or the Union soldiers who confiscated any decent horse flesh they came across during the violence of the war.

Behind Aster, Lia's parents, Richard and Natalie Merryweather, strode sedately into the room, moving around to take their seats, he at the foot of the table and she to his right. Richard was dressed in one of the somber suits he kept well-mended for his job as loan officer at the recently authorized Federal Bank in Huntsville. Natalie Hunt Merryweather's calm and reserve served her well in her role as a matriarch not only of the family but also for the town of Huntsville. She descended from one of the oldest families in the county and behaved accordingly. Lia's sister, Rose, followed their mother with a large basket of fresh rolls hot from the oven in both hands, evoking sounds of appreciation at the wonderful smell wafting along with her. Rose flicked an errant tress of hair over her shoulder as she turned to find her seat.

"All right, everyone, let's gather together for this special meal." Laura shooed the boys back into the dining room, drying their hands on their pants as they came. "Is everyone here?"

Richard nodded as he gazed at the family surrounding him. "I believe so. Come join us, Laura."

With a last perusal of her sons, Laura sidled around the table to take the seat to Samuel's right. "Let us say grace and share what we're thankful for."

"We do have much to be thankful for this year." Natalie reached to take the hand of Richard on her left and that of Travis on her right, then pulled back. "What's in your hand, son?"

"Isn't it pretty?" Travis held up a small piece of reddish-brown wood.

Samuel sighed. "Son, you shouldn't have brought that to the table. Now put it away."

"I want to widdle somethin' out of it. Can I, Dad?" Travis aimed hopeful green eyes at his father. "Please?"

"We'll talk about it later." Samuel gestured to Travis to pocket the wood. "Take hands and I'll say grace."

Sam's deep voice filled the quiet room as he said a blessing on the food before them. Lia kept her eyes closed until she heard rustling from across the table. Lifting her gaze, she met that of Travis, smiling at her as he held hands with his grandmother and next older brother, Theo. She canted her head and arched a brow at him, silently suggesting proper behavior, and he grinned in response before obediently lowering his gaze. The whipper-snapper.

"And thank you for helping the community mostly reopen the railroad in order to make receiving the simple offerings before us possible. Amen." Sam opened his eyes and scanned the expectant faces waiting for the signal. "You may eat."

Bowls and platters quickly passed from hand to hand, as the adults helped the younger children fill their plates. Between the sounds of appreciation, sporadic conversation followed.

"The volume of sound in this house is much better when the boys have their mouths full." Richard chuckled, his deep throaty laugh echoing in the quiet room.

"Indeed you're right. If only the town would rebuild the school soon, then they'd have a place to go during the week to use up some of that energy." Laura passed a bowl of tangy cranberry-orange sauce to Samuel. "And I'd have time for my other chores."

Richard wiped his mouth with his napkin. "We could lend the money to the town if they have the capital to secure the loan."

"Don't they?" Natalie glanced at her husband. "I'd think they'd want to find a way to educate the children, the next generation of leaders."

Richard shrugged. "They haven't confided their financial situation to me, my dearest."

"My impression from what some of my patients have told me," Samuel interjected, "is that there are limited funds in the coffers after the resounding whipping of the South. It will take some time for the government to stabilize and be functional, let alone to fund building projects."

Natalie laid her napkin beside her plate. After a few seconds, she nodded to herself and refocused on her family members. "Then we will need to help them out. I shall organize a Calico Ball before Christmas to raise the necessary funds to rebuild a school. Maybe even a bigger one."

Her mother was known for her charity works, and for her ability to get things done. But Christmas was only a few weeks away. How on earth could she manage such an impossible task on that schedule, with dry goods and foods so hard to come by? Lia had a sinking feeling she could guess but still...

Lia blinked slowly at her mother. "Before Christmas?"

"That's a splendid idea, Mother." Rose's expression revealed her excitement as she overrode Lia's astonishment. Her middle sister was always eager to jump into a new project. "I would enjoy designing dresses for the ladies to wear, ones that could then be useful to donate to other less fortunate women of the town."

"Yes, I'm sure everyone would enjoy having something new in their wardrobe for a change." Aster glanced down at her satin gown, one discreetly mended and refurbished throughout the war years. "I know I am tired of wearing the same rags for so long."

"But before Christmas? Can you do that?" Richard asked.

Lia shot a grateful look to her father for raising her concern more clearly. "That's only a few weeks, Mother."

"I can if I must. I will need a little while to formulate an appropriate plan. And I'll need help." Her gaze slid pointedly over every one in the room, a gleam in her tawny eyes.

Lia's heart raced when her mother's gaze stayed on her for several beats of her heart. A very familiar look, one foreboding and worrisome.

Suddenly, the dogs started barking out front of the house which stopped the conversation. Samuel stood and left the room, heading for the front porch to greet the visitor. Followed quickly by the scraping of chairs as the kids pushed back from the table and dashed after their father to see who had arrived, their pounding feet drumming across the wood floor. Who could it be? A shiver flashed down her spine as a premonition swept through her. Lia dropped her napkin to the table and rose to peek out the window. She spotted the three dogs on point at the end of the front walk as a rider approached on a black horse. They were not expecting company. In fact, very few people ventured so far from town unless for the purpose of seeing her doctor brother or her to buy a horse. But hopefully neither would be interrupting their dinner hour on a holiday without an invitation.

She clutched the curtain as the rider halted. No. It couldn't be.

Aster joined her at the open window and blinked in surprise. "Is that Bryce Day?" Aster nudged her in the side. "Your former suitor?"

Her face flushed hot. Nobody knew. And yet her sister's comment suggested otherwise. But no. That wasn't possible. No matter. She couldn't face him. Couldn't explain. His return would ruin everything. She needed space and time to think. "I-I have to go. Now." She spun away from the window, dropping the curtain back into place, and fled. Out the kitchen door, across the carriageway, and up the steps into her safe haven.

THE RUSTIC YET WELCOMING SETTING BEFORE Bryce recalled many fond memories but also emphasized his deep unease. Two magnolias, their dark-green waxy leaves glistening in the afternoon rain, stood accusingly beside the long drive leading to the barn. Those trees evoked piercing memories he'd be better to forget. Could not forget. Didn't actually want to forget. He slowed his stallion to an easy walk, giving himself just a bit more time to compose his aching heart.

His gaze drifted to the smaller white clapboard house situated to the left of Samuel's home facing the road. A welcoming place with a few bushes nestled around its foundation, a shaded porch with a couple of chairs for people to relax in while they waited to be seen by the good doctor. Only one story tall, he vividly remembered it contained three rooms inside. The doctor's examination room, a surgery room, and a good-sized room toward the back set aside for convalescing patients. And guests when not needed for patients. Where he'd spent many evenings alone with Lia, talking, touching, planning. Kissing, too. And more. Ah, so much more. He shifted in the saddle as he shook his head slowly.

The war had come between them. Divided them as cleanly as a knife through a watermelon on a hot summer afternoon. He'd gone to fight for the Union, with a desire to preserve it and everything his ancestors had fought for during the American Revolution. Without a strong union, a strong united country, how could anyone even think of settling down and starting a family like he longed to do? His goal was to establish a more safe and secure environment to raise a family and grow old with the woman he loved.

An environment like the two-story home standing before him. He slid his gaze over the larger structure. Sam had started with a typical dog-trot house, two living areas connected by a covered open porch. Over the years, he'd enclosed the central porch to add more interior space and added on to the upstairs to allow for sleeping quarters for his sons. The result was a white-washed clapboard house with sparkling windows to greet visitors riding up the winding lane to the farm. A wraparound porch featured several benches, chairs, and even a swing to encourage the family to gather. The large family stable behind the two houses had also expanded over the last few years, with more horses grazing in the paddocks at the edge of the forest beyond. He nodded to himself at the evidence of Lia's success with her breeding plans. He couldn't stop his gaze from sliding on to the other home on the property. The patriarch's house lived up to the name, even grander than Sam's fine home.

Richard and Natalie Merryweather deserved a lot of credit for establishing Hopewell, a beautiful property with a loving atmosphere for their children and grandchildren. The entire family resided together on the two-hundred-acre farm. Sharing most everything as a close-knit family would. Samuel had married Laura before the war and started his family. But what about the girls? Had Richard and Natalie's three daughters found husbands despite the fighting? Or were they still living within the brick and wood-frame building, surrounded by bushes and flower beds? Aster's skill with flowers was evident from the landscaping around the house. He'd bet she still lived at home. And Lia? Where was she?

His gaze lingered on the magnolias for another moment as he drew Jet to a halt, the tawny dogs milling around. Resting his hands on the pommel of his saddle, he grinned as a small herd of young boys flew through the front door, the shadow of a man following more slowly. The number had grown since he'd last visited his friend and his wife. Relief swept through him as his lingering concern vanished as to his friend's wellbeing. Sam had declared neutrality in order to serve all of his neighbors during the fighting, but that didn't mean his neighbors would agree with his stance. Several former—or remaining —rebels must still live in the area, probably defiant and angry after the end of the American Civil War. How long would they carry that particular grudge? Or would they come to accept the reality and move on? He hoped for the latter so he could work on making his dream of a quiet life with a wife and family a reality. A small hope but one that existed.

He didn't much care how long they were unhappy as long as they'd stop taking it out on those who had remained loyal to the country instead of the damn Confederacy. Why should he be called a traitor when he'd stood by the country he'd been born and raised in? The country he swore an oath to defend and had successfully done so amidst far too much bloodshed. If only the belligerent, stubborn rebels had realized their error in judgment then the tens of thousands of men wouldn't have been killed. The cause had stripped generations of men from the land. He mentally shook his head to chase away the angry ponderings. That was behind him, behind all of them too if they'd only see it and get on with rebuilding their lives. He grimaced at the thought of the effort it would take. Simply feeling right in civilian clothes had taken some getting used to, to be honest.

He'd waited and bided his time until he could safely get to the Union troops and sign up to defend the Union. He'd been forced to lie out in a cave for near a year, scrounging and hunting up food, dodging the rebel scouts searching for him and others like him. But finally his moment arrived. Bryce had joined up with the First Alabama Cavalry USA as soon as the Union troops occupied Huntsville in 1862. No more hiding and feeling like a hunted animal. He'd ridden and fought with them across the South, all the while aware that the state he called home harbored a different view and attitude toward the Northern "invaders."

A large contingency of Southern Unionists, people who remained in southern states that had seceded from the union, lived in north Alabama although they tended to lay low rather than broadcast their political views on the war. But the majority of the state sided with the Confederacy so they had to remain cautious. Lying out in the hills was safer than facing the threats, abuse, and hangings by the roaming rebels in search of supposed traitors to the Confederacy. Until the Union Army arrived and then they could safely sign up with the side they wanted to fight for. The war ended back in April 1865 and he was finally released from service in October. He'd pondered what his future might hold, especially considering his daft idea of ending his courtship of the only woman he loved. But he loved her enough to let her go. Then. Now he wanted to plan his future and strive to forget the past. If only that were indeed possible.

As the boys approached, he thought about how much had changed since he saw them last. The older boys he remembered as little boys. Now they'd grown and matured, showing hints of the fine men they'd soon become. They'd been so young when he'd left. A lifetime ago. So much had transpired during those years, some good as in strong friendships forged in the fires of battle but mostly horrific. Next in age to the twins, their next younger brother had been hardly more than a toddler with his chubby legs and cheeks. And the baby back then, who was now taking after his father's slender build and sharp eye.

The last of the boys was the smallest and youngest of the bunch. He was a new addition, not a boy he remembered. He'd always had a pretty good memory for faces, and thus knew he'd not seen this lad before. He looked determined to catch up with his older brothers, squinting his eyes and pursing his lips as he pounded across the front porch and down the stone steps into the yard. In his hand he carried something he obviously treasured as he held it close and enclosed in his fist.

"Oh, hello, Mr. Day." The lad shielded the lessening rain from his bottle-green eyes as he gazed up at Bryce. "It is Mr. Day, isn't it?"

The boy—Ian?—had grown in the years since Bryce had last laid eyes on him. Close-cut blond hair surrounded an open and interested expression. He'd matured certainly but remained a young, energetic firebrand of a lad. His twin, Michael if he recalled aright, skidded to a halt beside Jet, tentatively reaching a hand to stroke the warm neck of the horse. Jet, being a level-headed stallion, merely jangled his bridle and permitted the attention.

"Yes. Hello, Ian. Are your parents home?" Bryce shifted his gaze from the boy to the dog at his side and on to scan the front of the house and the adjoining stable yard. Then he saw a woman crossing quickly from the rear of the house away and across the yard. One with dark red hair. Lia?

"Yessir. We were having Thanksgiving dinner when you rode on up." Michael patted Jet once more and then shoved both hands into his front pockets.

Bryce lowered his gaze to meet the lad's. "Ah, I'd forgotten President Johnson had declared December seventh as a day of Thanksgiving. I'm sorry to interrupt."

The slam of a door drew Bryce's gaze up to see Sam marching toward him, down the front porch steps and the flagstone walkway with a huge smile on his face. "Don't be." Samuel maintained his smile for a beat, then scowled at his sons. "You boys, however, shouldn't bolt out the door without knowing who is approaching. You hear me?"

Sam's welcoming grin warmed the nervous chill in Bryce's gut. At least hist friend was glad to see him. Why had Lia left?

The boys murmured "yessir" in unison, but kept their heads up and shoulders back.

"Sam." Bryce swung out of the saddle and dropped the reins to ground tie Jet. The men clasped each other in a great bear hug for a brief moment and then stepped back to assess each other's condition. "You're looking fine."

"As are you." Sam's eyes glinted with happiness. "You've been away far too long. We thought you were dead."

"I thought I was a few times as well, but no such luck, I'm afraid," Bryce said on a chuckle. "I'm sorry it's been so long. Thank you for your very kind response to my inquiry as to a visit. You didn't have to."

"As I said, I think it's time and for the best. I'm glad you're here now and we can catch up on all the news."

"It's good to see all your boys are doing well, too. But who is the new addition to the family?" Bryce nodded toward the youngest who regarded him with curiosity as he held what looked to be a block of cedar. Bryce recognized the grain and reflexively reached in his front pocket to finger the small cedar carving he always carried.

"Oh, that's right. Let me introduce you." Samuel cleared his throat as he gripped the boy's shoulder. "Travis, this man is my friend, Mr. Bryce Day. Bryce, this is my son Travis."

"Nice to meet you, Travis." Bryce stuck out his hand to the boy who glanced at his dad for approval and then grabbed hold of the offered hand. "How old are you?"

"Four. Do you know how to widdle?" Travis stared up at Bryce with hope in his green eyes.

"I do. Do you?"

Crestfallen, Travis shook his head. "Papa won't let me."

Bryce solemnly regarded the disappointed lad. As a boy himself, he'd been fascinated by the old men sitting around the cracker barrel at the general store in the small town where he grew up. They'd play checkers for as long as the sun hung in the sky. Some would pull out a small knife and a length of wood and start cutting away the excess until they had something new in their hands. Bryce had watched the magic transform a plain piece of wood into a bird or a horse or any of a vast number of things imagined by the man holding the knife. Whittling seemed magical then and still did. The very idea of imagining something in your mind and finding it within a bit of wood in your hands seemed entirely mystical. He fingered the last thing he'd whittled, hidden in the depths of his pants pocket. His talisman kept him safe through many a trying time.

The front door of the parents' home across the expanse of lawn and carriageway closed sharply. The house where Lia lived, too. His lady love. She'd fled rather than come to him as he'd hoped. He sighed. He hesitated mentally over the endearment. Did he have the right to think of her in such terms? Probably not.

Sam shook his head, drawing Bryce's attention. "You're not old enough to handle such a sharp thing, Travis. I've told you, when you are old enough, I'll teach you myself." Sam ruffled the boy's hair, copper strands intermixed with brown and blond. "Now run along."

The boy was stubbornly persistent in his aims. Which reminded of him of his own childhood wants and demands. Ones his parents had quickly taught him to control or he'd feel the ramifications of his petulance. They'd been strict but he'd learned their lessons well. Still, the lad was very young. He had much to learn, including patience by the looks of things.

"But when will that be?" whined the boy. "I wanna widdle now."

"What did I say, Son?" Samuel's tone brooked no argument from his youngster.

"Travis, you'll need to be patient." Bryce winked at him. What a cute little fellow. The hope and sincerity in the child's eyes tugged on his heart. Sam was a lucky man to have such a son. All of his sons were treasures. "Trust me. I know your dad will teach you as soon as he knows you won't hurt yourself with a sharp knife."

"Listen to Mr. Day, Son. Patience is a virtue." Sam tilted his head toward Bryce, acknowledging his friend's support with regard to the youth's eagerness. He swatted Travis on the butt, chuckling. "Now go play before I find some chores for you to do."

Travis raised his brows, glanced once at Bryce, and then dashed off to join his brothers who were playing with small wooden soldiers in the mud beside the house.

"Oh no, Laura will not be pleased." Despite his spoken sentiment, pride and laughter shone in Samuel's eyes as he supervised his sons at play. "Their good clothes will need to be laundered yet again. Anyway, my friend, come on inside and have something to eat."

"Thank you. I feared you'd not be so welcoming after my long silence." He started to follow his friend and then paused. "I need to stable my horse first."

"I figured I'd hear from you eventually." Samuel acknowledged his desire to tend to his horse with a wave to follow him to the stable.

Just then, the front door of the main house opened and Laura stepped out onto the porch, a sedate smile on her lips. "Hello, Mr. Day. It's wonderful to see you again. We've plenty yet on the table. I'd be mighty pleased if you'd share with us."

"Thank you, Mrs. Merryweather." Bryce fingered Jet's reins as the smile on his face faded. Join the entire family and fend off questions as to what he'd been doing for the last few years. Why he'd ended communications with everyone. Nothing for it but to face the interrogation. "I'll just put Jet in the stable and wash up."

"We'll wait for you." Laura smiled at him and then opened the door and went back inside.

"Now you've been officially invited to our Thanksgiving dinner. Want a hand with the horse?" Sam asked. "I'm sure there's either a stall or a pen we can put him in. Come."

"Thank you. Are you sure Lia won't mind?" The words slipped out before he could think better of them. Of revealing just how much she was on his mind. How would she really feel about his horse in her barn? After all, she'd walked away from her own family at his arrival. His heart sank at the thought.

Samuel glanced at him and then shrugged. "Her priority is always the horse, so I'm pretty sure she'd rather we look after him before we take care of ourselves." Sam strode faster toward the stable, Bryce trailing behind as he drifted his gaze around the empty yard toward her house.

He had hoped to see her. He'd thought she'd at least greet him. But then again, what a idiotic thing for him to expect. He'd broken his promise to her. To come back for her. To love her always. Years had lapsed and he'd failed her. Why would she want to have anything to do with him?

The barn welcomed him with the sweet scent of fresh hay and the tang of horse manure. The most wonderful combination of aromas on earth as far as Bryce was concerned. One reason he'd jumped at the chance of serving with the First Alabama was so he'd have horses around him every single day. His beautiful bay, Lily, had served him well for several years before she'd been shot out from under him during a particularly heated skirmish. He still grieved her loss. He loved animals and found it pleasant to be accompanied now by the three dogs as they made their way down the barn aisle.

"This middle stall looks open. There's already some hay in the corner too." Samuel peered over the half-wall into the stall. "I'll grab a bucket and some water."

Bryce opened the latch on the stall door and swung it open into the aisle so he could lead Jet inside the roomy space. Pulling the door to behind him, he tossed the reins over his horse's neck and prepared to remove the saddle. The sound of water being pumped into a bucket filtered into the stable from the well out back of the building. He loosened and removed the saddle, hanging it on the stall door. Then started loosening the bridle and slipping it off. Draping it over the seat of the saddle, he quickly lifted both and carried them out of the stall. All the while he couldn't help listening for Lia's voice, for her to investigate who was doing what in her barn. He pushed the door closed just as Sam lugged in the brimming bucket of water.

Bryce quickly pulled the stall door open again to let Sam inside. "Where should I put these?"

"There's a saddle rack on the front of the stall that should hold everything." Sam hung the bucket on a hook inside the stall and then emerged to fasten the door closed. He met Bryce's gaze. "Unless you think your horse will bother them there?"

Bryce glanced from the finished leather in his hands to his stallion. "It's probably safer to have them away from his teeth."

"Follow me then." Sam led Bryce to a closed door down the aisle.

Pushing it open into the room, he stepped up onto a raised floor. "There's space beside Lia's tack."

His heart stuttered in his chest as he strode across the wooden floorboards to the spot his friend had indicated. At least his tack would be close to hers even if he couldn't. Impressive how she'd organized the tack room with brackets jutting out from the walls to hang the saddles on, and curved hooks for the bridles. He turned to see Sam smiling at him.

"Anything else?" Sam asked.

"Before we go in to dinner, I have a question for you." Bryce raised his brows as he folded his arms. "How have you managed to do so well despite the hardships and destruction of property?"

"It hasn't been easy. I've worked very hard to stay neutral, at least as far as my neighbors are concerned." Samuel glanced toward the open door but didn't make a move to leave. "It's best to stay out of it if you can."

"Unlike me, you mean." Bryce pressed his lips together as he wiped his hands on his pantlegs. "I was smack dab in the middle of the worst of the fighting."

"Really? What did you do?" Samuel crossed his arms as he regarded Bryce, his smile sobering into a more serious expression.

"My guys were chosen by General Sherman to escort him on his March to the Sea. That was the most elevated and most destructive part of my time in the cavalry. We were honored to be selected but the level of destruction wreaked all across the South to the Atlantic was horrifying. Necessary, but horrifying."

"You rode with Sherman? That is impressive. We heard all about his campaign to end the bloody war. Of course, he wasn't revered south of the Tennessee River as much as he was in these parts. Another example of why it's wise to not share your opinions too widely."

Memories of the weeks and weeks of riding, fighting with saber, pistol, bare hands flooded his brain. He'd relished the determination Sherman had to end the war once and for all. He succeeded in his aim but left behind much destruction and death in the process. Still, the war had ended and he could finally pursue his own dreams.

"I see. I'll come out in a while to rub Jet down and settle him in." Bryce pointed to the open door. "I suppose we should get inside before everything is stone cold."

"And before my wife comes out to chastise me for keeping you out here so long." Sam grinned as he ushered Bryce out of the tack room and shut the door. "I hope you're hungry because the women really put together quite a feast for us."

The women. Lia's mother and sisters, and Samuel's wife. They should all be at the table, too. But Lia had gone back to the other house. "I look forward to thanking them all for their delicious cooking."

If only *all* of them were indeed at the table.

CHAPTER 2

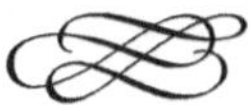

$\mathcal{P}$anic swamped her heart as she flopped onto her stuffed mattress. The precious floral quilt with its bouquets of red roses and yellow-centered white daisies scrunched in her hands as she fought to contain the fear sweeping through her. Dear lord in heaven, he'd returned. But why on that particular day? When everyone had gathered together to celebrate. She had no good excuse for her absence, for running away, but she couldn't have stayed either. She put the quilt to her mouth and screamed into the thick fabric.

She'd pushed thoughts of him far away. Down deep inside her memory. For her own sanity and her family's. No one need ever know how close they'd become when Bryce Day had first come to Hopewell five years before. Seeing him again surfaced every single memory of the weeks he'd spent visiting his dear friend Samuel. And wooing her.

Bryce Day had ridden up to Hopewell on a beautiful bay mare with white markings on her face and fetlocks. The mare move so fluidly, so lightly, Lia had stopped sweeping leaves and dirt from the porch to admire her. Then she noticed the rider, the well-built and handsome man who swung lithely from the saddle. He tied the reins to the hitching post by Sam's front walkway before spotting her watching him from the deep front porch. He'd doffed his wide-brimmed hat accompanied by the flash of a smile. His thick, medium-brown hair shone in the January afternoon sunlight. He nodded to her but then turned to stride up to the front door of Samuel's office, not his home. As he knocked on the door, she'd realized he had business with her brother and forced herself to resume her work. The good-looking gentleman had more pressing matters than a simple maiden's admiration.

Only later did she have the opportunity to meet him and when she did she'd felt an instant connection with him. Laura had invited everyone to join them for predinner cocktails that evening so they could introduce their guest to the entire family. Bryce's twinkling brown eyes roamed her from head to toe in a quick scan before meeting her own gaze. He'd smiled at her again and then approached her to greet her properly. The strangest experience of her life had been the sensation that came over her when he'd taken her hand in his. She'd felt, what exactly? Perhaps completed by his mere presence best described what had passed between them. But she didn't even know him. Only his name and that he was friends with Sam. He relinquished her hand after a few moments, longer than socially acceptable, and the intense connection slackened and left her sadder than before.

She needed to touch him, to confirm what she thought she'd experienced at his first contact. But she had to wait until another opportunity presented itself where she could finally, tentatively reach out her hand to lightly lay it on his arm to gain his attention. And there and then she knew they were meant to be together. Her inner senses rang with the truth of their shared destiny. With that certainty simmering inside of her, it had been so very easy to fall foolishly in love with him over the next several weeks they spent together.

Oh, the evenings of chatter and laughter beside the popping wood fireplace in the hospital of her brother's practice. They'd sipped a sweet port wine while they'd held hands, or he read poetry to her, or they simply talked about horses and his plans to build things. He'd studied as an engineer and wanted to see evidence of his existence on earth in the form of houses, buildings, bridges, anything and everything he could imagine. She envied his grand schemes to a point, but she never wanted to leave Hopewell to live anywhere else. Didn't want to leave her family. But she fell hard for him and one evening their emotions overcame them both and they woke up in each other's arms, their clothes scattered about the room. The first of many times they laid together.

Then the war broke out and he had to leave. They'd promised to love each other. He'd promised to write to her every chance he could while doing his duty to the country by fighting for the Union in that awful, bloody Civil War. He'd had to go hide from the rebels in order to keep his loyalty to the Union. She'd known he wouldn't be able to write every day, perhaps not even every week, but she hadn't thought he'd break off communications with her. She was left with nothing but heartache and worry about her own future. She had to make some serious decisions about her future. One without him in it.

Even after she'd set her life back on track, she'd wondered about him. What happened to him during the fighting? Did he stop loving her? Her heart broke at the realization their plans of a life together had ended.

She screamed into the quilt again, praying that nobody heard her sobbing hysterically at the remembered piercing pain. How could she ever explain what had caused her to run away from the family celebration? The pain of his betrayal and the months of grieving that followed, even though she'd not shared that grief with her family, echoed in her soul as she clutched the fabric to her mouth. Now he'd come back. What was she to do?

"Magnolia?" Tapping sounded at her bedroom door.

Drying her eyes on the quilt, she scrambled off the bed. "Mother?"

Coming to check on her, without any doubt. She must convince her mother that she was all right despite her panic. Couldn't let her mother suspect the depth of her anguish at their sudden visitor's appearance. She started for the door, stumbling over her kicked off shoes beside her bed. Drat. She sucked in a fortifying breath and pulled open the door, upset by the sincere dismay in her mother's eyes.

"My dear, are you quite well? You left so abruptly we thought perhaps you were ill." Natalie gripped Lia's shoulders with her hands to steady her before using one hand to angle her head this way and that. "You do look rather pale."

"I'm…" What could she believably say? "It's just a slight headache." More like heartache, but she couldn't say as much.

"Hm. Then you should rest and I'll send up some soup later. You won't want anything heavy for supper." Natalie inspected Lia's countenance for several seconds. "It was a shame you couldn't stay to visit with Mr. Day. I am relieved that he did survive the war despite our fears otherwise."

She inhaled sharply at the mention of his name, his presence and absence, and turned toward her bed. It was all too much. "I think I will lie down, Mother."

She pulled back the rumpled quilt to ease her stockinged feet under it, smoothing it across her chest as she lifted her gaze to meet her mother's worried one. Lia hadn't even removed her dress which would wrinkle it enough she'd have to iron it once she rose. No matter. She couldn't fret about such mundane things right then. She had bigger concerns. She didn't want to detain her mother any longer than necessary, not wanting to be forced to lie yet again to her. She didn't want the guilt inside to multiply.

"Lia, is there something wrong? What might have caused your… headache?"

"Perhaps the weather is about to change? I do not know." She closed her eyes, not wanting to see the suspicion in her mother's eyes. "I'm sure I'll feel better in a little while. You needn't worry."

Only, Lia had worries that wouldn't go away as long as Bryce Day remained.

* * *

LATER THAT EVENING, Bryce sat down to a simple supper with Samuel and his family. After the chaos of the earlier Thanksgiving meal, which had included Lia's parents and sisters but not Lia herself, the room was relatively quiet. Still, the noisy chatter of a loving family surrounded him as he soaked up the happy ambiance. Five young boys picking and squabbling with each other was music to his ears. If they didn't care for each other, then they'd not be acting in such a manner. He grinned to himself. All of the fighting and terror, the isolation and fear, had been to secure peace and prosperity for those he cared for. Seeing his friend's happy family tugged at his heart in ways he'd nearly forgotten.

He studied Samuel as Laura gently corrected the boys and urged them to eat and not bicker. The man's appearance hadn't changed significantly since they'd last spent time together. In his early thirties, his hair was still as brown, his eyes still as kind and compassionate. He might have lost a bit of weight, but he still looked healthy and fit. Life seemed to be good for him. His neutral political stance hadn't stood in the way of living a decent life and continuing to help others with his medical practice. Most likely because he'd wisely kept his politics to himself.

"You're looking well. Despite the shortages, I mean." Bryce relaxed back in his seat at the dining room table, peering at Samuel sitting at the head.

"Adam, what did I tell you about not wiping your hands on your pants?" Laura rapped her knuckles on the table. "Use your napkin, please."

"Yes, ma'am." Adam lifted the crumpled cloth and wiped his fingers, a mischievous light in his eyes.

"Now let the adults talk without your interruptions." Laura leveled a stern but loving look on her son. Then she lifted her gaze to Samuel. "My apologies, dear. Please continue."

With a nod, Samuel slowly spun his wine glass as he looked at Bryce. "We eat well enough, mainly thanks to my patients supplying our pantry in lieu of hard cash. And the stores in town are beginning to have more to offer since the rail is mostly open." He shook his head once. "It will take some time to rebuild any sense of wealth. Having the Federal Bank in Huntsville, though, has created a sense of stability so that will help with cash flow."

Cash in hand would make Bryce feel better about his own future. His pay during the war had been sufficient to survive but not enough to build a future. They'd even supplied him with a man to help him wrangle his two mounts, always keeping them ready for service. Saying goodbye to that man had been hard but the man deserved to lead his own life. Now he had his own mission to fulfill.

He'd yet to see his final pay from serving with the First Alabama Cavalry during the war. Not only fighting, but also working to destroy railroad bridges and then rebuild the ones the U.S. Army needed to move troops and supplies to strategic places. He pushed aside the memories of the fighting and destruction he'd witnessed and engaged in, focusing instead on the serenely content expression on both of Samuel and Laura's faces. They'd managed to navigate the war years with their home and livelihood intact.

Now that Bryce had been released from service, he needed a job. "I'm hoping to find sufficient work in town. Any suggestions?" Bryce rested his hand on the cloth-covered table, then slowly drummed his fingers as he waited for any insights or advice from his friend.

"You're an engineer, aren't you?" Samuel took a swallow of wine. "I'm sorry but I'm afraid I don't know what kind of work might be had that would use your skills."

"I've worked on the railroad tracks during the war. Both taking them apart and putting them back in place. And of course, the roads and buildings necessary. I've carpentry experience as well. There's much to be rebuilt, so surely someone could use my experience to their advantage." Bryce stilled his hand as he glanced at Laura and then back at Samuel. "Is there an architecture firm in town?"

"I don't go into town all that much, not since the war started. It's safer to stay put on the farm and not chance running into any die-hard rebels." Samuel shrugged. "Better to let the patients come to me if they can."

"That's smart. I hadn't considered safety when it came to staying in town, not now that the war ended so many months ago. I guess I rather unwisely thought feelings would have simmered down by now."

"Not yet. Most of them rebels have accepted they've been fairly whipped, but not all of 'em." Sam folded his arms. "There's a good number who I hear are still seeking their own revenge on the likes of us. You be careful who you tell about your cavalry service. Especially escorting Sherman across Georgia. Those men might take exception to your service all over your person."

"Duly noted." A ripple of trepidation quivered down his spine at the reminder of violence and lethal force used against him. He'd had enough of that.

He'd heard tales about how rebels had attacked the Southern Unionists. Beatings, hangings, burning their houses with them still inside. Destroying their livelihood any way possible. North Alabama had fared better in that regard than parts south of the Tennessee River where the rebel spirit thrived. The northern counties tended to be more loyal to the Union and even welcomed the Union occupation of Huntsville. The occupation actually protected the city from destruction since the Union officers living within the city had fallen in love with the area. But of course not everyone stood with the Union. Just how many men remained staunchly in support of the Confederate cause?

"Mr. Day, would you consider staying with us for a spell?" Laura smiled at him, pulling his attention back to the present. "I mean, I'm certain Samuel would welcome your company for as long as you'd enjoy staying."

Her offer didn't surprise him. She'd always been so very welcoming and friendly. She'd share whatever she had to offer. He'd heard of the hardships the people in Alabama had endured at the close of the war. The rampant destruction of mills and forges, livestock and water wheels, indeed anything which could be useful to the Confederates after the Union soldiers pulled out. The fact the farm stood intact and apparently untouched was some kind of miracle. That thought gave him pause. Perhaps more magical than miracle?

Lia and her sisters each harbored some remarkable abilities. He'd been impressed by Lia's talent with regard to riding and an uncanny way of choosing which horses to breed together. Her sisters also demonstrated eye-opening talents. Was one of those responsible for protecting Hopewell?

Right now, Hopewell would be ideal. A place to stay where he'd be safe and welcome sounded like an offer he couldn't refuse. Until he found work, acquired some little nest egg of money, he was nearly destitute. He could write home to his parents and beg a loan but he'd much rather find his own way. He intended to settle down with a wife and family now that the country was united once more. But he needed work, a livelihood, something with which he could keep a wife and start a family. Without that, no woman would accept him as her husband. He didn't need to think twice about whether to accept Laura's offer.

"Thank you kindly, ma'am." Bryce met Samuel's keen gaze. "I'd also enjoy staying and getting reacquainted after the lapse in communication."

"It's settled then. We'll get you all sorted in the guest quarters up front after supper." Samuel toasted with Bryce, clinking their wine glasses in salute.

Not only would Bryce have more chance to find out about opportunities in the area, but he'd have plenty of chances to see Lia. His heart sang at the idea of spending time with her. He'd be staying in the very place where they first declared their love for each other. He'd do so again, too. If she'd let him. Suddenly he realized that they hadn't even mentioned her during supper. Was she ill? Did he have any right to ask after the way he'd mucked up everything years ago?

CHAPTER 3

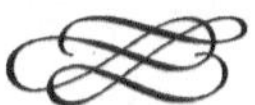

The weak winter daylight flowing through Laura's parlor window illuminated the serious faces of the four brothers the next morning but did little to remove the chill from the air. Sitting cross-legged on the carpeted floor in front of the cheery fireplace with its fragrant fire, they worked on their studies. As best they could, at least, while little Travis repeatedly peeked around the door to see when they could play, making childish noises to attract their attention in his desperation to have someone to play with.

Lia sat beside Ian, helping him sound out a difficult passage from the favorite book in his hands. His wavy blond hair lay neatly while he struggled to quietly pronounce the words aloud between flicks of his eyes to the doorway. She stifled the chuckle threatening to unravel their mother's best efforts to instruct them despite the lack of a proper school. The last school standing had been taken over as a hospital and then torn down for the wood planks and glass to make other structures. Families were forced to keep their children home and teach them as best they could.

She'd protested when her next youngest sister Rose reminded her about assisting her sister-in-law Laura with the boys' lessons. She wished she needn't see Bryce as long as he was visiting. But she couldn't break her promise to her dear friend and confidant Laura.

Laura roamed the room with slow strides, overseeing Michael's efforts with multiplication tables and Theo's work on addition. Her long skirts swept the faded rug with a faint swooshing sound. Adam tapped the chalk against his cheek as he stared at the slate boasting an array of letters in front of him to copy, a frown of concentration marring his features. While they all appeared industrious, Lia wondered just how much work was being accomplished between their sly teasing with their youngest brother in the doorway.

Indeed, Travis had a mischievous grin on his lips as he gripped the doorframe and peered into the room. He longed to participate like his older brothers. Only, he wasn't old enough to join his brothers with their educational efforts. Another few years and he'd be fighting to *not* be in the room instead of clamoring to be included. She mentally shook her head, clearing away thoughts of the future in order to focus on her nephew's reading struggle.

The grin and the tilt of Travis's head reminded her of his real father. No, she wouldn't even think about that man. She didn't want any hint of her true feelings to leak onto her face. Nor to be released into the world for others to judge her. Better to focus on the things she did want the world to know about her instead. She'd concentrate her thoughts on her horses, her family, and her love of books. Feeling calmer, she settled in beside her nephew to listen to him read.

"Travis Merryweather, what did I ask you to do?" Laura stalked to the open doorway and placed her hands on her hips.

"Go out and play?" Travis chewed on his lips as he aimed his green eyes up at her.

"So why are you lurking in the hallway?"

"I don't wanna play by myself. So I'm waiting for my brothers." Travis clasped his hands behind his back and fidgeted side to side. "I'm bored."

"What are you doing in the hallway, little man?" Bryce suddenly filled the doorway with his strong frame.

Lia blinked at the unexpected and unwanted sight, her heart

racing. She'd known from her sisters that he'd be staying and thought she'd prepared for seeing him again. Wrong. She was not prepared to be so near to him. She'd thought they had something between them but she'd obviously been wrong on that score as well. So much for her determination to not even think about him being on the property. How was she to ignore him when he loomed so large right in front of her?

"Waiting on 'em." Travis gestured to his brothers now sitting watching the exchange instead of working on their studies.

"Well now, it looks like they've got some work they need to finish before they can play. That's part of growing up." Bryce patted the boy on the head. "One day you'll understand."

"But I want to unnerstand now." The whine in the little boy's voice echoed through the silent room.

Lia sat motionless, hoping to avoid Bryce's attention for a little longer. She must compose herself and calm her thumping pulse. But inevitably, the man's gaze lifted from the boy to meet her reluctant one. Then it happened.

He smiled at her, a heart-tugging grin that bespoke the depth of feeling they'd once shared. His gaze softened the longer he held her enraptured. She'd forgotten the very physical draw she felt for the man. She recalled the delicious moments they'd shared standing by the magnolias so many years ago. The tender moments beneath the warmth of a comforter shared on a cold winter's night. Before the war swept them apart and asunder.

Laura's voice interrupted her tumbling memories.

"They won't be much longer, especially if you'll do as I ask and leave them in peace." She clasped the boy's shoulders and pulled him close. "I know you'd like to be in with them, but for now please wait on the porch. I'll send them out shortly." She gently turned him round and pushed him toward the kitchen and the back door.

"Yes'm." Travis sighed as he trudged through the house, his shoes thudding forlornly on the wood floor.

Lia caught Laura's eye with a rueful shake of her head. "He's so dejected."

"How about if I go keep him company?" Bryce lifted a brow as he looked to first Lia and then Laura. "I don't mind for a little while."

"Thank you, Bryce. I'm sure he'd like to talk to you if you have the time." Laura slowly pivoted back to the four boys looking up at her. "Now you boys finish up and then you can call it a day."

Bryce nodded once to Lia and then disappeared down the hall, trailing after Travis.

She let out a breath and rolled her shoulders once to throw off the weight of the remembered longings of the past. How sweet of him to console the boy. Only... She couldn't let him grow closer again. That wouldn't do at all.

* * *

LATER THAT MORNING, Bryce rode into Huntsville in search of a job. He'd fallen in love with the city when he'd first visited the area before the war. He'd worked then at the Easley Hotel as a carpenter and handyman while he'd stayed out at Hopewell. He'd had plans then to save up enough money to afford his own place then the war swept through. Working with his hands to shape wood into decorative or useful designs had satisfied something deep inside. But now he wanted to do something more than just repair windowsills and doorframes. Seeing a structure grow into something useful and appreciated swelled his heart. With all the rebuilding going on, surely he could find work that would bring more satisfaction.

The talisman in his pocket, a small piece of cedar wood shaped into a magnolia blossom, he'd whittled over many an evening after riding and fighting hard with his brigade. Lia had asked him to save the small block of wood to remind him of her, to keep him safe and bring him back to her. The chunk had called out that it contained a multi-petaled flower with a few wide leaves surrounding it. The blossom was polished to a sheen from his rubbing it when worried or lonely, or thinking of Lia, its inspiration. All of which was often during the previous conflict. He'd held onto it as she'd requested, not realizing how much he'd valued its presence until the war ended and he was still all in one piece. And finally he'd returned as he'd promised. Only she no longer welcomed his presence. Why precisely? What had happened after he left?

The city beckoned to him with its wide streets and many shops and stores lining the public square. Perhaps he could find work in one of them. But doing what? He didn't want to sell anything to anyone. He didn't want to feel like he had to pitch and persuade people to hand over hard-earned money. Union money that had proven difficult to come by since the war ended. All the Confederate script had become worthless at the conclusion of the war, likely even before the final surrender, leaving many destitute. He imagined over time the economy in the South would recover, but how quickly was anyone's guess. First the infrastructure for the creation and movement of agricultural products and livestock would need to be rebuilt. After the awful destruction at the end of the war, some of which he'd actively participated in under orders, time and money and many hands would be necessary.

He dismounted and secured the reins around a metal fence edging the street for that purpose. Jet stood among several other horses also waiting for their riders. He patted the furry neck, noting the depth of the hairy coat, a hint as to the cold winter ahead. Hopefully, it wouldn't be cold enough to snow, but anything was possible. He'd seen snow on the magnolias in front of Lia's house the last time he'd visited. When he'd first met Lia and fell in love with her. Such a rare, lovely sight—snow on magnolias.

Turning away from his horse, he perused the businesses on either side of the street. Trees stood here and there but their bare branches offered no respite from the sun shining brightly on the dirt streets. Buckboards and carriages came and went, horses stirring up the dust as they rattled past him. Several dry goods stores selling domestic wares and clothing were interspersed with a stationery and book shop and shoe stores. An inn occupied the majority of one side of the square, its kitchen housed next door in a separate small rowhouse type of brick building. The Eagle Saloon invited him to the northeast side of the square, but lunch would have to wait until he'd at least attempted to find work. He wanted to hold onto the cash he carried as long as possible, until he'd a means of replenishing the supply.

Striding across the busy street, dodging wagons and riders, he hurried to the book shop to see if the proprietor might offer him interesting work or maybe could tell him where he should look. Besides, he loved to read a good history and he'd be interested to see what other kinds of books the shop sold. Closing the door behind him, he scanned the warmly lit interior of the small store. Books sparsely lined several floor-to-ceiling shelves at the back of the room. Small piles of other books rested on a few scattered tables. A fire burned merrily in the Franklin stove in the center of the space. The uniquely satisfying scent of ink and paper filled his nostrils. A few people browsed a book or magazine here and there throughout the store. Perhaps working in a book store would suit. It was a comfortable and comforting place. He scanned the shop, feeling more and more at home. Lia would love perusing the variety of novels and histories available, a passion they shared.

"Good day, sir. How may I help you?"

Bryce peered at the red-cheeked, middle-age man approaching him. A bit of a paunch and thinning hair told of his age and his love of reading as well. "I'm looking for work. Do you need any help?"

The man's smile remained even as he slowly shook his head. "I'm afraid I can't afford to hire anyone right now. Most of the shops here on Commercial Row are in a similar state."

"Do you know of anyone who is hiring?"

Hope fought with disappointment as he held his breath in suspense. If so many businesses struggled to keep the doors open, he had little hope of finding work that paid enough to fund his plans. Maybe two or more jobs would be required for sufficient funds.

"Perhaps check with the Freedmen's Bureau around the corner or one of the hotels. They're thriving with the need to serve the people. The Bureau might find you work or hire you, either way." The man shrugged apologetically. "Sorry I can't be more help. Good luck."

After thanking the man for his suggestions, Bryce left the shop and stood on the street for a moment to gather his thoughts and make a new plan. He'd heard of the creation of the Freedmen's Bureau offices to assist former slaves in obtaining work and sustenance of every kind. What kind of work would they have for the likes of him? Not that he qualified as a freed slave, but maybe they could identify possible jobs for him as well. He heaved a sigh. If they needed help, then perhaps it was a good starting place.

He made his way down the street and turned the corner as the man had suggested. Over one door was a sign declaring that the "Bureau of Refugees, Freedmen and Abandoned Lands" waited within. Doubt swirled through his mind as he opened the door and went inside.

The place buzzed with conversation and the rustling of papers. Several desks were spaced about the large room, stacked with thick file folders and ledgers. At each, an official took down the information from the men seated across the desk. The atmosphere in the room was tense and suspicion seemed prevalent, the acrid scent of sweat permeating the air. Bryce didn't like the feeling of the place. He removed his hat and held it against his leg with one hand. After a moment, a man in a business suit approached him with a slight smile on his face.

"Good afternoon, sir. Can I help you?" The burly man stuck out his hand in greeting.

Bryce clasped his hand briefly but firmly. "I'm looking for work and it was suggested that I come see you."

"I see. I might be able to help you. We have a listing of available jobs. What skills do you have?"

"I've worked as a carpenter and a handyman at a hotel here in town...before the war."

The man glanced sharply at him. "And during the war?"

How much should he reveal to this man of his activities during the fighting and destruction? He knew how to wield an axe, a crowbar, and even explosives to dismantle and destroy. He also knew how to wield a hammer, a saw, and a paintbrush to create something beautiful. He had experience with both, the creation and the destruction of many kinds of structures and infrastructures. But Sam had reminded him to keep that information quiet. A constant anger simmered inside at having to obfuscate his perfectly legitimate service during the war or fear violent reprisals from actual traitors to the country. Despite his anger, he chose to be circumspect and not court trouble. But one day he might not be able to hold back.

He swallowed the ire. "I worked more as a railroad worker than anything else. Though I'm not sure that's where my talents actually lie."

"Most of the jobs I have are agriculture related, so I don't think I can help you." The burly man grimaced as he glanced around him. "With the crop failures the last couple years, food stores are critically low and importing food stuffs is expensive. I don't suppose you'd want to work at planting, or raising livestock?"

Bryce surveyed the others in the room and noticed most of the black men were dressed in faded jeans and rough shirts. Newly freed from slavery, they needed help with the basics of living far more than he did. While he enjoyed working with his hands, digging in the dirt and herding cattle and hogs didn't appeal to him as a livelihood. Now if it involved horses, he'd be interested. But they were not typically a food source in these parts so chances were slim of finding such a position.

He tapped his hat back on his head. "No, sir. Thank you for your time."

Back on the street, he looked about him with a sense of dismay. He'd hoped to have at least a lead from the bureau. What now?

CHAPTER 4

The afternoon sunlight began to fade as Lia worked with one of her horses in the corral behind the barn. Puttering about the stable and pastures always brought joy to her soul. Merely standing near to one of her many horses could soothe any agitation she felt. She could forget about any worries or concerns for a time while she enjoyed working with the animals. They provided solace in troubled times.

"Easy now, Merrybell." Lia gently lifted the leather straps around the filly's nose, drawing the bridle up until the metal bit slipped into her mouth. "That's it, girl. Now I just need to fasten the buckles and you'll be all set."

She quickly buckled the throatlatch to hold the bridle in place. Merrybell briefly rubbed her jaw against Lia's shoulder. Lia gently pushed her away but smiled at the filly's affection. The young horse had accepted the bit far easier than she'd dared to hope. But then the three-year-old had always trusted Lia and adjusted to new ideas and experiences with ease. Lia patted the dark chestnut neck before leading the horse around the corral while she grew accustomed to wearing a bridle. She spotted Travis and Theo running toward her, excitement in their eyes.

"Aunt Lia, what'ya doin'?" Travis climbed up on the corral fence, gripping the top rail with his hands.

"Are you breaking in that horse?" Theo asked, following his brother's example and resting his folded arms on the top rail.

Lia kept the filly moving as she smiled at the boys. "I'm teaching her to wear tack. She's doing right well, don't you think?"

"What about the saddle?" Travis tilted his head as he pressed his lips together. "You gonna ride her bareback?"

She chuckled at the idea. "I'll break her into wearing a saddle after she's comfortable with the bridle and having a bit in her mouth. One step at a time."

She enjoyed the interest the boys showed in her horse training. Perhaps one day they'd be old enough and interested enough to help her with other horses. She loved her nephews and did what she could to teach them about handling horses. They'd learned to ride as soon as they could walk, but riding well without hurting their mount would take more time for them to really perfect. She was eager to continue their education about horsemanship and husbandry as they grew more mature and capable. Already they showed signs of becoming fine equestrians.

"When will you ride her?" Theo shifted his arms on the rail as a frown settled on his brow. "I want to see that."

"In a day or so, I think. She should be ready by then." Lia halted the filly and patted her neck again. "I think she's done enough for today."

Her objective with the filly was to teach her the basics and slowly begin her education of the rider's cues to communicate with her. Over the next few months, she'd teach her everything she'd need to know. Mostly working from the ground to begin with, then as she matured from the saddle. Slow and steady progression would maintain her willingness. Lia had high hopes for this particular mare so she wouldn't rush her training. Reaching up, Lia unfastened the throat-latch and slid the bridle off the horse's head. Then she picked up the rope halter and slipped it in place. She led the horse to the gate and soon had her outside, turning her out in the pasture nearby.

She watched the mare take off at a gallop, racing about the field and enticing the other five mares to join her. Such a glorious sight. Horses running free across the field, bucking and cavorting. They took another lap around the fenced pasture and then slowed to a trot, then a walk. Merrybell shook her neck and then lowered her head to graze. The other horses soon followed her lead and calmly tore at the grass. Lia turned away to stride back to her nephews.

"You boys want a snack?" She draped the cotton lead rope and halter over one shoulder.

"I do!" Theo yelled.

"Who's that?" Travis pointed to the carriageway where two men rode toward the barn.

Surprise jolted through her at their sudden appearance. Lia hung the halter on the corral fence as she stopped by the two boys, now standing on the ground in front of the corral. "I don't know. Shall we go see?"

The three walked down the lane toward the men. One of the men wore a wide-brimmed hat and peered at her with brown eyes. The other's blue eyes pierced her, his appearance familiar. She'd bet they were interested in buying a horse since she'd run an ad in the *Huntsville Advocate*. She couldn't imagine any other reason for them to be so far from town on a pretty winter afternoon. And approaching the barn instead of the house where her brother saw patients.

They reined to a stop. The blue-eyed man spoke first.

"Good day to you. You're Magnolia Merryweather."

"Yes. How may I help you?"

"Don't you remember me? We used to go to the same school way back when. My name is Dylan Blackwater and this other fella is Eddie Lackey. I'm looking to buy a new saddle horse. I understand you have a few for sale." He swung out of the saddle and held the reins in one hand. "I'm thinking a gelding will suit my purposes."

"I do have a few you can look at." She stared at the slender man as he towered over her. He really did look familiar but she didn't really remember him. School had been many years before and a nuisance taking her away from her horses. So she hadn't paid much attention to the other students, just focused on accomplishing her work and returning home. But if he was interested in a horse, then she'd see if one of hers would serve his purpose. "They're in the field over there. If you'll follow me."

Eddie dismounted and led his horse alongside of Dylan's. "I live not far from here and didn't know you were a horse breeder. That's mighty unusual work for a woman."

How would he know what was usual or unusual for a woman's efforts on her own family property? Just because nobody asked didn't mean a woman didn't earn money from many different ways all while remaining at home. Horse breeding and training was her way.

She halted and searched his face for signs of scorn. She found only pleasant interest, as if he'd like to ask her more about why she was breeding horses and selling them. Not that she'd answer him if he did. "Where do you live?"

"A few miles east of here. I hear Dr. Merryweather has a guest staying with him, is that so?" Eddie inquired, a gleam in his eye. "Who is it?"

The rumor mill was hard at work apparently. Lia detected the curiosity flaring in his eyes. She wouldn't satisfy his greedy question. No point in feeding the rumor mill. "A friend. If you'll come this way, I'll show you what I have for sale."

She led the two men away from the barn and closer to the forest to the pasture where six horses grazed, five geldings and her prize stallion. Theo and Travis trailed along, hands deep in their front pockets as they walked. She gazed at the herd, proud of their gentle natures and pleasing conformation. Just seeing them placidly grazing made her happy and at peace. She stopped at the gate and started telling the men about them, detailing how much training they each had undergone to date. The boys plunked down on the grass, picking blades with a sharp yank. She tried to ignore their attempts to make whistles, only yielding shrill squeaky noises as she continued telling the men about the horses.

"Any of those are available except for the big red bay stallion. He's not for sale."

She gazed at the beautiful Morgan horse she'd kept for the past ten years. It hadn't been easy to keep him hidden away from all those soldiers out searching for horse flesh during the war, but she'd managed to hide him in the woods on more than one occasion with the help of a few words of protective illusion. She'd not wanted to lose such a fine horse to be used in the military. He was her stud which she had crossed with her Quarter Horse brood mares to have such docile offspring like Merrybell. Mostly they threw chestnut foals, but once in a while a Palomino colored foal would appear as well.

"I'm sorry to interrupt you but I get the distinct impression you really don't remember me." Dylan turned to look at her more closely, his hat shading his eyes. "Is that right?"

"I'm sorry, but I really didn't pay much attention to my fellow students back then." She crossed her arms in a reflexive defensive movement. The man was far too attractive for her peace of heart. Not in the same way that Bryce attracted her, on a cellular level, but definitely he was a fine example of the male of the species. "I had other things on my mind."

"I know, but I had hoped." Dylan's ebony hair hung about his shoulders, sleek and glossy. His piercing blue eyes assessed her, warming the longer he gazed at her. Full lips and light stubble on his jawline enticed her but she refrained from reaching out to touch his face. He was a good-looking man. There hadn't been too many men about town during the war, most were off fighting somewhere. Those left in the area were either already married or maimed. Seeing a healthy male returning her interest was unusual as a result.

"You've done well for yourself, Miss Merryweather." Eddie interrupted the moment as he peered at the horses moving about the field. "Any of these could work for you, Dylan."

"I think I like the chestnut one with the white blaze. He's got a good eye, like he's interested in the world around him." Dylan pivoted toward the fence to study the horses more closely. "I'll take that one."

"You don't want to ride him first?" Lia frowned at him, unsure whether to sell him a horse he hadn't even sat on once. Surely, he'd want to test the horse's gaits and tractability under saddle before handing over significant money to buy one. "I'd rather you know if you're a good match for each other before you buy any of them."

"Well, if it doesn't work out then I'd have a good reason to come back and see you, wouldn't I?" Dylan glanced at her, his eyes twinkling with humor. "I'd like to have a reason to return if you'd like for me to as well."

His flirting with her made her heart flutter. She hadn't been the object of a man's interest in a very long time. Now that the war had ended and the men had come home, perhaps she should think about looking for a man to be her husband. The number of marriages listed in the paper each week had increased over the last few months, an indicator of the love stories abounding in the vicinity. Why couldn't hers be included in that number ere long? Nah, she'd much rather not go down that primrose path.

"I think I would like that." Even if Bryce would object. Not that she cared. She had made no promises to him or anyone she must keep. She held out her hand to Dylan. "Let's shake on it."

* * *

BRYCE PUSHED AWAY from the table, refraining from patting his stomach in satisfaction as he stretched out his legs and crossed his ankles. Laura served up a delicious mess of vittles. Sam was a damn lucky man. He reached for his ale, swallowing a mouthful of cool bittersweet. After his unproductive afternoon searching for a job, he'd returned in time to help Sam with rehanging a gate on the garden fence behind the house. Then they'd been called for supper. He figured the dark winter evening ahead would be perfect for reading a good book.

"My friend, might you have a worthwhile history or biography I could borrow this evening?"

Samuel laid down his fork and knife on the plate in front of him. "I have a small collection you can browse. I wish there were more but the war interfered. Especially the interruptions to the inflow of manufactured goods."

Bryce understood what Samuel referred to because he'd been part of the effort to interrupt production of anything which would aid the rebels. The South had once been a primary producer of agricultural products and livestock. Bryce had been ordered to tear up railroad tracks, bridges, crossings, everything and anything that would stop the flow of commerce in any direction. Then to ensure the Rebels didn't benefit from any of their efforts, they'd wreaked havoc on mills, tanneries, forges. The Union troops had protected Huntsville up until the end of the war, but then turned around and destroyed much of the buildings and businesses across the northern part of the state. But of course when the Union wasn't in control, the Rebels also pillaged their neighbors for food and supplies, attacked their Southern Unionist neighbors and burned their houses and barns. The ultimate result was the practical annihilation of resources the state could count on to restart or rebuild its economy.

"I thought the tracks were open, aren't they? That should allow for the exchange of goods with the North." Bryce folded his arms as he relaxed in his chair.

"I saw a notice in the Advocate that the Memphis and Charleston, the line that runs east and west through Huntsville, is open if questionable except for the Decatur bridge out west. They're working on the bridge but in the meantime have only a pontoon bridge across the Tennessee River to cart goods and people on the trains from one side to the other."

Bryce shook his head. "What a job that must be. How long before they finish the bridge?"

"I don't know but not soon enough. It slows the flow of goods east and north to sell and then to purchase manufactured goods to bring back into our region."

"Mama, can I be excused?" Michael pushed his napkin onto the table by his plate.

"Me, too?" echoed around the table from the other four boys.

Samuel and Laura had quite a large family, and all of their five children were smart, polite boys. Even if they did have a tendency toward mischief. Didn't most boys? Bryce hadn't been any kind of saint growing up. His father had whipped his backside more than once for his misbehavior. Especially if he'd lied about what he'd been up to. He'd learned not to tolerate lies for any reason, which had stood him well as a general life principle. Something he'd teach his own children one day. He considered his host and hostess for several moments. Looking back, he didn't envy his parents. He and his two brothers had been handful enough. Imagine five boys under ten years old in one house to raise.

"Finish your vegetables first." Laura arched a brow at her son. "While you finish, why don't you boys tell us what you want for Christmas this year? Keeping it within reason, of course."

Bryce firmed his lips at the change of topic. She had a point. The men's discussion could wait until after dinner had concluded. Besides, he should contribute his own gifts to the family. "I'm curious to know what kinds of gifts you'd like, too."

The back door squealed open and then slapped closed, drawing Bryce's attention to the open doorway connecting the dining room to the hallway. Who might be coming in the back door this time of evening? Then he heard her lovely voice. Lia hummed as she approached, her footsteps quick and all business. She appeared in the doorway, her simple, yellow cotton dress emphasizing her fine figure. Her features remained striking, alluring. She rushed into the dining room without meeting his appreciative gaze.

"There you are, Sam." Lia shoved a small stack of greenbacks into her brother's hand. "Another contribution to the family finances. I sold a horse to a man just a few hours ago. That's your share."

The move set Bryce back on his heels, so to speak. Why would Sam's sister be giving him money? He silently watched the exchange, a frown weighing down his brows. Was Sam in more financial trouble than he'd let on? He seemed to have enough food for his family, patients to either pay him or bring him other foodstuffs in payment.

"Uh...thanks. Congratulations on selling one of your horses. I know how much that means to you. It's helpful. Want to join us?" Sam gestured to the room at large.

Bryce met his friend's embarrassed gaze. What was that about?

Confusion battled with surprise inside him. He'd known that she'd started breeding horses with the intent of training and selling them. That wasn't shocking. The fact that she'd managed to sell one that day also didn't raise his brows. What did was the fact that Samuel accepted a share as if she owed him. For what?

Lia scanned the room with a happy smile on her lips until she met Bryce's quizzical expression. "Oh, I'm...I'm sorry to interrupt. I just want to give you what I owe... I mean, I'll come back later."

"Don't leave." The words popped out of Bryce's mouth before he could reconsider the wisdom of them. He'd caught glimpses of her from time to time, but always there were others around or she was too far away to have a conversation. He wanted to change that equation. Needed to create the opportunity to begin to rebuild what they once shared. "I mean...there's no reason to hurry away if you have some particular business with your brother. We're about finished with supper, and just about to learn what the boys want for Christmas."

He'd given her a reason to stay. To linger in the same room as him. Would she take it? She could remain and join in the conversation, or she could follow through with her idea of leaving them alone. Indecision reflected in her eyes as she skimmed her gaze around the others in the room. Stay, give him chance to learn more about her. What happened to her during the war. What her hopes were now for her future. Whether she'd had a relationship with any other men while he was out of the picture. The last thought being the most important and most troubling to him.

"I agree with Bryce, Lia. You should hear what the boys want for Christmas." Sam aimed a pointed look at her. "Have a seat."

"Very well." Lia sighed and squared her shoulders before sliding onto the chair beside Laura. "So, what do you boys want from Santa?"

"Oh, do you think Santa Claus will come this year?" Theo asked, his eyes bright. "He didn't come the last few years because of the war."

Now that was something Bryce hadn't considered. It made sense that there wouldn't be much to count as toys or treats for the holiday with everything so hard to come by for everyone. Inflation and lack of facilities combined to put quite a damper on gift-giving and merry-making for everyone. But surely they did something to acknowledge the special day. After all, Alabama had led the way to declaring Christmas a holiday back in 1836.

Samuel smiled faintly as he addressed his son. "I understand that he has allowed that now the fighting is done, he will get back to delivering gifts to you kids this year. So wish away."

"I want candy." Theo rubbed his belly and smacked his lips. "Nothing better in this world."

Bryce chuckled along with the other adults in the room. Lia also laughed at her nephew's happy grinning face.

Adam piped up. "I want a new rifle, Mama. One with a better sight on it."

Laura nodded and then shifted her gaze to Michael. "What about you?"

Michael considered for a few seconds. "If it's not too much to ask, I'd like to get a new book to read."

Bryce liked the boy's bent toward education but Adam's hunting rifle would also provide food for the family table. "Any particular topic, Michael?"

"Whatever Santa thinks is best will be fine with me."

"Alright, what about Ian?" Laura aimed her easy expression at him.

"Could I maybe have a guitar? I'd like to learn to play one." The gleam of hope lit up the boy's emerald eyes.

"Be sure to ask Santa then." Laura smiled gently at Ian and then shifted her gaze to the youngest son. "What about you, Travis?"

Travis wiggled on his seat as he glanced nervously at his father then back to his mother. "Would he maybe bring me a widdling knife?"

"Oh, Travis." Samuel shook his head at the boy. "I think you should ask for something more your age."

Crestfallen, Travis dropped his chin, looking down at his hands in his lap. "I'll take a toy train then…"

Oh the poor, unhappy little guy. Bryce stifled the grin tugging at the corners of his mouth as he met Sam's amused yet somewhat annoyed expression. The boy really had a one-track mind, and not for railroads despite his settling for a toy train. Whatever had inspired him to want to handle a knife? He didn't dare ask or risk perpetuating the lad's persistence in the matter.

"I saw that both Murray's Stationery and Dentler's Confectionery have a supply of toys, so perhaps you can find a train there." Bryce grabbed up his ale and took a swallow.

Lia's gaze drifted to Travis, then on to Adam, Michael, Ian, and finally Theo. Then she met Laura's gaze with a flash of raised brows.

"We'll need to make a trip into town then won't we, Laura?" Lia smiled at her sister-in-law. "We have a few weeks yet until the big day to let Santa know what the boys would enjoy."

Interesting that she looked at everyone in the room except him. Although the more he thought about it the more he realized that she had every right to ignore him, or avoid him, or even despise him. He'd broken his promise to her. She knew he'd done so for her benefit because he'd laid it out. He'd ended their relationship in her best interest. Which he could only imagine must have hurt, broken her heart and her trust in him. But now he'd come back and wanted to reestablish that relationship. What he needed to do was find a way to talk to her, to tell her how stupid he'd been. Then with any luck she'd find a way to forgive him.

CHAPTER 5

Waiting proved one of the hardest things Lia endured. She'd rather be outside with her horses rather than sitting in the parlor as her mother Natalie had requested. Rose played the piano, her fine talent on display. Aster stood at the window, peering through it to the brown and gray world outside. Laura occupied one chair by the fire, her knitting needles click-clacking away as she worked on gifts for the upcoming holiday. Lia remained in her seat, hands clasped in her lap, by sheer force of will.

The room had witnessed many a family gathering over the years. Cozy and welcoming, a red sofa and matching side chairs were grouped around a low cherrywood table before the snapping fireplace. Two windows overlooked the front carriageway, floor-length azure drapes flanking the sparkling glass. Aster had refreshed the vases positioned on the side tables with flowers from her extensive and varied garden nestled among gathered reeds. Portraits of her parents as well as one of George Washington graced one wall. Her father had revered the nation's first president for as long as Lia could remember. Thus it was no surprise he'd sided with the American government instead of the Confederacy. An unpopular stance for her home state, but one she fully supported.

Lia had washed up after working with several of her younger horses that morning but remained wearing her split skirt and casual blouse for riding. Her tall boots gleamed dully in the firelight, worn and scuffed but serviceable. Now that luncheon had passed and the afternoon progressed, she hoped her mother wouldn't tarry with her sudden family meeting. She had one more horse to work with ere she could relax for a while before she helped with dinner preparations. An intriguing novel called to her and it was a perfect day to curl up on the front porch and read for a spell. If only her mother would reveal her urgent and pressing business.

Suddenly, Natalie sashayed into the small parlor. "All right, my dears, let's get down to business, shall we."

"We've been waiting on your pleasure, Mother." Rose turned away from the ivories to smile at Natalie but it was tense and impatient, belying her easy banter.

Natalie sank onto a chair by the fire, a piece of paper and pen in her hands. "I see you're as eager as I am to plan this gala event."

Aster crossed the floral carpet to sit beside Lia on the horsehair sofa.

Lia pursed her lips. "Are you talking about the calico ball?"

"Indeed! I think it should be a Christmas Calico Ball the night before Christmas Eve. After all, nobody will truly want to be out and about on Christmas Eve except to be with their own families. Which means..."

"We don't have much time at all." Aster edged forward on her seat. "That's only three weeks from now?"

"More like two plus a few days." Natalie surveyed the stunned faces around her. "What?"

Laura shoved her sewing beside her and rose quickly to stare down at her mother-in-law. "How can the five of us plan and put on a ball in such a short span of time?"

"Easily. You must remember I've thrown many a ball in my lifetime. They're not all that difficult. We just need to divide and conquer. The first thing we must do is make a list of everything that needs to be done." Natalie laid the paper on the table in front of her, tapping it twice with a manicured nail. "We'll need a location for the dance, an invitation notice put in the *Advocate*, tickets printed, decide on the cost of those tickets…"

"Whoa, Mother. Slow down." Aster jumped to her feet beside Laura, her skirts swirling about her ankles as she folded her arms over her chest. "Are you writing those tasks down as you say them? Because I won't be able to recall such a long list."

Chuckling, her mother nodded. "I've already written most of them down. But what I need help with right this minute is making sure the list is complete."

Lia sat back on the sofa, regarding the astonished yet enthusiastic expressions of her sisters. The snap and pop of the logs in the fire punctuated the silence for a long moment. The slow ticking of the mantle clock marked the passing seconds. It had been years since they'd planned a ball of any kind, but with such short notice this one would prove a real challenge.

"What about the dresses and the men's accessories?" Rose leaned forward, getting into the spirit of the planning. "We'll need fabric and notions so they complement each other."

"We should be able to find them in town, given the advertisements in the paper claiming new shipments of everything." Natalie arched her eyebrows. "Having the railroad open again has relieved the lack of dry goods at least. With the fighting behind us, the men have come home again, and now we should celebrate."

"Have you noticed the increase in the number of marriages listed in the paper lately?" Aster asked, sliding a glance toward Lia.

Lia blinked at her but didn't rise to the bait. Just because more eligible men were out and about didn't mean she would marry. Not right away. Dylan's handsome features floated into her mind's eye. He seemed interested in her, returning her slight interest. Still, it was early yet before she could even determine whether he was worthy of her notice. In all probability he likely fought on the losing side. His loyalties were probably not the same as hers given how few unionists could be counted in the state. How would that bode for a relationship?

For that matter, would Dylan ask her to the ball? Or to dance at the ball? Oh, goodness. What if Bryce also attended? How would that play out? She'd have both men in the same room. That wouldn't do. She'd have to steer clear of Bryce as best she could, despite the fact he was staying in her brother's hospital across the way. Not give him any hope toward restarting the close relationship they once engaged in before he left. And that he ended. She sat up straighter, firming her resolve. She'd have to focus on that fact in order to keep her mind clear where he was concerned. She had no intention of pursuing a relationship with him. Indeed, she didn't even want to regard him. Or maybe she shouldn't go to the ball and then she wouldn't have to worry about any of the potential pitfalls.

Laura shook her head as she sank back onto her seat. "I'm happy for those who can finally start their lives together. I can only imagine how many weddings had been delayed due to the men being away."

"How many won't happen because the men didn't come back?" Aster asked with a slow shrug. "Such personal tragedies must be more numerous than we can count."

Natalie tapped her finger on the paper to bring their attention back to her. "Let's not get maudlin, we haven't much time as we've already discussed. Now, what are we forgetting?"

"Food. Who can we get to cater the event? And on such short notice." Lia pressed her lips together as she glanced at her sisters. They looked confused. "I mean, gathering the necessary quantity of foodstuffs and beverages to feed a crowd when so much is limited right now could prove quite the daunting prospect."

"That is a good point to raise but I'm sure we'll come up with someone." Natalie waved away Lia's concern with a flick of her hand. "Your father may even know someone. Which brings me to, who will we task with which items on this growing list?"

Laura sighed as she got to her feet and gathered her sewing. "I'm afraid I can't commit to much at the moment. I have Christmas to prepare for my young'uns. Not only hosting the family dinner but also the decorating and gifts, such as they may be."

"We'll need a sponsor and a hostess for the ball, Mother. Will you and Father serve as sponsor?" Aster tilted her head as she smiled at her mother. "You're the perfect choice, I think."

"Yes, as it's my idea I think that is quite right and proper." Natalie wrote on her paper before meeting Lia's gaze. "And Lia, will you as my oldest daughter serve as hostess?"

Her heart and faint hope sank like a stone in the lake. So much for not attending. Unease swelled in her chest as she thought about how she could navigate her duties without encouraging Bryce's sentiments toward her. Or Dylan's. She had no choice. Lia drew in a long, silent breath and nodded once. "Of course."

* * *

SNUGGLING deeper into her wool cloak, Lia turned the page of the novel. What would the hero do about the dastardly situation he'd found himself in? The heat of the day, such as it was, had quickly siphoned out of the air. She'd had a busy and productive day, working with her youngest bay gelding to train him to handling. He was a beautiful horse, too, with his dark red coat and black mane, tail, and legs. He'd make for a pretty ride. She was taking her time in preparing him to eventually be a docile and willing mount. But she didn't want to think about all that right now. She only had a few minutes to enjoy some solitude while she read before she'd have to go back inside and help fix dinner. She focused harder on the page in front of her, shunting aside everything else in her surroundings.

The wind rustled dry leaves across the expanse of the front yard and carriageway, their rattling trying to distract her attention from her oppressed hero. A nicker from one of the horses floated on the breeze. The scent of wood smoke wafted past her nostrils from the continuous fires burning to warm the homes. She inhaled deeply, savoring the aroma as it evoked a lifetime of fond memories. Her desperate hero set out on a quest to attempt to avert disaster, drawing her attention closer to the narrative. Only a few more pages to finish the chapter and then she'd go inside and return to her chores.

Bootsteps interrupted her reading, lifting her eyes from the page to watch in silent dread as Bryce crossed the porch and dropped into the other chair. He glanced at her, nodding in acknowledgement, then swiveled to survey the area in front of her house. She stiffened despite her resolve to avoid him, to not give him hope of resuming their once loving relations. She returned to reading, or attempted to, but his proximity claimed every iota of her awareness. He'd brought both the smell of leather and of sawdust with him. She blinked at the combination and turned to study him.

At first, he ignored her contemplation but after a few moments he met her inquisitive stare with a slow smile. "Good afternoon, Magnolia. How has your day fared?"

"Well, thank you. What have you been occupying yourself with to leave you smelling like sawdust?"

"Do I? My apologies. I've been helping Sam with cutting some fence boards."

"How industrious of you. And just how long are you planning to stay here?" She wanted to slap a hand over her mouth but refrained from such an impolite and telling response to her own unfortunate question blurted out from desperation.

He shrugged and slid his gaze away from her to linger in the direction of the pair of magnolia trees, their glossy leaves shining under the late afternoon sunlight. Those trees had stood witness to the origins of her family on this land. Her father purchased the acreage before he'd even proposed to her mother and had shaped and developed the buildings and structures on it to suit the needs of his growing brood. When his only son took a wife, he'd insisted they build nearby. Now all of Richard and Natalie's children and grandchildren lived on the property.

"Those magnolias are so beautiful. I've recalled them fondly while I've been away." His gaze sharpened on hers. "Their beauty was enhanced by that unexpected snowfall that day when we'd first..."

"That was a cold day in January, that's for sure." She cut off whatever he was going to say. She couldn't relive that day, that moment, to go back to having feelings for him. Trouble and disaster would follow as surely as the fog melting with the morning sun.

He folded his arms and let his eyes scan the perimeter of the property from his vantage point. "I've always thought of you as more beautiful than the rare beauty of the snow frosting the magnolia trees." He swiveled his head to capture her astonished gaze. "You do know that, don't you?"

Surprise washed through her at his claim. He'd not said as much to her before he abandoned her. Sure, he'd spoken of loving her forever, but nothing about her being a rare beauty, for pity's sake.

"How could I? You've never even hinted at the matter." She closed her book and laid it on her lap before crossing her arms under cover of the warm cloak. "You left and reneged on your promise. You left me."

Her heart broke yet again and fell into a million fragments. She'd not thought about the devastation she'd grappled with privately for so long. She'd forgotten the pain. Forgotten the anger. And most of all, forgotten the love they'd shared. She had to in order to move on with her life. Against her will, the bits and pieces of her heart cried out at the reality of their supposed relationship. Severed and shattered.

"Seemed like the right thing to do given the war and all," he muttered, dipping his chin as he scanned the distance. "Least, that's what I thought at the time."

"But why? I had promised to wait for you, to love you. And you told me to go on with my life."

He swung his troubled gaze around to peer at her. "For your best interest, seeing as I might not have survived the war."

The thought had crossed her mind too many times to tally. She'd feared he'd be killed but to have him sever the tie between them at the very moment when she'd come to face her gravid situation. She hadn't wanted to, but she had to face reality. She had to let him go, mentally and emotionally, in order to merely function with any semblance of normalcy. The worst, most grievous part of the affair was that she couldn't share her grief with the rest of her family as they didn't know about him. About them. Only Laura and Samuel were in on her secret out of sheer necessity. But she couldn't tell her loving, concerned family for fear of unraveling her crafted story to protect her and her illegitimate though dearly beloved child.

"I received your note ending us. So I had to let you go." She clenched her arms around her waist, holding back the tears that suddenly threatened to fall from her stoic eyes. She would not cry. Not any more.

"I'm sorry, Lia. I really thought it was the right thing to do. It seemed like the right thing to do at the time. But now I see that I was mistaken. Can you ever forgive my stupidity? I've never stopped thinking about you, imagining you sitting just like you are, praying for your safety and happiness. I've loved you for years and expect I will love you for the rest of my life. It took far too long for my liking to be able to come back and tell you that. Can you ever forgive me? Please?"

She sucked in a startled breath and held it, pulse pounding in her ears. Sincerity echoed through his declaration of love, his plea for forgiveness. The bits of her heart started to stitch themselves back together into a patchwork quilt of longing. But what he asked, forgiving him in order for them to start where they left off, would collapse her carefully constructed house of cards.

CHAPTER 6

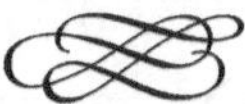

$\mathcal{A}$ quiet Sunday afternoon gave Lia the perfect opportunity to clean and polish her saddles and bridles. She hummed "Silent Night" as she applied saddle soap to the seat of an English saddle, rubbing it in with a circular motion. The stalls stood empty while all of her charges roamed various pastures outside. Such a lovely day for them to enjoy the winter sunshine and blue skies while they searched for whatever tender grass they might find in the dead of winter.

She switched to singing another favorite, "O Come All Ye Faithful," as she finished with the saddle. While working alone she could belt it out without anyone complaining if she went off key, too. She sang the traditional Christmas hymn with all the emotion she could muster. She didn't want to relive the fraught moment when Bryce had declared he loved her. And her lack of response.

She hadn't known what to say to him. She harbored feelings for him. But she couldn't admit it without giving him hope of rekindling the flame that once burned so brightly between them. Her feelings remained sorely divided on that score. So she chose to ignore the topic, to ignore him.

She lifted the clean saddle she'd been so fortunate to be able to purchase before the war, gleaming with a fresh application of oil to prevent the leather from drying out, and carried it across the tack room to hang it back on its saddle rack. She perused the array of saddles and bridles, blankets and pads acquired slowly and carefully and neatly stored in the small room. She moved to straighten a stack of saddle pads then heard approaching hoofbeats outside. She finished adjusting the pads and then went out of the tack room to investigate.

Dylan Blackwater swung out of the saddle and landed with a muted *thud* on the dry dirt entrance to the barn. "Miss Merryweather." He tipped his hat and then dropped the reins to ground tie the chestnut gelding he'd bought from her the other day. "How fare you on this fine afternoon?"

"I'm well, thank you. I see you and Rowdy are doing well together." She stopped at the doorway of the stable and skimmed her gaze over the horse to verify he remained fit and sound.

"I've come to congratulate you on the fine training you accomplished with this horse." Dylan strode toward her, tapping his hat into place as he stopped in front of her. "We're getting along grandly."

"I'm relieved to hear as much." His decision to not ride the animal before purchasing him had concerned her, but he was obviously an experienced horseman so she'd allowed it. "Thank you for letting me know. It relieves my mind."

"It's such a nice day for a ride, too. But more importantly, I wanted to see you again."

She saw the eager light of interest in his eyes. It made her feminine heart pound with an inner joy at being appreciated by the handsome young man. What woman wouldn't feel something with a man gazing so at her? But no, she couldn't encourage his attentions any more than she would Bryce's.

"Now you have achieved your aim. I hope you have a pleasant ride home." She had more work to do and really didn't want for this flirting conversation to continue. Would he take the hint? Or would he push his own agenda forward? She started to turn away, shifting her booted feet, only to stop as he continued speaking.

"Why are you out here all by yourself?"

"Because I wanted peace and quiet to take care of a few tasks. I like my alone time." She folded her arms as she searched his eyes for a moment. "I appreciate you stopping by but I do not want to detain you."

"What if I want to be detained?" He reached out to pry one of her hands loose from its grip on her elbow. "I can't stop thinking about you, Miss Merryweather. I'd like to get to know you better."

She pulled her hand free of his grasp. "We don't have anything in common, other than my horses." She imagined he and his loved ones most likely supported the Confederacy like most everyone within the state. She couldn't imagine they'd get along if they began discussing that particular history. He'd probably fought on the wrong side during the war after all. The losing side. "I can't imagine you'd like what you might learn about me."

"Because your father and brother are unionists?" He nodded slowly. "That's not your fault and so doesn't matter. We can ignore all of that and see how we get along, can't we?"

"It's not just my father and brother's view, it is mine as well." She glanced over his shoulder at the sound of horses approaching. Samuel and Bryce returning from an errand in town. "You should go."

Dylan pivoted to see who she was looking at and then aimed his vibrant eyes at her again. "I'm not afraid of your brother or his friend, whoever he is. I can take care of myself. And you, if you'd permit me. I would like to court you, to see if we might be a good match."

The pair of horses halted outside beside Rowdy to give Samuel and Bryce a moment to dismount. Then the two men led their horses toward the barn. Lia stepped to one side, Dylan shadowing her movement. Bryce stared at Dylan with suspicion blazing from his eyes.

"Is that Rowdy outside?" Samuel asked as he put his mount into a stall and then returned to stand beside her. "This must be his new owner, then." He held out his hand to shake with Dylan. "I'm Doctor Samuel Merryweather. And you are?"

"Dylan Blackwater." They briefly shook hands as Bryce joined them. "And you, sir, are?"

So obviously she wasn't the only one who didn't recall Dylan. Sam must not have remembered him from school either. More concerning was Bryce's reaction. Lia sensed the distrust and concern emanating from Bryce as he extended a hand to Dylan. Animosity simmered beneath the surface. Anger? Jealousy? The two men had never set eyes on each other so what caused Bryce to react so negatively toward Dylan? Perhaps Lia's reluctance to reply to Bryce's declaration had something to do with it. Darn. She hadn't meant to cause him grief or hurt. But she probably had.

"Captain Bryce Day." He squeezed Dylan's hand hard enough that Lia saw him wince. "You shouldn't be in here with Miss Merryweather unaccompanied."

Ah, that was the problem. Her reputation had been threatened. Men. So naturally he had to push Dylan's proverbial buttons by insisting he use his military rank instead of his civilian honorific. Well, two could play at that game. "He is a client, *Captain* Day."

Bryce shot a dark look at her at her audaciousness and then returned his hard gaze to address Dylan's smirk. "You've already bought a horse, what else did you want?"

Dylan squared his shoulders at the challenge in Bryce's glare. "If you must know, sir, then I will tell her brother." Dylan swung around to address Samuel. "I wish to court your sister."

Samuel took a step back. "I see. Well, it's not up to me to give you leave to do so. Lia? What say you?"

"Lia. Please." Bryce growled low in his throat but then fell silent.

His hands fisted at his sides. Lia sensed his disbelief, his worry, and most of all his fear. She drew in a long breath as she debated how to respond in the face of the two men's silent pleas aimed her way. She still loved Bryce, but she couldn't tell him that. Not at the moment. Not like this, if ever. The two men were likely to come to blows over her. She couldn't tolerate the idea.

"You both are acting childish." She peered at Sam, trying to convey the depth of her feelings without words. At his nod, she turned to speak to Dylan. "We've already discussed this, Mr. Blackwater. You should go before something bad happens."

Dylan studied her for a moment before glancing at Bryce and then back to her. "I take it Mr. Day is also a suitor?"

"Yes." Bryce ground out the one word. "And it's Captain to you."

"Which army?" Dylan lifted his chin to stare at the other man.

Samuel intervened. "That's neither here nor there any more, gentlemen. But I agree with my sister that you should leave, Mr. Blackwater." He pointed at the barn doorway. "Now."

Bryce's fists clenched harder, making Lia fear a fight was about to break out right before her eyes. She wouldn't be witness to bloodshed. She huffed a sigh as she met Bryce's glare. "I cannot condone this sort of behavior. Good afternoon." She stormed out of the barn and marched herself home, not looking back.

* * *

Bryce confronted Dylan, hands still clenched, eager for an excuse to take a swing at the invader. "You're walking a dangerous path, Mr. Blackwater."

Dylan drew himself up straight. "The danger is yours, I believe. Since you're so chummy with the good doctor, that must mean you have the same sympathies." He spat in the dirt of the barn aisle.

"Mr. Blackwater, your business here has concluded. Please leave." Samuel stared at Dylan. "Now."

"I'll go because I don't want to have anything to do with the likes of you traitors." He spat again and then turned and stalked out of the barn.

Yet he desired to court Lia? The bastard obviously didn't realize Magnolia and the other women in the family had established their own loyalties not just reflecting their men's views. As the sound of hoofbeats faded, Bryce finally shook off the rage and anger simmering inside of him. The anger was replaced with confusion and concern. Had she welcomed Blackwater's plea to court her? Or did she send him away? How could she even contemplate becoming entangled with a man like Dylan Blackwater?

"Well, you brought this on yourself, my friend." Samuel smacked Bryce on the shoulder with an open hand.

"How so?" What did Samuel know about what had transpired, or hadn't, between he and Lia? Perhaps she said something to her brother after leaving Bryce to abruptly go inside the house. She'd merely said she'd had to help her mother.

"You broke her heart." Sam held up a hand to stop Bryce's next comment. "You did. She didn't say anything but I know you two once shared something. I could see her waiting, watching, hoping. Then your note breaking it off. And she'd just discovered… Never mind."

"Discovered, what?"

"It's not important at the moment." Samuel eyed him. "You professed your love, then said never mind and left her high and dry with a broken heart. What did you expect she'd do when you came back without any warning?"

He had envisioned her falling into his arms with joy to have him back. Hoped she would willingly accept his advances. Instead she'd pushed him away.

"I hoped she would forgive me so we could try again." Bryce rubbed his stubbly jaw. "I even told her I love her, but she didn't forgive me nor return the sentiment. I thought she'd be better off forgetting about me."

"Did you now?" Sam shook his head. "She loved you, probably still does. You never forget your first love."

He never forgot her. He'd thought about her every single day, no matter what hell he was living through. All he had to do was reach into his pocket to find the magnolia blossom and peace would wash through him. She'd blessed the piece of wood before handing it to him, begging him to carry it with him as a shield and a reminder. The talisman truly had protected him and brought him back to her. Though it had worked differently from what either of them had thought.

"I don't think she will forgive me or give me the chance to make this up to her." What could he do to make it right? What would be enough? "What do I do now?"

"As her brother, I can tell you she can be very stubborn. So, talk to her about how you feel but be patient. She'll need time to think through everything and to see your earnestness."

"I'm not feeling very patient at the moment, especially not with Blackwater nipping about." An urgency flowed through his veins at the thought of another man courting his woman. Of someone else feeling her lips under his, of exploring the mysteries of her body instead of him. He needed a plan of attack of his own and fast. "But I'll try."

* * *

Low clouds hung in the late morning sky as Bryce strolled out of the mayor's office. He'd hoped for a lead, and he'd found one, weak though it might be. The mayor had suggested he talk to the folks at the railroad, where it turned out his old commander, Major Charles Smythe, who'd become a casual friend of sorts during the war, was some kind of manager. Maybe he'd have some ideas.

Smythe had made a good reputation for himself during the conflict and had apparently landed himself a cushy job with the Memphis and Charleston Railroad. As the yardmaster, he ensured the trains carried the right cargo when they departed for other cities. Bryce intended to visit him at the Huntsville Depot the following day. But working for the railroad? So many awful memories clung to his time working on railroads during the war. Bryce pulled in a long breath and eased it back out along with the odiferous scents of sewage in the gutters and steaming horse dung. Then he sucked it back in again when he spotted Richard Merryweather's carriage pull to a stop in front of the elegant and obviously popular Easley Hotel not fifty feet from where he loitered on the side of the dusty road.

The side door popped open and Richard emerged, quickly stepping to the ground. He offered a hand up to his wife, to help her navigate to the road with her long skirts carefully clasped in one hand. Then, joy of joy, Lia poked her head out of the doorway and soon stood beside her mother. Bryce stared at her, his heart filling with a combination of hope and hesitance. After their conversation and then her walking away from him, she'd seemed less open to accepting his presence. A situation he must work to change. She looked lovely in a garnet-red dress and blue cloak, a somber blue hat edged with narrow lace on top of her head. Her gaze swept the road and then landed on his with a slight smile of recognition. Her smile drew him to her.

"Mr. Merryweather." Bryce tipped his hat to Lia's father. "It's a pleasure to see you all here in town."

Richard spun slowly to address him, his appraising glance inching over Bryce's tense frame. "Mr. Day, good day to you as well. Are you thinking of getting a room at the Easley?"

A subtle suggestion to not stay with Samuel any longer than necessary? Bryce blinked away his suspicion. More likely simple curiosity. "I've been visiting various businesses in search of work. What brings you to this fine establishment?"

"Ah, yes. I know you're in search of a job. I do wish you success in finding adequate employment." Richard proffered his arm to Natalie, who laid her hand on his arm. "We're in search of a location for the calico ball my wife is planning. Hugh Easley owes me a favor so I'm hoping he'll be able to accommodate the event."

Lia squared her shoulders and moved closer to her mother, aiming serious eyes his way. "Given the short time we have to organize everything, I hope he can as well."

Thought and words fled Bryce's mind at the tempting features of the woman he'd loved, though from afar, for years. He'd dreamed of her, relied on his memory of her to see him through many a long, cold night. He'd do whatever he must to win back her trust, her acceptance, her love. He couldn't be separated from her again. She meant the world to him.

"We should go in. Dear?" Richard led the way into the hotel double doors without further discussion.

Bryce belatedly offered his arm to Lia, delighted when she accepted after a hope-crushing hesitation. Pleasure filled his heart as he walked with her into the decorated foyer of the hotel. Beautiful, gleaming marble floors showcased opulent gold side chairs and mahogany casual tables. Oil paintings of various leaders graced the walls. Potted plants created privacy screens for gentlemen's conversations as they conducted business. The guests sauntering through the large room reflected the wealth of the establishment. An oasis of comfort and money after the years of hard times and want. They halted beside Richard and Natalie, who were already in conversation with an older gentleman Bryce recognized as Hugh Easley, the proprietor.

"You say you want the ballroom? Are you sure?" Hugh Easley folded his arms on his paunch of a stomach. "Perhaps you want to see it first."

"Mrs. Merryweather, would you want to inspect the ballroom for its suitability?" Richard asked, a gentle smile on his lips.

Natalie shook her head as she met Hugh's quizzical expression. "I'm confident the space will be perfection itself, Mr. Easley, so there's no need, but thank you for the offer. Is it available on the twenty-third by any chance?"

Hugh blinked at her, tapping his fingers on one elbow. "Oh my. I am not sure, but..."

Natalie angled her head with a lift of her brows. "Mr. Easley?"

Abashed, Hugh left his mouth hanging open for several seconds before snapping it shut. Then with an obvious effort, he managed to put a smile on his face and nodded. "Of course it's all yours, Mrs. Merryweather, as always. I am at your service."

Bryce witnessed first hand the matriarch working her own kind of magic to acquire what she desired. He'd forgotten how revered and respected Natalie Hunt Merryweather was by the populace.

A radiant smile lit Natalie's expression. "Why, that's wonderful news. We all appreciate your donating the space to the cause, Mr. Easley. Thank you so very much."

"Oh, Mrs. Merryweather, and Mr. Merryweather, I didn't realize you were here. My apologies for not greeting you properly." A woman in a dark dress with white shirtfront approached the small group lingering in the bustling foyer. Her brown hair was coiled into a bun at the back of her head, emphasizing her intelligent gaze as she greeted the group.

"Magnolia, Richard, you remember my friend, Mrs. Hugh Easley.

Margaret, it's been too long. If your patients needs allow, I hope you'll join me for tea later this week."

"I recall Miss Merryweather and your kind husband." Margaret nodded in greeting to Richard then turned to Lia with a gentle, inquisitive expression on her face. "How are you faring, my dear?"

Lia faintly stuttered a greeting to the other woman. Bryce shot Lia a look of concern at her inelegant response. Was something amiss? Lia stared at the woman as if she wished her to disappear. Apparently, Mrs. Easley was some kind of physician given the reference to her patients, but how she'd managed to attain such a title was a mystery. The medical schools traditionally only allowed men to attend, but a few schools had changed their admission policies to allow women to become doctors. It would be unusual for the woman to be a true doctor, but it was possible. Perhaps Lia was reacting instead to the likelihood the woman was in fact merely a midwife and not a true doctor. But why had Lia gone so pale? Unless… But no, she would have told him if they'd created a child together. She was an honest woman, after all.

"I've been well, thank you for asking." Lia cast her eyes about the room and then dropped her gaze on her father. "Perhaps we could get a bite to eat? I'm famished."

"You are looking rather peaked." Natalie sidled over to her daughter and slid an arm around her waist. "Please, Richard, I believe Lia needs nourishment."

Bryce smoothed the frown from his brow. "I understand the Easley has fine fare. Shall we adjourn there?"

Richard nodded. "A good idea. Hugh, is that agreeable to you?"

Hugh grinned at the large party, likely seeing dollar signs. "Indeed. Follow me." Placing a guiding hand on the small of Margaret's back, he encouraged her with a gentle push to join the two women in wending through the busy lobby toward the airy and bright dining room.

Bryce fell into step behind the women, Richard and Hugh chatting boisterously in front of the small group. Concern sifted through his confused brain. Not only for his own future, but also for Lia's wellbeing. Something seemed off but he'd be damned if he knew what. After everyone was seated around an oblong table positioned in the front window of the hotel dining room, he took a moment to really look at each of the others. Richard kept a steady gaze on his wife and daughter, while Lia wouldn't meet Bryce's eyes no matter how long he studied her. Instead, she flicked glances around the table, inevitably returning to Margaret's relaxed countenance.

"Hugh, tell Bryce what you told me earlier." Richard waved a hand in the air, encouraging his friend to speak up.

"About the availability of open positions?" Hugh lifted a crystal goblet and sipped the amber beverage. Swallowing, he set the glass back down and nodded as he pinned Bryce with his scrutiny. "It's rebounding but finding work that pays in money and not in kind is the challenge."

"Barter? I can't work for chicken feed." Bryce struggled to relax tense back muscles, struggled to keep a frown from his features, and mightily struggled to not ask Lia what on earth had her acting so strangely. "I've been all over town and still don't have any really good options."

"What about the Freedman's Bureau? They're supposed to be in the know of work." Hugh stared at Bryce for a long moment. "All things to everyone, in fact."

His tone revealed much about his attitude toward the organization. Pile on the upcoming Christmas holiday and the hope and expectation of the children for Santa Claus to bring them gifts when there was little money to be had. No wonder everyone seemed somber and worried. He thought of the five little boys back at Hopewell, each longing for something specific and no doubt costly. Inflation had risen to extraordinary heights during the war. If he could find good paying work, then he'd happily contribute to their gifts this holiday season. But he had to find work that paid in real money.

"Nothing there for me. I am not even certain what kind of job I'm looking for." Bryce pressed his lips together as he contemplated a bleak future without two dimes to rub together. "I did hear the railroad may be an option."

"Ah. Well, if that falls through or isn't sufficient, you're an engineer, and from what I hear highly trained and experienced with building things. Maybe start your own firm? Consult with others who want to rebuild. Tell them what they need to do, to consider, and such." Richard shrugged lightly as he trailed his gaze around the table. "I'm sure you could manage your own business, right?"

"It's a possibility." Bryce opened his mouth to continue but snapped it shut again as Blackwater approached the table. What on earth did he want? He plastered a neutral expression on his face as best he could. "Richard, you have a guest coming up behind you."

Richard shifted to look over his shoulder, his quizzical expression changing into a welcoming smile as he pushed back his chair and stood to greet the new arrival. "Mr. Blackwater. A pleasure. Do you know everyone here?"

A faint inhale of air drifted to Bryce's ears, compelling him to search out its source. Lia sat rigidly, a tight smile on her lips. If one didn't know her as well as he did, they wouldn't discern the faint interest glinting in her eyes. She'd been comfortable—too comfortable—with Blackwater the other day. He blinked as he contemplated her reaction. Then he turned back to peruse Blackwater more closely.

His name suited his dark good looks and his brawny build. He must work with his hands more than pushing papers around on a desk. His mouth was set in a hard smile as he swept the group with his regard, hesitating when he met Bryce's gaze, and finally softening when he met Lia's. Then he resumed his conversation with Richard. "I believe I have had the pleasure. What brings you here today? Anything I can help with?"

Richard shook his head and then addressed the group, his eyes lingering on Bryce. "Mr. Blackwater is a fine real estate agent in town and has been helping me identify some potential properties to invest in with my meager savings. In fact, Mr. Day here may soon be in need of a house of his own if all works out for him."

Blackwater speared him with a sharp, greedy look. "I'm sure I can help you find a place to call your own home, Mr. Day. Feel free to contact me when you're ready."

Bryce stiffened as the man emphasized the honorific, apparently refusing to respect Bryce's preference of being addressed as captain by that particular man. He couldn't take him to task in the present circumstances, but one day... He inhaled a calming breath and let it out slowly. "Mr. Merryweather is correct that at some point I will need a house but not at present." Bryce felt Lia's awareness of the tension tingling in the air spanning the table. He glanced her way, surprised by the frown marring her features. The atmosphere grew more and more electric until he though the candle on the table might ignite it like a bomb. In fact, he detected a faint shimmer like water vapor on a hot summer afternoon. Combined, he felt uneasy with the growing group. "I'd appreciate any leads on employment in the area, however. I am in search of a new career now that the war is over."

Blackwater grimaced as he stared hard at Bryce and then shrugged off whatever he'd been thinking. "If I hear of anything, I'll be sure to let you know. I can understand why someone who relied on military service would find times difficult. Especially if they were on the wrong side of the question."

Bryce fisted his hands in his lap, ready to defend himself and the other unionists at the table if overtly threatened.

"I-I'm sorry but I must beg to be excused. I've developed quite a headache." Lia braced both hands on the edge of the table as she pushed back and stood.

Blackwater seemed startled by her sudden declaration and acted as if he'd like to intercede. Not while Bryce was present. Lia was his true love, or would be if he hadn't upset her so much. But he had a plan for making up to her if she'd permit him.

"What about luncheon?" Natalie asked, as she stood to place a steadying hand on Lia's waist.

"Yes, food may help." Margaret considered her with a worried expression. "I'm sorry you're not feeling up to snuff."

"I can't eat now." Lia shook her head slowly with wide eyes, her gaze landing on Bryce. "I'm afraid I do not feel well. I'd like to go home."

She'd effectively summoned him to her aid with the desperation in her eyes. Bryce rose to his feet in one fluid motion, stepping quickly around the table to stand beside her. Her father seemed taken aback by his sudden move but didn't forbid his proximity to her. He'd do whatever he could to please Lia. He addressed the group at large. "Please allow me to escort her home while you all enjoy your meal. My horse can handle us both."

"Is that what you'd like, my dear?" Richard asked, his tone cautious.

She worried her lip for a brief moment, her eyes fixed upon her father. "Oh, yes. Please. I am not well."

"Very well. Mr. Day, if you'd be so kind." Richard sat back in his chair and indicated for Bryce to do as his daughter requested.

"I will see you home, Lia. Come." He thanked heaven that she was not adverse to riding astride so he could take her home forthwith. Trying to locate a suitable carriage for hire on the spur of the moment would likely prove difficult.

He escorted her from the room and out to where his horse stood tied. He'd out-maneuvered Blackwater, left him standing with his mouth in a hard line. He felt as if he'd won a prize. But all the while he and Lia rode home, he wondered about her strange reactions over the past hour.

CHAPTER 7

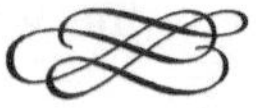

Cinnamon and nutmeg scented the air as Lia rolled out pastry dough for the apple pies she was helping Laura put together. With so many hungry mouths in one family, it would take more than one to satisfy the horde. After Bryce had left her on her front porch before riding back to town, she'd waited until he was out of sight before striding briskly over to talk with her sweet sister-in-law. She needed a heart-to-heart talk to ease the worry in her soul.

Relief at avoiding any deep or revealing discussions in the presence of the gossipy midwife still reverberated through her core. Not that anyone else at the luncheon table would have assigned such label to Margaret. Thankfully, they did not know the extent of Margaret's knowledge about the child. Would she ever think of her in a different light? And having Bryce part of that gathering only made the entire experience more fraught with emotional peril. Only Laura could help her make sense of everything tumbling out of control.

Rubbing a floured hand over her brow, Laura sighed. "Christmas is only a few weeks away and I don't have anything for the boys. Or Sam. What am I going to do?"

"They told you what they'd like."

"Yes, but we don't have the money. You heard them rattle off what they wanted, things like an instrument and a book, both expensive and hard to come by right now. I may have to resort to making tarts for each of them just so they get something." Laura rolled out the pie dough in a large circle with long, even strokes. "You know, of course, what the youngest wants, to whittle. That's not going to happen. But we'll get him something else he'll like. If we can afford anything, that is."

Laura and Samuel's youngest son so longed for a whittling knife and everyone in the family knew it. Not that he'd get one yet. Perhaps at some future Christmas. Lia bit back her dismay at the thought of forgoing yet again the traditions of the season they'd once enjoyed. Years ago. Before the war destroyed everything, including their sense of peace and prosperity. No more elaborate dinners and extravagant gifts of fine clothing or accessories. The swaths of evergreen garland across the mantle with red and gold candles providing a comforting ambiance. A tree harvested from the neighboring hills and decorated with carved wooden cardinals, tatted white snowflakes, glass balls of different colors, small gifts, and golden-flamed candles, with toys for the children arrayed beneath its green boughs. Platters and tiered stands of meats, cheeses, fruits, and nuts to enjoy. Without steady income, those days had vanished like the smoke from the rifle barrels that helped take it away.

"The drought has not helped matters." Lia dusted the dough with a bit of flour. "But at least we are not reliant on crops of cotton and corn to survive. People will always need horses, after all. As long as I can continue to raise and train quality stock, we should be all right in the end." That aspect of her future remained a source of both pride and comfort. But the child...and Bryce... What about them?

Laura arranged the pie crust dough onto the pie pan then laid the rolling pin aside. "Sam worries about the bartering and how that will make things more difficult. I don't know that it will not get worse." Grabbing a handful of sliced apples, she arranged them in layers in the pan.

"Oh, please tell me things will get better now. I know it's naïve to wish for things to return to as they were, but with good fortune perhaps we'll be able to restore the flow of goods and produce so we can live more easily. Everything seems to be such a struggle right now."

"Imagine the poor souls who have even less than our men can provide for us." Laura stopped to peer at Lia with concern flickering in her eyes. "The calico ball your mother is putting together will be appreciated by so many. I will do whatever I can to help."

"As will I. Not that I think I have as much to offer as my mother, mind. The community looks to her for the direction of their efforts."

Her mother managed to pull off seemingly miraculous events by merely asking for others to pitch in. Her subtle magical touch encouraged their willingness to be part of the effort. As a result, everyone seemed to feel good about their involvement.

"Oh, how are you feeling? Did your…headache ease?" Laura shook her head once and grimaced as she returned to placing sliced apples with a sprinkle of cinnamon and nutmeg on each layer. "I shouldn't have permitted you to stay on your feet. I'm sure that couldn't have helped."

Guilt swept through Lia at her sister's words. Caught in another lie, small though it might be. When did Lia begin lying instead of sticking to the truth? "If you'll promise to keep it to yourself…"

Laura glanced at her when she paused. "What is it?"

"Truth be told, I didn't actually have a headache." There, she'd admitted her fib. Now, how much of her concern should she share with the one woman who totally understood the situation?

"I thought as much." After dusting her hands off, Laura wiped them on the apron protecting her dress. "You didn't appear ill to me when you came home with that handsome young man of yours."

"My…man? I don't have a man." Lia's face grew warm. Laura knew of the past close—mayhap too close—relations she'd enjoyed with Bryce. "I just didn't want to remain in the presence of both Bryce and Dylan. It was far too uncomfortable." For reasons she wouldn't allow herself to contemplate.

"Having two men vying for your attention? Romance novels are written on such a theme." Laura grinned at her and then started rolling out the top crust.

"Neither of them are mine. Just keep that firmly in mind." She finished rolling out the bottom crust and transferred it to the waiting pan. "I don't want a man."

"Pshaw. Of course you do. You need a husband, now that there are men to choose from once more. You're what, twenty-eight years of age now? You cannot live with your parents forever."

The war had provided the perfect excuse for why she hadn't attracted a husband. But now the men had all been released from military obligation or paroled after being captured in the last months of the fighting. All the men were free to live their lives as best they could manage. Which, like her sister-in-law pointed out, meant claiming wives to raise their children and manage their household. She'd always assumed eventually, one day far into the future, she'd end up in such a role. The war had let her push that likelihood farther down the road and let her pretend she could live life on her own terms. But Laura burst that balloon with her insightful observations.

"They have not given me any indication they are unhappy with the arrangement." Lia studied Laura's unbelieving expression. "Have they?"

"I only know that I look forward to the day when my boys are grown and living on their own so that Samuel and I might have some peace and quiet in our days." Laura winked at her. "If you understand my meaning."

"No, I...oh. Yes, of course." Heat flared in Lia's cheeks. Relations between husband and wife were private and rarely even hinted at among family members. "I will have to think on what you've said and see what I might do about it."

Laura smiled at her. "Bryce is quite repentant for hurting your feelings by breaking off his courtship with you. He's mentioned it to me several times now, as how he hopes to make it up to you. I'd give him a second chance if I were you."

"I'm not interested." The pat answer came out quickly. She wasn't interested. Or was she? His handsome visage arose in her mind's eye and she felt a twinge of guilt and regret in her heart. She still loved him despite her denials. Should she give him a chance? No, she couldn't allow herself to put any sense of her feelings towards him into the world around her. No one must know. Hers and her son's lives would be ruined. "It's not so simple."

"I know what you're saying." Laura laid down the fork she'd been using to flute the edges of the crust in order to peer seriously at Lia. "Nothing is ever that simple, but you have to decide what it is you really want and then go after it. You cared for Bryce once and I think you still have feelings for the man. Give him a chance to explain, to apologize, to make things right. You both deserve that much."

"But what about…"

"Everything will work out. You have to have some faith."

Swallowing back the denial that clawed at her throat, Lia nodded. "I'll think on it."

* * *

AFTER DROPPING Lia off at home, Bryce rode back to town to meet with his former commanding officer who now worked for the Memphis & Charleston Railroad Company. Major Smythe had resigned his commission as an officer in the First Alabama Cavalry before Bryce got out of the service. Charlie had suffered a deep saber slice to his left leg in the last months of the war, which nearly cost him the leg. Left with a limp, he was grateful to have survived the war so didn't fuss about the inconvenience of not being comfortable in the saddle any longer. Bryce reined Jet to a halt outside of the three-story, red brick depot on Church Street and swung to the ground. Patting his horse on the neck, he tied him to the hitching rail and went inside.

The well-lit lobby welcomed him as he crossed the wood floor to the Agent's Office. Charlie emerged from the office as Bryce neared. Seeing him in civilian clothes still took a bit of an adjustment after they'd served for years together wearing blue uniforms while in the

Union Cavalry. He'd also grown a trim beard and small mustache after getting out, so he looked very different as he made his way toward him.

"Bryce Day, as I live and breathe." Charlie stuck out his right hand to shake with Bryce. "I'm damned glad to see you looking so well."

"And you too." Bryce scanned his former commander to assess his attitude toward him. "I've come to talk to you about possible employment. I heard that the railroad is looking for capable engineers to help with maintaining the tracks and crossings. Is that true?"

"Yes, indeed." Charlie slapped Bryce on the shoulder. "You've come to the right place. I'm doing the hiring and I know you're qualified. I'd welcome your talents and skills."

"What does it pay?" He couldn't give away his time, so hopefully the salary would be sufficient. He'd made seventy dollars each month while in the Union Army plus money to keep two horses and a servant. He'd need to make at least that much to support himself and his horse. Otherwise he'd have to continue looking. He waited impatiently for Charlie to answer him.

"We're paying the going rate for railroad workers, $2.75 per day for six days work each week."

He did some calculations then shook his head. Sixty-six dollars a month just wouldn't make ends meet adequately. "I'm afraid that's not enough. I have plans I need to finance. I'll keep looking for something that pays better."

"What kind of plans?"

Bryce studied the other man's inquisitive expression. How much should he share of his personal aims? Partial information might prove enough. After all, they were friends after everything they'd endured together.

"That wife and family I wanted to start a few years back." He folded his arms over his chest. "Now that the war is over, I'm going to try again."

"That lass is still waiting for you despite everything? I'm amazed but glad for you."

The man's tone set Bryce's teeth on edge. Did he really want to work for him again? Yes and no. At least he would know what he was getting himself into with Charlie as his boss. But the low pay closed that door. "I'll have to keep looking. I'll see you around, Charlie."

"Wait. What if I could do three dollars?" Charlie held out a hand as though to physically prevent Bryce from walking away from his offer. "Will that work for you?"

Good thing he was good with math. That increase would bring his monthly pay to seventy-two. Enough for a start. "Yes, if you can then I would be grateful for the work."

"Done. You can start tomorrow. We've got a lot of track to upgrade and improve after the lean war years when we didn't have the materials needed to do so."

"We destroyed more track than we put down." Relief flooded Bryce's chest. He'd found a decent job, one he at least had experience with and which would allow him to live well. Even save some if he watched his spending. He'd simply have to be content with the prospect of working for the railroad until something better came along.

Charlie frowned at him as he shook his head sharply once. "I wouldn't go around talking about what we did in uniform if you want to live well in these parts."

"What do you mean?" Bryce stiffened as he cast his gaze around the bustling space. Was there nowhere in town he'd feel safe from harassment? He'd known coming back to a state which had seceded from the Union would be difficult, of course. But he hadn't realized it would be a threat to his personal safety once the conflict had been settled. "Should I carry my gun?"

"Definitely. Most men from around here are not happy with the way the war ended, if you get my meaning. There are some who resort to violence of one kind or another when they encounter unionists like us. I'd just keep it quiet about our war experience but be prepared."

"I see." He'd served with honor and pride in defense of his country from those who sought to destroy it. But he could see why Charlie was cautious in a former Confederate state. Like Samuel had advised as well. The fighting had ended but the rebel sentiments hadn't gone away. "Very well. I'll be back tomorrow."

Now that he would have steady income, time to start seriously working on his plan to win back the love of his life and his future.

CHAPTER 8

*H*er mother had some interesting ideas floating about in her head. Lia could only stare at Natalie, blinking slowly. "Did you really say that you think I should sew my own dress for the ball? Me?"

"Why on earth not? You've made other dresses over the years." Natalie folded her hands together on her lap. "Haven't you?"

Rose shook her head, golden curls swishing across her shoulders. "Not that I remember. I should know since I think I've been making her clothes for years."

Natalie cast disbelieving eyes at her oldest daughter. "I was unaware of that fact. I suppose I shouldn't be surprised."

Aster sauntered into the sitting room where the sisters and mother often gathered to work on their sewing. The sunlight flowing through the clear glass windows across the front of the house ensured good visibility of whatever project they were working on during the day. Several comfortable stuffed chairs, each featuring a different needle-pointed floral pattern, were grouped around the room. Each of the sisters had worked on the patterns to create their namesake flowers for the seat coverings. Lia was rather proud of the final result of her magnolia blossom, its creamy petals nestled among forest green leaves. Small wooden tables sat between the chairs, handy for holding the stitching or knitting materials close to hand.

Sinking onto the yellow rose patterned chair near to Lia, Aster surveyed the others with a swift glance. "What shouldn't surprise you, Mother?"

Lia shrugged with a twist of her mouth. "That Rose makes my clothing instead of me doing it myself."

"Oh, that." Aster flicked a hand in the air to dismiss the thought. "Lia cannot be trusted to stitch a dress she wouldn't be embarrassed to wear."

"Thank you, Sister." Lia grimaced with good humor. "I do know my limitations."

"I have no problem making you a ball gown, Lia." Rose crossed her ankles and leaned forward toward Lia. "You know I enjoy sewing and making the outfit suitable to the wearer."

"I appreciate your talents and gladly welcome the idea of you taking care of the gown for me." Lia refrained from biting her lips with an effort. She was nervous about the calico ball but didn't want to let on to just how much. Her sisters wouldn't let her live it down if she did. She longed to change the subject, but she had no hope of doing so since her mother had insisted they discuss plans for the event. Best to simply get it over with so she could do something else and not think about what might happen. "What other details must we settle?"

"Centerpieces for the tables," Aster chimed in. "And garlands to decorate the mantel and columns. I can put something together if that's all right?"

"Would you? Thank you, dear." Natalie nodded enthusiastically with a smile. "You're so creative with decorations and plants."

"She certainly is." Lia agreed with her mother but knew it went deeper than simple creativity. They didn't often discuss the sisters' special talents but they were all aware of them. It was better to not risk anyone outside of the family suspecting their gifts. Even when visitors were not present, they tended to only allude to their talents. "I'd be happy to help you gather whatever you need."

"And I'm happy to have all of you helping me with this quick event planning." Natalie smiled at each of them. "One day you'll need to step into my shoes."

"What? No. That's not possible, Mother." Lia shook her head, shock ricocheting through her chest. Was her mother considering stepping down as the town's matriarch? "You're not quitting, are you?"

Natalie waved a hand in the air. "Not on your life. I enjoy myself far too much to stop with my charity work. But one day..."

"Are you not feeling well?" Rose asked, rising from her seat to cross the room to her mother.

Natalie chuckled and indicated for her to resume her seat on the aster chair with its pale-blue, daisy-like flower motif. "I'm fine. I just plan ahead and part of that planning is teaching you girls how to do what I have been doing for so many years. Now, we also need to discuss who is going to cater the event. Someone in town who can handle a rush order."

Her mother's casual mention of the sisters taking the reins of the charity work for the area made Lia realize just how much Natalie did for the community. She'd been aware of it in a vague sort of way, but she hadn't contemplated the extent of her efforts. Tapping her daughters to carry on her volunteering efforts seemed the natural thing to do. Lia would want to instill the same willingness to give back to the community through volunteer work to her own children one day. She wished she could be closer to her son, but no, she couldn't think about that. She couldn't risk putting his existence out into the universe for fear everything would unravel. Better to focus on what she could do to help with the Christmas Calico Ball plans and try to squash any wayward motherly impulses.

"Perhaps Father will have some suggestions when he returns from town this evening." Aster stood and smoothed her long skirts with both hands. "I need to go start supper or we won't eat until very late."

"Your father will be expecting a hot meal upon his return. I'll come help you." Natalie rose from her chair and followed Aster out of the room.

"Well, now that our planning meeting has obviously come to an end, I'm going outside." She had time to work with one of the younger mares before supper. "I'm heading out to ride Gem in the forest for a little while. She needs to be out away from the barn and the other horses to learn not to be barn sour."

"Be careful, Lia. I've never liked it when you go riding alone."

She dismissed her sister's concern with a flick of her fingers. She'd ridden alone, under a protective word or two, many times without any issues. Today would be no different. "I'll be fine. The war is over so there shouldn't be any soldiers out and about to fret over."

* * *

BRYCE TROTTED along the trail winding through the countryside surrounding his friend's home. The dense forest stretched away on either side of the trail, the trees standing sentinel to the infrequent passersby. He didn't meet anyone else on the stretch of the trail branching out of town leading toward the outlying area where Hopewell nestled up to the forest. The day had been a successful one and he felt light of heart for the first time in many years.

Not only had they secured the ballroom for the upcoming dance, but he'd secured a decent job with adequate income. He couldn't wait to inform Lia of his good fortune and then begin to woo her back to him. He wanted nothing more than to call her his wife and start the family they'd once promised to have together. Before he'd made the mistake of breaking his promise to her. A mistake he deeply regretted and would work hard to make up to her. If she'd let him.

Jet rounded a wide looping curve in the trail and Bryce slowed to a walk when he spotted another rider approaching him. The Palomino was a beauty. Her coloring, a golden body with flaxen mane and tail, striking in the shadows of the forest. The woman riding flowed with the horse's movement such that he could tell she was a natural horse-woman. As if she were one with her mount. The Palomino slowed to a walk as the woman noticed him. The trail was narrow enough that to pass they'd have to negotiate who moved off the trail to allow the other to continue. He'd be a gentleman and do so, of course.

The woman reined to a halt twenty paces away from where Jet stepped off the trail. Her auburn hair was held back in a casual ponytail. After a long moment, she urged her horse into a walk, slowly closing the distance between them. Bryce watched her coming and suddenly recognized her. Magnolia. His Lia. Just the person he most wanted to see, to talk with. What was she doing out in the woods alone?

As she neared, the mare grew agitated. Dancing and jigging instead of calmly walking. Lia kept a firm hand on the reins and talked soothingly to the horse but the mare wasn't listening to her assurances as she drew closer to Jet. He bet the mare was in heat, the way she was acting as she approached his stallion. Jet wouldn't try anything untoward as long as Bryce was on his back, but the mare didn't know that.

"Lia, go back," he called out. "You shouldn't be out here by yourself with that mare."

"She has to learn to behave." Lia pressed the mare forward, keeping her eyes aimed in the direction she intended to continue going.

Suddenly the mare gave a little crow hop of a rear, sending Bryce's heart into his mouth as Lia grabbed mane to stay in the saddle. "Lia, don't. Go back!"

Still she kept urging the mare forward, to walk—or rather jig—past Jet. Bryce signaled his horse to sidle farther off the trail but the mare again reared, this time with more force. Lia grimaced as she focused on getting her mare to cooperate and settle but stayed with the horse as she balked about walking any closer to Jet. She met Bryce's worried gaze. "She trusts me. Just stay quiet and let me work with her for a minute."

"If you're sure…"

Staying quiet as she'd directed proved harder than he'd imagined. Jet stood like the gentle giant Bryce had trained while the other horse pawed and jigged as Lia inched her closer and closer to what the mare obviously perceived as a threat. Then Lia asked her again to proceed but the mare flatly refused, rearing and pawing the air with her front hooves. Lia quickly grabbed for the mane but lost her grip and fell hard onto the ground.

"Lia!" Bryce watched as the mare turned and bolted back the way they'd come. He jumped from the saddle and ran to Lia. "Are you hurt?"

She huffed as she scrambled to her feet, her split skirt brushing her tall boot tops. "You had to mess up my afternoon, didn't you?"

Taken aback by her seething anger, he hesitated to offer his hand. When he did, she shook her head. What was wrong with her? She blamed him? "I didn't do anything to cause your mare to react in such a way."

"You're being here is all it took. You and your big black horse." She swiped her hands across her buttocks to dislodge any leaves or sticks which might have stuck to her clothing in her fall. "Why can't you just go away and leave me alone? Why did you come back, anyway? Just go away."

"We need to talk, Lia. I came back for you." He couldn't let her walk away from him. In fact, she'd need him to give her a ride home after her mare's sudden departure. He grabbed her arm to keep her from walking away in reality. "I'll give you a ride."

She jerked her arm free from his grasp. "You're infuriating. I don't want to ride with you nor talk to you. You've ruined my day with your presence. Now if you don't mind, I need to walk home and see to my horse."

She took several steps before he spotted her limping and rushed after her. He caught hold of her hand and drew her to a stop. Felt her trembling, which made him worry all the more. He whistled for Jet who came trotting over to them. "It's a long walk home from here, Lia. Ride with me. Give me a chance to explain everything to you once and for all."

Surely after she heard his reasoning she'd understand why he'd done what he did. And how much he sincerely wished he'd kept his promise. Looking back on what went wrong provided clarity to what had been a confusing situation to his mind. What was the right thing to do when he was fighting a war and could in all likelihood be killed? So many men died in the war that had just ended recently. It had been only eight months since the surrender, after all. He seriously thought he'd be one of them on more than one occasion, which gave support to his decision to let her go and not try to keep her for himself. Now he could see that she'd been devastated and heartbroken. Because of what he'd done. A huge mistake he needed to mend.

"Why? What is it you expect from me, Bryce?"

"I want us to try again. To start over and rediscover the love we shared, that I hope we can still share. Will you give me the chance to explain?"

She glared at him, glanced at the trail winding away toward her home, then met his gaze and finally nodded once. "I hope whatever you have to say to me is short and to the point."

"I'll try." He clasped both of her hands in his and tugged her to him. "But will you let me tell you just how beautiful you are? How much I missed you and wanted to be with you always?"

"Then why... No. I don't understand."

"I never stopped loving you, Magnolia." He peered into her watery eyes, saw her desire to believe him. Her slightly parted lips beckoned to him, invited him to taste of her. "May I kiss you? Please?"

She closed her eyes and nodded once. So he lowered his head to press his lips to her softness. Relived again the swell of joy at being intimate with her. He pulled her closer, wrapping his arms around her so she couldn't escape until they finished their long kiss. Then he eased back and retook her hands, gave them a squeeze as her lashes lifted and he saw the effect of their shared moment of desire. Rekindling the love they had for each other. He could see it in her eyes. Hope for a future with her flared bright and warmed his soul.

"Come, I'll take you home." He mounted Jet then reached down to help her swing up behind him. "Hold on to me. I don't want you to fall again."

After a pause, her hands grasped each side of his waist. No wrapping her loving arms around him. But a start toward her forgiveness. "The most important thing you need to know, Magnolia, is that my feelings for you have not changed. And that I'm deeply sorry about ending our courtship. It was a stupid mistake, one I deeply regret. I kept the talisman you gave me, whittled it into a magnolia blossom as a constant reminder of you and all you represented. I came back to you, for you, for us. I love you and always will. There. Was that short enough for you?"

She drew in a long breath and her hands tensed on his sides. "Yes. I appreciate you telling me that. Now let's go. Gem will get to the barn and everyone will be frantic about me."

"Please forgive me, Lia." He urged Jet into a trot, and after a few strides Lia's arms wrapped around his waist for a more secure hold on him during the bouncing gait. "I'll do anything to make it up to you. I need you in my life."

"Just ride. I'll think on it but know I can't make any promises. I don't want to talk right now."

Maybe not now, but soon they needed to air out all of her grievances with him so he could lay out a strategy to meet her demands and win her forgiveness. To win her hand in marriage as he'd dreamed of doing for so many years. He'd hold his peace for the moment, but only so he could refine his plan. He'd convince her to give him another chance so they could have the future they'd once dreamed of together. Somehow.

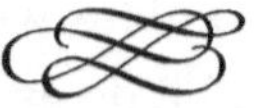

CHAPTER 9

"I think it needs something more…"

Lia lifted her gaze from the scrap of paper she'd been staring at for far too long to look at her mother. "Such as?"

Natalie grimaced as she shrugged lightly. "I simply don't know. Something to really highlight the cause more?"

Rose tapped a finger on the kitchen table several times. "You didn't put in that guests will receive not only a fun evening but also the warm feeling of helping their neighbors during this difficult time."

Lia blinked up at her sister. The ad for the Christmas Calico Ball could only be a few lines. How was she to include all of what Rose spat out? She studied what they'd already agreed on. Then she read it out loud:

"Get your tickets to the Christmas Calico Ball to be held at the Easley Hotel! Dec. twenty-third at eight p.m. Benefit for a new school in Huntsville. See Mr. Hugh Easley to buy your tickets today."

"Mother, do you think Mr. Easley will mind handling the ticket sales for us?" Aster asked, a puzzled frown marring her pretty features. "We should inquire with him first, don't you think?"

"I'll handle him. He is already set up to sell things so I'm sure he'll be happy to oblige my request." Natalie sat back in her chair and folded her arms. "But I still feel like we need something to really make people want to come out to support this cause."

"Could we give them something they'd want to have on Christmas Day?" Rose asked slowly. "A fruitcake perhaps?"

"Which reminds me, we haven't found a caterer yet." Natalie sat up straighter and laid her hands on the table. "We must have food to serve or no one will want to attend."

The back door opened, a breath of rain-scented morning air ushering in Bryce. Lia stilled in her seat, her entire senses overwhelmed by his presence. After their revelatory conversation the day before, she'd been thankful to not see him. His appearance in her kitchen shook her to her toes. The incident that led to her fall echoed in her mind. Embarrassment had made her lash out at Bryce. Irrationally, given his assistance, which just spiked her embarrassment more. With Bryce reappearing in her life, insisting on being part of it again, were the Fates conspiring to reveal her secret? But neither he nor her whole family would guess the truth of her son and who his real father might be. Would they?

"What are you lovely ladies planning to cater?" Bryce asked, pulling the door shut with a soft *thud*.

"The Calico Ball for Christmas. You know, the one at the Easley later this month?" Natalie folded her hands in her lap. "You were there when we arranged the venue."

"Yes, I recall. I am delighted to have the opportunity to dance again. It's been a long time." Bryce perused the faces around the table, ending with a long look shared with Lia. "I hope you will save me a dance."

The back door opened again, and Samuel peeked in before stepping inside. "There you are, Bryce. Did you come for a snack, too?"

"No, I came to see how Lia is feeling today after her fall yesterday." Bryce glanced at Lia as he finished his statement. "I hope you're not too sore?"

"I am perfectly fine, thank you." She wouldn't admit to the bruise on her hip nor the pain in her leg from the rock she'd landed on. She'd recover in a few days and nobody would be the wiser. She refused to think more about the fall and the ensuing embarrassment she'd felt. She'd do what she always did and focus on what she could control and not on the past.

"I'm relieved to hear that." Bryce strode over to the stone fireplace, holding out his hands to warm them by the crackling fire. "What are you ladies working on?"

"The ad for tickets to the ball." Aster stood and moved to the free-standing cedar pantry, pulling open the door. "Sam, did you want your usual snack?"

"You know I do." Samuel walked around the group at the table to join his sister in front of the treasured piece of furniture Grandfather Merryweather had built many years ago. "I love Mother's sugar cookies. They really hit the spot."

Aster handed him a stack of the delicate cookies and he bit into one immediately. "You're too much, Sam. Go on with you."

Lia watched her brother devour his snack in short order. Mother's cookies always melted in her mouth, they were so light and buttery. The recipe only existed in her mother's brain, so she was the only baker who could make them. But she made a lot of them when she did bake cookies once a week in order to keep Samuel, as well as the younger boys, happy. A steady supply occupied one shelf of the pantry so everyone knew where to find them. One of many happy traditions they shared.

"I'm heading into the paper later today if you want me to take that ad with me." Sam pushed the last piece of cookie into his mouth and wiped his fingers on his pants leg. "I mean, we need to get it advertised soon, right?"

"Yes, but it still needs something we haven't figured out yet." Natalie sighed as she looked down at the paper again. "What's missing?"

Bryce moved around to stand beside Lia as he leaned over the table to read the ad himself. "You said it as I walked in. You need to let folks know who is catering the event so they can get excited about the refreshments."

He was far too close for her composure. Lia held herself very still.

No part of her would bump into him. Touching him, despite how close he stood, was out of the question. Despite his sleeve nearly brushing the back of her hand. She felt her face flush as she recalled hugging him the day before after the mind-blowing kiss they'd shared. She couldn't risk such a reaction in front of her family. She slowly pulled her hands into her lap as she carefully turned to look up at him. "But we don't know who will be catering."

"You'll want someone who will do a fabulous array of foods and beverages to make the tickets attractive." Samuel cocked his head to one side as he looked around. "What about Ernest Dentler on Eustis Street? He's pretty popular. I imagine he'd jump at the chance to give back to the community that has kept him in business."

Lia had seen his advertisements in the *Huntsville Advocate* over the years. He'd started his confectionary and bakery years before the war and had managed to keep it open despite the shortages and hardships during the fighting. He offered a wide variety of fine French candies, cakes both plain and ornamented, crackers of all kinds, nuts, raisins and fruits, too. He took orders for balls, weddings, and other large events in the city and surrounding areas as well, so Samuel had offered a good suggestion.

"That's a fine idea. We'll need to go see him to determine his availability." Natalie pushed back her chair and stood. "It looks like I'll need to go to town tomorrow to make some arrangements. Anything else I need to do?"

"I'll need fabric to make the gowns," Rose said, also standing. "It will take some time to cut out and stitch together as well as do any finishing we want."

"Remember to keep them pretty but rather plain so that the ladies who receive them after the event will not feel awkward wearing them during the day."

"I will, Mother." Rose pushed her chair back in and rested her hands on its back. "Lia should go with you to pick out the cloth she wants to wear. I'll stay here and work on Aster's gown, the one she wanted remade into something nicer."

"Yes, it's one of my newer dresses but the color simply looks awful on me," Aster explained. "I think it will be perfect with a few tweaks here and there for someone else to wear."

Lia studied the text on the page. "I think if we want to get this ad in the paper as soon as possible, then we'll need to leave off who is catering and hope people will care more about the cause than the caterer."

"Once you're satisfied, I'd be happy to take care of placing the ad and having the tickets printed," Samuel offered.

"Thank you, Son. So tomorrow, Lia and I will be going to town to ask Mr. Easley about his role selling tickets, Mr. Dentler to see if he is willing to do the catering, and to buy fabric for Lia's gown. Once we settle all of that, then Samuel will place the ad and get the tickets. We're making good progress. Thank you all for pitching in to help pull this together so quickly."

"I'm happy to help anyway that I can, too." Bryce laid a gentle hand on Lia's shoulder, drawing her reluctant attention. "You only need to ask."

Funny how he was so willing to be in her life now when he'd eschewed the opportunity during the war. He'd explained his reasoning but his abandonment still stung. He'd asked her to reserve a dance for him, which meant he intended to be at the ball. She wouldn't be able to avoid him no matter which way she turned. At home, or in town. With her family or in public. How utterly disconcerting.

"That's very kind of you, Bryce." Natalie smiled sweetly at him. "I'll let you know."

Lia remained silent as the group dispersed. She had nothing to add that wouldn't sound petty and unkind. After everyone had left, she heaved a sigh of relief. Then she had an awful thought: what would transpire between Bryce and Dylan if both attended the ball?

* * *

FROST GLISTENED on the rooftops and grass the next morning as Bryce arrived at the depot to report for his first day on the job. He tied Jet to the hitching rail out front and went inside the busy building. The large waiting area was crammed with low benches stretching across the floor, passengers seated at various spots. In the back he could see baggage and boxes piled and waiting. The schedule board by the ticket booth told him no trains were due for another hour. Despite the recent war, the trains had managed to stay busy with people and products. He crossed the wood floorboards to the agent's office in the left rear corner of the depot.

"I'm looking for Mr. Smythe. Is he here?"

"Is he expecting you?" An elderly man wearing a black vest over a white shirt and black trousers peered at him from the desk in the corner of the small office. He pushed back from the desk and stood, approaching Bryce.

"Yes, I'm the new engineer he hired yesterday. Bryce Day."

"Ah, yes. Go on through that door and up the steps to the second floor. That's where his office is."

He pointed to a closed door at the rear of the office so Bryce thanked him and went through the door. He found a set of steps that led up and quickly mounted them, taking them two at a time to burn off some nervous energy. At the second floor, he stepped into a large, dark-wood-floored area with several rooms. Taking a guess, he strode into the largest of the rooms to find it crammed with a large table surrounded by chairs in the center with desks positioned in front of the large paned windows to either side of the large fireplace at one end, and a couple of others at the opposite end. A heavy door stood ajar in the corner but Bryce couldn't see where it led from the entrance to the room. Seated at the desk by the small door, he quickly spotted the man he was searching for.

"Good day, sir. Reporting for duty." Bryce hesitated at the doorway, unsure whether he'd be welcome inside the office.

"Come in. Glad you're here." Charles stood and came around the desk by the open door to shake Bryce's hand. "But we're not in the army anymore. Just call me Charlie and leave it at that. The less we bring up the late war the better."

"Yes, sir." At his new boss's arched brow, Bryce corrected himself. "Charlie. What is all this?"

"You're standing in the headquarters of the Memphis and Charleston. I've set you up with a desk on the other side of the hallway with the other lower ranked employees. All I ask is that you stay out of the paymaster's closet where we keep the valuables." He waved to the open door which turned out to actually be a vault door, made from thick metal and featuring a hefty locking mechanism. "The paymaster will have your neck if he catches you or anyone else in there. Ready to get to work?"

Bryce dragged his attention back to Charlie. "Yes. What do you want me to do first?"

"I need your engineering experience most. There's a trestle east of town that is a bit questionable as to its structure. How much it will hold, which worries some of the railroad conductors enough they don't want to drive a long, heavy cargo train over it. I want you to assess its current weight maximum and suggest ways to improve it so the conductors are satisfied it will hold their fully loaded trains. Can you do that for me?"

"Of course. Just tell me which one and I'll ride out and inspect it."

"I'll show you. Let me grab my hat." Charlie lifted his wide-brimmed hat off the coat stand by the door and tapped it on his head. "Let's go."

The two men rode for nearly an hour before Charlie reined to a halt and pointed ahead. "That one up there. See how some of the boards look like they'll fall at any minute?"

Bryce nodded as his trained eyes scanned the aging trestle spanning a wide stream. Not too high to work on but it would require wading into the water to reach the middle portion. Several of the wooden boards supporting the tracks hung such that he doubted they were being held in place by more than one nail at either end. Others split down the middle with part about to drop. In fact, it looked much like it had been hastily rebuilt so that it wasn't going to last much longer. He'd helped rebuild many such bridges while in the army. But this one hadn't been done right. No wonder the conductors refused to bring heavy loads across it. The resulting delay in receiving manufactured goods from up north and the east only added to the shortages the area experienced from disruption during the war and the recent drought. That would impact Mrs. Merryweather's ball, too. He wasn't going to let that happen.

"It might need to be rebuilt entirely. Let's get closer." Bryce urged Jet forward until they reached the base of the low bridge.

He dismounted and then grabbed hold of one of the dangling boards and pulled. The wood not only came away far too easily but it also crumbled into pieces from dry rot. He spun around to meet Charlie's horrified expression, dusting his hands off as he walked back to remount.

"You need to close this until we can rebuild it entirely. It's not safe as it is." The image of a passenger train crashing through the trestle into the water below had him shaking his head. "Immediately. I'll get to work designing its replacement and we can have it back up and safe again in a couple weeks."

"What do we do in the meantime with the trains scheduled to come through here?" Charlie rubbed a hand on the injured thigh. "There are several every day with people and products not only trying to reach Huntsville but points west."

"You'll need to have trains operate on either side until we're done." Bryce continued studying the crumbling structure, concern for the safety of all uppermost in his mind. "We can put in a temporary pontoon bridge to let people walk across and board a different train on the other side and we'll just have to have some men to unload the cargo and carry it over as well. Like they're doing in Decatur until they can finish rebuilding that much larger bridge."

Charlie gripped both sides of his forehead with one large hand. "I'm getting a headache."

"You know I'm right." Bryce heard a distant rumble and glanced to the dark skies.

"Yes, I know." Charlie let out an exasperated sigh. "Fine. Let's get back to town so I can send out a telegram and you can start planning the replacement. And before that storm hits. There's absolutely no time to waste."

"I agree. You know, this may actually help my hostess' efforts to help the town as well." Bryce swung up into the saddle and the two men started back to town. "In fact, you might consider sponsoring some aspect of the event."

"What event?" Charlie wore a heavy frown on his face but he seemed genuinely interested.

"Mrs. Merryweather is planning a Christmas Calico Ball for Christmas Eve Eve. You could promote the railroad and increase its popularity by funding something, like the catering perhaps or maybe some party favors."

"I do like the way you think, my friend." Charlie's frown cleared a bit as he nodded. "I'd be happy to see what we could help with."

"I'll let her know when I get home this evening. She'll be very pleased."

"You won't be getting home early, that's for sure. I want those plans on my desk by this afternoon, so we can determine what we'll need to rebuild that trestle. And fast."

Bryce was already figuring out how he'd redesign the failing trestle with one more sturdy and sound. He pictured crossed boards of wood along with the framing to create the best foundation for the tracks on top. Calculating the exact length needed would require a return trip with a measuring rope but he could give his boss an estimate that would likely be close to exact. After all, he'd been doing this type of design work for years. Meshing the design with the requirements for timber and nails proved both challenging and fun. But the "fast" comment could be a problem. To build it right would take time.

"How many hands will you hire to get the work done?" Bryce asked as they turned onto Church Street and the depot.

"As many as you need. Four?"

"If you want this done in a month, that would be enough. But if you want this done in weeks, then I'd double that number and make sure they are experienced so we don't have to waste time training them."

"I'll start on that as soon as I send that telegram. Follow me and I'll show you where to put your horse."

"Good. I don't like leaving him tied up all day." Bryce followed

Charlie across the street to the stable adjacent to the neighboring hotel just as the rain started falling in earnest.

They dismounted and waited for the stable lad to emerge to take the reins. Then they strode back across the street, water sluicing off their hats and down their backs, and through the rear door into the depot which was bustling with passengers waiting for their train to arrive. A train which might not arrive after all, or at least not in the way they'd hoped. But the inconvenience was far better than risking a catastrophe.

Bryce removed his dripping hat and held it at his side. "Point me to my desk and I'll get started."

They hurried up the back steps to the second floor and Charlie led him into a smaller office across the hall.

"Here you go. Hang your coat and hat on a peg. I've got you a desk set up in the corner by the window." Charlie chuckled as he led the way into the room. "You'll have plenty of light and I'll be able to keep an eye on you as I come and go."

"Like old times, then." Bryce shook his head. "You supervising my excellent work."

Charlie guffawed. "If you say so. Have a go at those plans. I'll send that telegram now and tell the conductors about the plan for the next undetermined amount of time. They won't be pleased."

"They'll be uninjured and alive though." Bryce pulled out the chair and sat down, opening the drawers of the desk to inventory its contents.

"Good point." Charlie sighed as he gripped the doorframe. "I just wish there were another way."

"I'll get to work and let you know how long I think this will take by the end of the day." Bryce nodded at his boss. "You're doing the right thing even though it's difficult."

"I hope so." Charlie pointed to Bryce's desk. "Now get to work. If you need anything else, ask me when I get back. I want you to be operating at peak efficiency on this project."

After Charlie left, Bryce found several pads of paper in the right-hand drawer and several pens and pencils in the center one. Behind the pencil tray, he found a ruler and a protractor. Charlie really had set him up well so he could begin designing straight away. He bent his head and put pencil to paper.

CHAPTER 10

After a light lunch of cold chicken on a warm biscuit, Lia drove her mother in the covered carriage pulled by a pair of her young geldings into Huntsville. She had high hopes for the pair to make a fine team for carriage work or perhaps a coach if they muscled up a bit more as they matured. She'd dressed up the black carriage with a big red bow on the front in honor of the season, a touch which made people smile and wave as they passed. The dirt streets showed where the light rain slowly turned dust to mud. The greener of the two horses shied at a flapping cloak as a passerby hurried past. She settled the pair with firm hands on the reins and a quiet word, pleased as they settled once more into an easy rhythm.

"Where to first, Mother?" Lia turned the carriage onto Clinton and slowed to a walk.

"Mr. Dentler. He'll need the most time to prepare a delicious feast for the gathering."

Lia halted the carriage in front of the confectioner's shop. They went inside, inhaling the glorious aromas of fresh bread, sweet candies, and cinnamon. Only one other customer, an older woman Lia didn't recognize, shopped for goodies. Natalie strode briskly up to Mr. Dentler with a huge smile on her face. Ernest Dentler, for his part, looked every bit the baker he was. A splattered and floured apron wrapped around his girth, and he wore a white chef's hat to signal without any doubt his role in the bakery.

Lia watched, amazed, as her mother transformed from the reserved yet vivacious woman she knew to one gregarious and outgoing. How did she manage to pull on a different persona so easily? To assume the role necessary to persuade another to do as she desired. What a unique and useful talent to have. When the day eventually arrived that Lia and her sisters stepped into her role, then how would they achieve the ends their mother had so easily? A perplexing question.

Natalie extended her hand to the shopkeeper. "Mr. Dentler, how lovely to see you again. How is Wilhelmina faring after her bout with illness?"

Mr. Dentler grasped her fingers briefly, with a nod of appreciation. "Mrs. Merryweather, thank you for asking. She's up and about again, thank goodness. Now, what can I help you ladies with on this rainy afternoon?"

"I understand you cater balls and such?" Natalie clasped her soft purse in front of her with both hands. "Is that true?"

"Yes, indeed." Ernest's eyes lit up at the prospect of a large order. "Are you sponsoring a ball?"

"I am." She elaborated on the charity and the need to raise money to build a new school. "Would you be available to cater it for me?"

"When?"

"Christmas Eve Eve, at the Easley. I realize it's short notice, only eleven days from now, but surely you can help with this charity ball to encourage everyone to come out for some fun and to help their neighbors over the holidays. Can't you?" She batted her eyes at him slowly. Steadily wearing him down with her forceful personality, her will. And a feather touch of her magic.

"Please, Mr. Dentler," Lia added. "You've come highly recommended."

Ernest straightened his spine and smiled at the pair of women. "Indeed? Well, then of course we must satisfy the hungry populace and give them a feast for the history books. I'll even be generous and do it for my cost."

"Oh, thank you, sir!" Natalie laid a hand on his upper arm for a second. "I'll expect your proposed menu tomorrow. And make it festive, please. Farewell, Mr. Dentler. Come, Magnolia." Natalie spun about and hurried toward the door. "Come, dear, we haven't much time."

Blinking in surprise, Lia shrugged at the baker and quickly followed her mother outside and into the carriage. No one ever said no to her mother. She wasn't ugly about how she made her requests and demands. Effective, yes. Definitely. But a consummate Southern lady with her manners and demeanor.

"Now for Mr. Easley." Natalie settled back in her seat, dripping water on the floor of the vehicle. "He shouldn't be any problem either."

"I'm sure you're right." Lia chuckled then clucked to the horses.

Within a few minutes they'd crossed the center of town and parked at the livery for the hotel. Thunder boomed above as they scurried inside, laughing apologetically as puddles of rainwater formed on the tiled floor of the foyer. The doorman handed them each a small towel to blot their faces and hands while another man quickly mopped up the water.

"My dear Mrs. Merryweather, what are you doing out on a day like this?" Margaret hurried up to stand by Natalie. "And good day to you, Miss Merryweather."

Lia inclined her head in response to the greeting but didn't interrupt the ensuing conversation between the two older women. She knew her place and it wasn't to be in the middle between the two more important matriarchs of town.

"Mrs. Easley, how fare you?" Natalie asked, recovering her composure swiftly despite the rain glistening on her dark-red cloak.

"Oh, well enough I'm sure." Margaret shrugged lightly in her pretty, medium-blue cotton dress with a small motif pattern, puffed sleeves, and a ruffled bodice. "And Magnolia, how is the little one faring?"

Lia stiffened as she struggled to remain calm. She did not want to talk about her son. Especially not with the midwife who helped tend him when he'd become ill upon returning to Hopewell. Not that his existence was a secret. She drew a calming breath, reassured by recalling the woman didn't know all the facts. Memories of the questions asked during the boy's treatment echoed in her mind as she pasted a smile on her lips. The woman's curiosity was as great as her girth. She'd wanted to know too much about the child, where it had come from, its parents. Questions she couldn't answer honestly but with the pat replies agreed to with Samuel and Laura. Their explanation of his arrival had been readily accepted by her family but not so much by the midwife.

Her palms dampened within her gloves as memories long buried surfaced of when she'd been in the throes of labor. Of the contraction pangs, arriving in shorter and shorter intervals. She hadn't realized what she was feeling at first but Laura had recognized the signs. The pain increased with the frequency until she couldn't contain her screams. Mercifully, birthing the child didn't take long, only half a day instead of the horrific lengths she'd heard tales of. A month after he was born, the midwife at Laura's sister's place in the mountains of Tennessee had declared Lia and the boy able to travel and so they'd returned to Alabama.

Only it wasn't a week before Travis came down with a fever and rash. Margaret was summoned post-haste to attend to him and she quickly took charge. Lia's mother of course came also to see her friend and to be available to assist if needed. Between moments of distress over the child's condition, Margaret chatted about who did the boy look like, and did he have the same hair color as the father or mother. Lia opened her mouth to say it was none of her business, but then Laura had asserted that she and Samuel were the parents, couldn't the midwife see the likeness? That shut the midwife up but she didn't look like she believed the claim of parentage. Finally, her mother had taken Mrs. Easely aside and then the midwife blessedly stopped asking questions.

"He's well, thank you. But we've come to ask your husband a

favor." Lia swiftly changed the subject away from her son to the purpose of their visit before the midwife said more that could endanger the secret Lia kept. One she sensed wouldn't remain a secret much longer.

Natalie glanced sharply at Lia before forcing a calm regard aimed at the other woman. Did she suspect there was more to the story than what Lia had told her? She should probably have a conversation about it with her mother. Surely she'd understand and not reject her out of hand. But why? No good would come of such a revelation.

"Oh? Then let us go find the good man." Margaret looked at Lia with a question in her eyes but thankfully she didn't ask it.

Instead, she led them across the foyer to the office behind the registration desk. Lia worked on gathering her composure close as she followed the other women. Inside, Mr. Easley sat behind an immense carved wood desk stacked with files and papers, and littered with several pens and clips.

"Mr. Easley, you have visitors," Margaret announced.

He glanced up at his wife and then at Natalie and Lia. "Ladies, welcome. What can I do for you?"

Lia's heart still raced in her chest but relief from her near miss soon helped to slow its pace. She let her gaze sweep around the room, noting the oil paintings of various important people like George Washington and John Adams gracing the walls. Two padded chairs flanked the desk for guests to use. A good host, he'd ensured he had several lamps and candelabras lit to provide a welcoming environment and the light he needed to do his work.

"Mr. Easley, would you please be in charge of ticket sales for the Christmas Calico Ball? I trust your ability to adequately handle such a task." Natalie smiled at the man, clasping her cloak around her as she waited for his reply.

"Sell tickets? Well..." Hugh rubbed a hand over his jaw for a moment as he regarded Natalie with a serious expression. "I don't know whether I'm the right person for the job."

Natalie raised her brows as she widened her smile. "Why of course you are, sir. You are already set up to take money and keep it safe." She eased around to the side of the desk. "Please? For me?"

"Honestly, Hugh, don't tease the lady so." Margaret chuckled at her surprised husband's expression. "You've already said you wanted to help."

"I did." Hugh nodded as he shrugged. "So then, I will do it, Mrs. Merryweather."

Her mother had the entire town wrapped around her pinky. That was the bald-faced truth. All she had to do was pay them a compliment and ask for their help and *voila*. She got her way. If only Lia enjoyed the same level of respect or dignity her mother did. She couldn't rely upon her reputation to pave her way to easy acceptance and respect.

"Thank you, kind sir! I deeply appreciate your assistance. I'll have my son bring the tickets around as soon as he gets them printed." Natalie tapped her hand on the desktop before turning to Lia. "Come, daughter, we have one more stop to make."

"In this weather?" Hugh shook his head. "You should head for home. I can hear the thunder now."

Natalie waved away his concern. "I can't let a little storm interfere with my schedule. Thank you again, sir. Come, Lia."

Lia smiled at the couple before following her mother out of the office and back across the large foyer to the front doors of the hotel. The doorman swiftly opened the door to allow them back onto the street. As they hesitated before making a dash for their vehicle, Lia turned to her mother. "You were quite brusque with him, weren't you?"

"Time is wasting. I didn't want to dither with him about such a simple request." Natalie glanced away and then settled her gaze on Lia. "I don't understand why you didn't want to say more to Mrs. Easley about Travis. Why were you so brusque with her?"

Lia swallowed, fear of discovery uppermost in her mind. She hadn't told her mother the truth. Only two others actually knew that Bryce was the father of her son. Everyone else thought, because she'd told them, that he was Laura and Samuel's son. Not the truth that she and Bryce had lovingly created the child. And that she'd never told him about being with child let alone he had a son. Now, it was too late to change any of it without seriously affecting her son's future.

"She just seemed rather nosey today." Lia held her breath, hoping against hope her mother would let the matter drop. "Shall we go to Wilson & Company to choose the fabric for my ball gown?"

"Margaret Easley has a right to inquire about her patients." Her mother studied her for a long awkward moment. "Or is there something else you're not telling me?"

Lia swallowed hard at the stern look in her mother's eyes. "Whatever do you mean?"

"The truth always emerges whether you want it to or not, my dear." Natalie pressed her lips together as she contemplated her daughter for a long moment. "One day, you'll have to confess your secrets one way or another."

A cluster of men in overcoats and hats brushed past them where they stood under shelter for a minute or two. Lia caught a look from one of the men, as if he was curious about their conversation. "This isn't the place to have this exchange. I'm going to the carriage."

Without waiting for her mother, Lia made sure the way was clear and then stepped into the street to hurry back to their waiting carriage. She stepped up to the seat under the protection of a roof, the vehicle rocking as her mother followed closely behind. Once she was settled, Lia lifted the reins.

Clucking to the horses, Lia steered them down the street and back to the town square. "I hear what you're saying, Mother. I do. But right now I can't say any more about what is on my heart." She stopped the vehicle and looked at her mother. "Let's just concentrate on getting ready for this ball, alright?"

"Alright. You know you can speak with me about anything that is troubling you. I love you and want to see you happy." Her mother gave her a brief one-armed hug. "Now let's go find the perfect material for your dress."

Lia followed her mother out of the carriage and back into the rain, pushing the conversation as far out of her thoughts as she could. She shivered as the temperature dropped, turning the cold rain into a mix of sleet and snow. She hurried after her mother to the warmth of the store. All she wanted to think about was the pattern and color of fabric. She didn't want to even *think* about the consequences of actually telling the truth to anyone about her son's parentage. Not now. Not ever.

* * *

WHEN BRYCE finally arrived back at Sam's house, it was in a cold onslaught of sleet and snow from the sudden cold snap. He stabled Jet, making sure he had some hot mash and a good rub down. The boys were out front of the house, trying to catch snowflakes on their tongues, the dogs frisking about in the flurry of flakes. He waved to them, then quickly strode inside the hospital to warm himself. Odd, that. Staying in the hospital ward again. It wasn't too uncomfortable either. As long as he kept the sweet memories of his time with Lia at bay. Instead he focused on the facts and figures and designs floating through his brain, still wrangling with the best replacement for the trestle. But Charlie seemed confident in Bryce's ability to craft something durable and affordable. A tall order with a short time to accomplish it.

The large room where he slept held four beds, one in each corner with a table and chair between. One window looked out the back of the building toward the main house and the woods beyond. A fireplace in the front wall was open to the examination room at the front, serving to warm the small building with its glowing aromatic flames. The pine boards used in building it still gave off a slight new wood scent. He pulled off his hat, outer coat, and gloves and tossed them aside. He moved to the fire to warm his hands as he pondered his next steps.

Knowing he had steady income spurred Bryce to want to start his own household, his own family. If he had his way, he'd do so with the love and help of Magnolia Merryweather. Just like they'd once planned before everything fell apart during the war. Before he'd made the biggest mistake of his life. Well, he'd have to clean it up and soon.

He turned away from the warmth of the fire to cross to his cot and sank down on it. Unbidden, the image of Lia coming toward him in only her shift, a hesitant smile on her lovely lips made him still. She'd been so sweet and willing and so unsure of herself. He'd made gentle but passionate love with her because of the love they shared. The belief in a future that he nixed in the bud after making promises of the heart. Promises to always love her and be faithful to her. Promises he'd kept even though he'd stupidly, idiotically told her to forget him. He raked his fingers through his hair and cursed out loud.

The more he pondered his course of action the more he realized how strong his feelings for Lia remained. Despite the length of time they'd been apart, he'd never let go of the dream of holding her close, of sharing a life with her. He could envision the wealth of children they'd have once they married. Married. He was so certain of that eventuality even though she'd been resisting his presence. If Sam was correct, her resistance wasn't due to lack of love and caring for him but more an uncertainty as to whether she could trust him to not break her heart again. Whether she could rely upon him to love and support her in return. He merely needed to convince her of his sincerity and the depth of his feelings for her.

In fact, there was no time like the present.

He put his coat and hat back on and went outside, shoving his hands into his pockets as he did. He glanced at the barn but he knew Lia wasn't there. So he crossed the yard to knock on her door. Stamping his feet to both knock off the light snow and to warm his feet, he waited on the covered porch as footfalls sounded inside. In a moment, Lia pulled the door open and motioned for him to enter, surprise lighting her eyes.

"It's freezing out there. Come inside." She stepped back but he shook his head.

"No, come out with me for a walk in the snow. I want to talk and not with anyone else listening. Is that all right?"

She hesitated, scanning the yard with the snow falling lightly onto every surface. Then she stared at the magnolias, her drifting gaze stilling for several seconds. "Let me get my cloak."

Lia disappeared inside only to return in a flash swaddled in cloak and hat and mittens. "Let's go."

He helped her down the slick steps and they strolled toward the forest, her hand in his possessive clasp. How should he start? He had one burning question but was reluctant to baldly ask it. He needed to ease into the discussion with more subtlety and care. She'd run away if he presented his desperate desire to be with her. He must frame his thoughts in proper style and order so she'd fathom his need for her. Indeed, he'd make her see how sincere his desire was to court her, to love and adore her. Forever.

As they turned at the back fence, he drew her to a halt. Snow glistened on the leaves of the trees, on the fence boards, and sparkled on the grassy expanse. "Isn't it beautiful?"

"And cold." She hugged herself, pulling her hand free from his grasp. "We should keep moving so we don't freeze in place."

He chuckled as he took hold of her arm to steady her and to satisfy his compulsion to touch her. To be with her. "How I've missed your sense of humor."

She cast a quick glance up at his face. Her eyes lit with merriment as she studied him. "I've missed you, to be honest."

Hope warmed his chest as he smiled at her. "I haven't seen you much of late. Have you been avoiding me?"

She glanced away with a sharp exhale of air. Then met his gaze with damp eyes. "You noticed."

"I notice everything about you, sweetheart. My feelings for you never wavered." He lifted her chin with his fingers so he could see her pretty features more clearly. "Never."

"It's too late for us, Bryce. Don't you realize that?" She pulled free of his hand and looked away, then started pacing toward the pair of magnolia trees.

He caught up to her, taking her arm again. He couldn't help himself. He needed her. She must understand just how much. As they neared the magnolias, he vividly recalled their first kiss standing next to them. She'd been so eager, so pliant, so loving. When their lips touched, he'd known she was the woman for him. Everything about her called to him. Her sense of humor. Her intellect. Her compassion. But then to experience the feel of her and the impact to his entire being as a result, just confirmed his instinctual need for her. His never-ending love for her.

He guided her to the magnolias and pulled her around to face him. "Lia, my love, I want to ask you…"

"Bryce." She tossed her head once, the caution in her tone filling him with anxiety.

"Lia, Samuel told me you probably still have feelings for me. Is that right?"

She gasped as her eyes widened. "He shouldn't have told you that."

He hesitated, detecting her reluctance in her stance and her voice. Time to change the subject to another topic. But he couldn't live with himself if he didn't tell her how he felt about her. If he didn't ask her whether they even had a chance of reviving the passion for each other they once shared. If it made her happy to not be together, a thought that sent a shaft of pain through his core, then he'd walk away. He'd die inside but he'd do it. For her. He'd do anything for her.

"Lia, do you think that—"

The boys blasted past where he stood with Lia's hands in his. Pushing through them. Pushing them apart. She staggered backwards and sat down abruptly in the snow. Bryce caught his balance with a flung curse at the rambunctious rascals.

"Watch out where you're running, boys!" He hurried over to offer a hand to Lia, who accepted his help with a wince. "Are you alright?"

Concern flooded through his heart at the surprise and shock on her face. He pulled her to her feet and steadied her with hands on her shoulders for a moment.

She swiped at her backside with both hands, brushing away the remaining snowflakes. "I think so."

"I'm relieved to hear as much. Those boys…"

A shadow passed over the ground near them as a horse appeared with a man in the saddle. The man got off the horse to rush toward

Lia. "I saw what happened. My dear, please tell me you're not injured?"

Startled by his sudden appearance, Bryce blinked as he assessed the other man. The real estate agent. Dylan Blackwater. The man who wanted his girl. Having another man who was tall, dark haired, and good looking to boot who challenged Bryce in height and muscle made his hackles raise. The man was worse than a plugged nickel, showing up when not wanted.

Bryce quickly sidled up to Lia and wrapped a supportive arm around her waist. "And how can we help you?"

Dylan stopped midstride on his way toward Lia to confront Bryce's challenge. "I came to see Miss Merryweather." He took a step closer and Bryce glared at him. "This doesn't concern you, sir. If you'll excuse us?"

"Whatever you have to say to Magnolia you can say to me as well." Bryce didn't look away from the other man, silently warning him off. "We're very close."

Dylan lifted his chin to look down his nose at Bryce. "Is that so? Well, I am 'close' to Miss Magnolia as well. In fact, she's considering my request to wait upon her." He glanced at her for her confirmation.

Bryce held his breath the longer it took for her to respond. He stood there staring at her, hoping for her to reinforce his claim to the other man. That she was not interested in Blackwater but in him. Prayed for the hope that they could in fact explore and renew their relationship with an eye to a future shared.

Lia glanced first at Bryce and then at Dylan then shook her head. "Now, now. There's no need to be so antagonistic. We're all friends here. I don't recall agreeing to either of you courting me, so you have no right to be upset. Now if you'll excuse me, I'm cold and wet so I'm going inside. Good night."

She spun without waiting for Bryce to escort her, picking her way across the snowy yard and on inside her home. Bryce rounded on the other man, ready to tell him more about how inappropriate his actions were. Then he ducked the punch thrown at his jaw. He jumped back out of reach as another fist whooshed past his ear. Then he lunged at the man, knocking him backwards into the snow to straddle him and punch him in the mouth.

"Get off me!"

"Only if you get out of here once and for all." Bryce pinned the man's shoulders to the ground. "Agreed?"

A growl emanated from somewhere deep inside Dylan's throat. "Hmph."

"I'll take that as yes." He rocked back and grabbed the shoulders of the surcoat in both hands, bringing him up to a standing position with him. Then spun him around and shoved him toward his horse.

Dylan staggered over to grab the saddle and haul himself up. Grabbing the reins, he glared at Bryce. "Don't think this is over. It isn't. Not by a long shot."

"Yes, it is." Bryce propped his fists on his hips and lowered his darkest most aggressive look at his rival. "Now git."

He watched the man wheel his horse about and gallop away. He'd messed up with Lia. Again. He'd made a damn enemy. He'd engaged in violence. He sighed and started walking back to his bunk. What next?

CHAPTER 11

The fabric flowed over Lia's head as she stood on the low box in the center of the sisters' bedroom. The swish and rustle of the smooth forest-green poplin settling around her hips and ankles elevated her mood. Or perhaps Rose's unique touch had been sewn into the seams of the gown. She marveled at the imitation Valencia white lace trim with its delicate flower pattern edging the bodice and sleeves. Such a beautiful touch her sister had added.

"You've done wonders in such a short span of time." Lia caught Rose's attention with a smile. "You're so talented."

Rose examined the fit, tugging here and smoothing there, as she moved around her model. "You're easy to sew for with your lithesome figure. Plus…" She paused to lean closer to examine the stitching at the back of the waist. Then straightened with her hands on her hips as she peered at Lia. "I know you and what you like. Now, do you think we should add some ribbon or perhaps some small bows around the collar?"

"I think it's perfect the way it is." Lia grabbed the sides of the billowing skirts and swung them back and forth for the sheer pleasure of hearing the fabric rustle. "And whoever receives it after the ball will likely feel just as happy wearing it as I do at this very moment."

"That's the hope." Rose dropped her hands to clasp in front of her. "You'll probably have a full dance card now that so many eligible men have returned to town. Like your Mr. Day."

Lia let the skirts fall back into place as she sobered. "He's not mine."

"He could be. I think he wants to be yours unless looks and actions deceive."

"I don't know that I want him to be, but I believe you're right in your perception of his intent."

He'd said as much on more than one occasion despite her best efforts to dissuade his attentions. She simply couldn't risk the dangers inherent in the idea of him courting her, learning more about what had transpired while he was in the cavalry and away from home. Away from her.

"Why not resume your earlier courtship now that the war is over and he's safe and sound. And home." Rose gripped Lia's upper arms as she searched her eyes. "I think you still care for him. Don't you?"

Lia swallowed her denial, knowing that would be telling another lie. One was too much to bear. She recalled her mother's admonition about eventually telling the truth. Would she feel embarrassment or relief if such a time ever arrived? A bit of each most likely. Relief might actually win out though, given how guilty she felt hiding the truth from everyone.

"Is that enough? Just because I still have feelings for him, is that enough to warrant risking my heart all over again?"

"I believe so. Hold still. I want to adjust the fall of the bustle." Rose pulled Lia in for a brief hug, close to the gentle scent of her signature lavender, and then released her. She turned away to her sewing box to retrieve her pin cushion. "What about that other fella, the one who came to buy a horse?"

A quiver shook Lia's composure at the thought of Dylan Blackwater. The man moved with such panther strides, smooth and confident. Some might consider him even more handsome than Bryce, with Dylan's height and breadth but also devastatingly beautiful blue eyes. His physique, tall and slender, made him look so regal in the saddle as he moved easily with the horse's gaits. Pretty is as pretty does, but she didn't have any real feelings for the man. Not like what she felt for Bryce. Her heart fluttered as she realized what she'd just admitted to herself.

She had been resisting the idea that they could start up their previous relationship so easily. But why not? It made so much sense. She liked him. He liked her. They'd had something very honest and special once. She wanted it back in her life. She wanted *him* back in her life. And the way he kissed her... She pressed her fingers to her lips as the memory of their last shared kiss swept through her mind. But what had her sister been implying about Dylan?

"Mr. Blackwater is a buyer. Nothing more." At least not at the moment. He had indicated he wanted to court her, to dance with her at the ball. She frowned as she went over in her mind their interactions. "Well, he has inquired about courting me, but I don't have any interest in allowing him to do so. He's not for me. Why would you think he is someone I should entertain?"

"You needn't. But know that every single red-blooded male in the region probably has their eye upon you with the same interest that your Mr. Day has expressed." Rose chuckled as she put the last straight pin in place. "There. Now let's get you out of that dress so you can go be with your horses."

Her sister knew her so very well. "Will you help me?"

"Of course. But tell me who this Mr. Blackwater is and how you two became acquainted." Rose glanced at Lia before swiftly unbuttoning the row of buttons down the front of the bodice.

"Well, he just rode up one day inquiring about my horses. Turns out we apparently went to school together and now he's also working with Father about some potential investment property."

Rose stopped fussing with buttons and ties to stare at Lia. "That's all?"

"Yes, why?"

"I thought there might be more to it than that." Rose gently hugged Lia and then smiled at her. "I can see why you're keeping him at a distance then. Get out of that dress and go ride. Clear your mind."

Lia gave Rose a weary smile but a rising sense of joy filled her at the idea of taking a ride or working with one of the horses. "I like the way you think. Thank you again for my lovely gown. I'll wear it with pride."

"You'll be beating the men away with your fan, I'm sure." Rose grasped Lia's shoulders and spun her around. "Now put on your riding habit. Let me make the final adjustments to the gown while I have time this morning."

Moments later, Lia strode out of their shared bedroom. As she closed the back door behind her, she sucked in a bracing breath of cold winter air. She couldn't wait to be in the saddle and forget about her men troubles.

* * *

THE MORNING FLEW by as Bryce prepared for the day ahead. He'd spent several hours with his design, fiddling with angles and materials. Trying to determine the difference in expense between them since his boss had indicated that cost could curtail the project. He glanced at his pocket watch suspended on a chain at his waist and cursed. Stacking the pages together, he laid them inside the leather portfolio he used to protect the designs. Closing the portfolio and shoving on his hat, he made for the door.

As he neared the open barn doors, he heard a female voice. Lia. Funny how just hearing her tender tone lifted his heart. He tucked the portfolio firmly under one arm as he marched through the doors. Lia stood in one of the stalls with a young horse, running a curry brush over the chestnut coat. He slowed his pace, not wanting to startle horse or rider. She glanced up at his approach with a welcoming smile that warmed him from head to toes. He returned the smile, wondering what had changed to make her so receptive on this late morning. Not that he was complaining. In fact, maybe this was the perfect opportunity to ask her to be his date.

He leaned against the stall wall, trying to appear casual and not in the hurry he should be in. He cringed inwardly as he thought of

Charlie impatiently waiting for his arrival. Bryce should be saddling his horse and riding out but instead he was calmly chatting with the woman he wanted to be his in every single way possible.

"Good morning, Bryce. You heading out?" Lia tapped the bristles against her flat palm to clean the brush out.

"Soon. What are you up to?" She smiled at him again which made him happy in ways he hadn't felt in a very long time. He couldn't pull himself away from her. Not yet.

"Saphire and I are about to go for a ride to see what she thinks of being alone in the woods without any of her other buddies." She patted the chestnut neck and then came out of the stall. "I think she has a lot of potential to be a wonderful companion for a fine lady."

She scooted past him to lift a blanket and saddle from the rack standing in front of the stall. He stepped toward her to help her but she shook her head once at him and went back into the stall. Of course she was fully capable of handling a saddle. He wanted to smack himself on the forehead for being so patronizing even if his offer to help came with the best intentions. She arranged the blanket on the mare's back with one hand and then added the saddle, cinching the girth in efficient movements.

"She's quite a beauty, too." Bryce gripped the top of the stall wall with one hand, wanting to go in with Lia but aware she wouldn't desire his assistance with her horse. "You do have a way with animals, don't you?"

She nodded as she went to the hooks mounted on the wall to lift a bridle from one. "Mother says I have a natural affinity with them, but horses seem to be most sensitive to my touch. We understand each other in some way I can't explain." Lia eased past Bryce back into the stall to bridle the horse, tugging and adjusting the straps until they lay smoothly and snuggly around the mare's head.

Bryce moved to the stall doorway to meet her when she emerged. Before she mounted and rode away from him and he'd miss his chance. She nearly bumped into him as she came through the doorway.

"What's the matter?" Lia asked, blinking up into his steady gaze. "Did you need something?"

He needed many things. Her trust first and foremost. He had to win back her belief in him, that he wouldn't disappear on her again. He saw no future without her. He craved her, pure and simple. He needed time to convince her of his devotion. The first step came from the question burning in his heart.

"I need to ask you a question." He paused, swallowed, took a breath. "May I escort you to the Christmas Calico Ball as your partner for the evening?"

* * *

OH DEAR. He stood there, tall and handsome, kind and generous, and oh so very tempting. She had admitted she still harbored tender feelings for him. She'd hoped for easing back into their previous closeness. If she accepted his offer, let him escort her to the ball, he was laying claim to her. Nothing casual came from his asking to court her, starting with the ball. She knew his ultimate goal, could see it in the hope gleaming in his eyes. Her heart thundered in her chest as she held perfectly still, swiftly sifting through possible paths forward.

The one path that she dismissed remained confessing everything to everyone. Her calm and composure quailed at the mere thought. Even though part of her reluctantly allowed that her mother may well be right in her encouragement to do so even as she herself was in the dark as to what that particular truth might be. But the ramifications would be huge. Once Bryce learned he was Travis' true father, he'd want to claim his son. As was his right as a man, a father. Even if the law didn't see him as obligated, since they were not married to each other, his sense of responsibility would dictate his involvement in his son's rearing. Then Travis would lose the only father and mother he knew, people who loved him, encouraged him, and had a solid future planned for him. Replete with the quality of education and the resources to fund what his dreams and plans may be as he grew and matured. He'd be confused by learning he had other parents, too.

Bryce had work but not even a home to call his own. And she, as an unmarried woman with a child from her love of a man she wasn't even engaged to, would lose any claim to the fine reputation she currently possessed.

Perhaps even worse than all of that, her family would never trust her again. How could they? *Why* would they? She'd lied to them for years, a lie of omission to tell them that she'd been pregnant and birthed Travis while she purportedly accompanied Laura to her sister's to have an imaginary child of her own. But she wasn't ready. She needed to think, to sort through the best way to go about it. Because obviously, eventually, without question she would have to do so. She sucked in a long breath and let it out through her nose, delaying her response even longer.

"Lia?"

She wouldn't lie, not to him, not again. A valid reason for not accepting his offer is what she required. Suddenly she recalled her mother's request. She eased a soft smile onto her lips as she shrugged lightly. "I can promise you a dance, but my mother insists that I attend to her until we arrive and everything is working as she wants. Will that suffice?"

The spark in his eyes dimmed as he pressed his lips together for a long moment then bowed to her. As he straightened, he returned her smile, though it didn't quite reach his eyes. "Very well. Perhaps more than one though I expect your dance card to be full since you'll be the belle of the ball."

His evident disappointment nearly had her caving on her determination to protect her son at all costs. She'd hurt him, which made her own heart ache inside. Never did she want to cause him pain or grief. But this situation she'd gotten herself into was for higher stakes than just a loving relationship between the two of them. Travis's happiness and future were on the line. As his mother, clandestine though it may be, she couldn't do anything that would knowingly hurt either of those aspects of his life. But she could soften the blow she'd just given to the man she loved.

"Bryce." She held out both hands toward him, glad when he gently clasped them with his own. "I'm looking forward to dancing with you as much as possible."

He squeezed her fingers as the spark relit in his eyes. "I am counting the days until I can hold you in my arms again."

She closed her eyes in anticipation of that moment. As much as she'd denied him, her heart wouldn't permit her to lie to herself any longer either. She loved him. Her heart called out to him, to be with him. She must resist until she could figure out a way to make everything right. She simply needed a little more time. Opening her eyes, she searched his and then squeezed his hands.

"Give me time to accept and adjust, Bryce. Please?" She clung to his hands, willing him to understand and agree.

"I will wait as long as it takes, sweetheart." Bryce tugged on her hands, pulling her closer to him until only a few inches separated them. "But I need something in return." Then he lowered his head to press his lips to hers.

Sensations and memories fought for supremacy throughout her being. She closed her eyes against the onslaught and held fast to his strong hands as he lengthened the kiss, slipping his tongue inside her mouth to slowly dance with hers. She was forcefully reminded of how special their attraction had been. How potent and all-consuming. Then thought fled as the kiss continued, obliterating everything around them. Only they existed in a separate world from reality for what could have been hours of bliss. Then slowly, carefully, he eased back to smile down at her. She blinked at him with an answering smile of her own.

"Sweetheart, I ask only one thing while I'm waiting." He wrapped his arms around her and held her close. "That you don't see any other men until you've decided where your heart lies. Agreed?"

"Other men?" She couldn't think clearly and definitely didn't know of any other would-be suitors. "I'm confused."

"Dylan Blackwater comes to mind. He seems rather taken with you."

She pulled back, putting space between them so her mind could clear. "Dylan is merely a buyer of my horses. He's never been anything more than that."

"But you do have a history with him, as was apparent at our last meeting the other day. Exactly how did you become acquainted with the man?"

Oh dear. "I…went to school with him years ago." That much was true. "And of course, he's a new client now."

Bryce reared his head back and frowned deeply. "Is that all?"

"Yes. You'll have to trust me on that." She frowned up at him. "Can we change the subject? I really do not wish to talk about this."

"But he wants to court you. He said as much." One brow slowly arched as he studied her expression for several seconds, his countenance hardening with each passing moment. "Knowing that changes how I feel about that dolt. I hope he has the good sense to steer clear of you, and me, in future."

"I told you, he's a buyer. That is all." Should she warn Dylan to stay away from Bryce? Given the look on his face, perhaps so. But still, she had her business reputation to consider as well. "You'd have me turn away good money for no good reason?"

"His money probably isn't good." He gentled his thunderous expression. "But if you say there's nothing more between you than horse buying, I'll believe you."

Bryce managed to sound reasonable but she sensed his anger held in check. Dylan shouldn't plan to attend the ball for two very good reasons. First, Bryce simply wouldn't tolerate his presence. Second, she couldn't handle having both men in the same room especially knowing that Rose had seemed to see a level of interest in Dylan that Lia herself hadn't picked up on. What would Bryce interpret from the other man's appearance and behavior as a result? She recalled how they nearly came to blows upon their first meeting and resolved that she would dissuade Dylan from attending. If only he'd listen to her. Which he had no reason to do.

She could only try.

CHAPTER 12

The ride into town did nothing to defuse the burning anger in his gut. A part of him chided that he was being unreasonable, but only a very small part. He couldn't help but keep an eye out for Blackwater the entire way. In his present state of mind, the man best steer clear. He wouldn't be responsible for the condition he'd be left in when Bryce finished with him. Bryce handed off his horse to the lad at the hotel stable, grabbing his saddlebag and marching across the street to the depot. One glance at his expression had everyone avoiding him as he strode across the waiting room to the stairs and up to Charlie's office.

Charlie sat at his desk, the midday sunlight pouring through the paned window to highlight the ledger open before him. A fire burned in the large fireplace beside him. He raised his eyes to peer at him as Bryce stopped in front of the desk. "What's the matter with you?"

He opened his portfolio and pulled out the carefully drawn design for the new trestle. "Nothing to concern you. Here's what I propose we build." He laid the paper on the ledger. "The number and size of the cross-beams will ensure the new trestle will support four times what the present one can carry."

Charlie lifted the page to peruse the details of the drawing. "I like it. You've not only improved its capacity but its appearance as well. And the cost?" Charlie placed the page on the ledger and met Bryce's gaze.

"With the current prices of building materials and hardware, I'm thinking it's about this much." He withdrew another page detailing the kinds and quantities and resulting prices and put it on top of the design. "While pricey, this will last for many years."

Charlie huffed as he lifted the estimated expense of the new trestle. "I'll have to get authorization for such an amount but we're gonna have to bite that bullet. We need to reopen that trestle very, very soon or it will be my job."

"Seriously?" Bryce cocked his head to one side, not having considered his boss might lose his job over any delay in the rebuild.

"And yours if mine goes." Charlie stood and picked up both pages. He pointed to a chair as he came around the desk. "Wait here. I'll be back in a few minutes with both authorization to proceed and the work crew I've hired to do the work."

Bryce settled onto the wood chair and tried to find a comfortable position. He could see out the large window to the gray sky beyond. The view seemed as cold as it felt as a result of the dull backdrop. In the distance he could see the many small houses the Memphis and Charleston had built to house its employees within a short walk of the depot. He'd been offered to live in one but since he had a place to stay he had declined. Off to the right he could see the roundhouse where the train engines were turned around to travel in the opposite direction on the tracks. He'd always appreciated the design of a roundhouse but had not had the opportunity to work on building or planning for one.

With less than two weeks until the big holiday of Christmas, he wanted to save as much as he could to buy Lia the perfect gift. At the moment, he'd only set aside a few dollars but after pay day the following week, he'd have enough to see about finding a solitaire engagement ring. He clung to the hope she'd take him back and he wanted to be prepared for the moment when he felt she'd accept a proposal of marriage. What could be more romantic than to propose during the festivities of Christmas?

Once he could claim her as his wife, then any other potential threat to her would fall under his protection. He'd defend her to the death.

"In here, gentlemen." Charlie led a group of eight men into the large office space and indicated for them to take seats around the meeting table. Then he motioned to Bryce to join them. "Bryce, if you will."

He rose and moved to take one of the last chairs at the table, scanning the other curious faces peering back at him. All were deeply tanned from working out in the sun. The workmen displayed their profession in the rugged jeans and coarse woven shirts as well as sturdy leather boots on their feet.

"Mr. Bryce Day, I'd like you to meet your work crew." Charlie went quickly around the table, introducing each of the men to Bryce in turn.

He didn't remember all of their names, but he'd work on that over time. "Nice to meet all of you." Bryce nodded to each man in greeting then turned to Charlie. "So you received authorization to proceed?"

"Indeed. I will have the materials ordered and delivered out at the site as soon as possible. Perhaps you'd like to show these men what they'll be working on and where."

"I'm happy to." Bryce pushed to his feet but Charlie indicated for him to wait. "Something else?"

"I've also arranged for the M&C to sponsor the catering at the calico ball Mrs. Merryweather is organizing. The board is pleased to be supporting such a worthy cause as a new school. Educating our children is an important mission for all of us."

"I'll be sure to let her know of the decision. Thank you."

"She will receive an official letter confirming their decision. Please let her know to look for that at the post office."

"I will. Is there anything else you need to tell me? Or can I take these men out to the work site?"

Charlie waved him off with one hand as he handed him the couple of pages Bryce had given him earlier. "Go. I'll let you know when to expect the materials."

Collecting his portfolio along with the pages, Bryce tucked everything into his saddlebag. He pivoted and then addressed the men, clustered at the door of the large office space. "Meet me at the stable across the way, and we'll get started."

*　*　*

"WE'LL BE REBUILDING this trestle from scratch." Bryce gestured to the standing structure with a flick of his hand. "And like Mr. Smythe said, we won't have much time to do it but we need to do it right. Understand?"

The group of men nodded and muttered in response.

"I'm told you all have experience with railroad construction. Right?" Bryce scanned the stoic faces around him. No response. "Right?"

"Yessir." A man with a trimmed beard and bushy mustache shifted his weight to one leg. "We all have worked together on tracks and trestles both."

"What we don't know is whether you really know what you're talking about." Another man with thick brows and piercing eyes stepped toward Bryce. "Just how much should we trust your design?"

A thin and wiry man crossed his arms over his narrow chest. "Yeah, just b'cause we's told you know what you're about doesn't mean we believe it."

"That's a fair point, sir. You're Stephen Brenner, aren't you?" Bryce waited for the man's nod before continuing, using the pause to quickly formulate his response. "I'm a trained and experienced engineer. I graduated from university before the war."

He hoped that would satisfy their curiosity and their doubts as to his qualifications. The shifting of eyes to assess each other's reaction told him they needed more. Rather than offer more about his training and experience he hesitated, waiting to learn what they needed yet to know. Be circumspect, Samuel had warned him.

"And during the war?" The bearded man rubbed a hand over his bristles. "What were you about then?"

The men's gazes fixed on him, some with arched brows, some with crossed arms. His Adam's apple slid harshly in his throat. He could lie or obfuscate the truth but that went against every fiber of his being. He'd done nothing to be ashamed of. He'd been a good soldier and done his job as he'd been ordered to do. Thankfully, he'd not been asked to do anything against his own moral code. Even if the results of his actions led to the destruction of property. The end result of peace made it worth the horrific memories haunting his dreams.

"I worked to build railroad tracks and bridges, just like you men. Now, let's agree that we all know what we're doing and we can rely on each other to do a fine job to make the bridge safe for trains to cross."

"Which side were you on?" Stephen asked after a moment.

"The war is over, sir. We don't need to relive it here." Nor did he want to have that particular conversation because he sensed the leanings of the men in front of him. Despite being hired by Charlie who served with the Union, these men apparently were rebels and proud of that fact. "We can start tomorrow morning at eight to tear down the existing trestle, salvage anything worthwhile."

"I don't like you dodging his question like that." The bearded man spat on the ground.

Bryce stiffened, sensing a shift in the attitude of the men from wary to antagonistic. The threat to unionists was real indeed. He'd thought the violence had ended with the war but no, the deep-seated anger really did still remain in the rebel hearts.

What could he say that would settle the matter once and for all? "Look, I know you all have a right to know you can trust me. Short of showing you my diploma and escorting you to where I've built other things, I don't know how to prove to you I know what I'm doing."

"Were you infantry?"

"Cavalry." He caught his breath after the single word blurted from his lips. The crew shifted and shuffled their feet. "Now, can we get to work?"

"I don't recall seeing you in my unit." Stephen hocked up some spittle and spat on the ground. "Who'd you ride with?"

"A lot of good men doing their best." If he said he rode with Sherman, they'd beat him to a pulp.

"I see. You're one of them unionists, aren't ya?" Stephen clenched his fists at his sides.

"We're all unionists now, gentlemen. The country has been reunited as one. The war is over and now we have a job to do to help rebuild the infrastructure destroyed during the fighting. You do want to get paid, don't you?"

Stephen spat again but relaxed his hands. "Yessir, I guess we do."

The others muttered but stayed put. Obviously Stephen was their de facto leader. As long as Bryce didn't rile him then the work could proceed. Bryce wished Charlie had forewarned him about the men's loyalties during the war so he could have tried harder to avoid the entire conversation. Perhaps he'd settled the concerns or perhaps they just wanted time to decide how they'd respond. Either way, he doubted that the matter had been put to bed by his milquetoast response. He'd sounded rather patronizing to his own ears so how had they interpreted his little speech?

"Then I'll see you all at first light tomorrow right back here." At least they hadn't turned ugly toward him once their leader had accepted him as the job boss.

Still he wouldn't relax his guard around any of them. He'd learned enough during his service to know when a threat to his personal safety existed. He wouldn't put it past any of them to act out against him if he provoked them. Which he had no intention of doing, of course. He wanted them to complete the work quickly and well. They shouldn't be worried about him in that equation. The glances they tossed at him as they mounted their horses and rode away told him that his hope of their acceptance might be premature.

CHAPTER 13

*T*he next morning, Lia found herself out in the forest with Aster in search of decorative foliage for the centerpieces and other garlands. The frost was thick on the grass but the snow had melted away. Typical in the southern state where the temperatures may dip to freezing but quickly warmed again. Still, the chill in the air made Lia very glad for the heavy wool cloak about her shoulders.

"I think we'll find some Jackson Brier up ahead a ways." Aster drove the small dogcart along the worn path through the woods. "We can use it as a kind of runner on the tables."

"Will it last until the ball?" Lia kept an eye on Merrybell as her sister worked the traces. Merrybell was one of the nicest fillies Lia had bred and raised. With a chestnut coat, striking white socks, and a pretty star on her forehead, she was also beautiful. Unease flickered in her belly at having someone else driving her young horse, but it was good training for the three-year-old.

"Yes, and beyond. I want to get a jumpstart on figuring out how much I'll need and how I'll use them together." After another few moments, Aster gently pulled on the reins to halt the cart. "Over there. See up there in the tree? Come on."

Together they stepped out of the vehicle and grabbed shallow baskets out of the back. Aster pulled on leather gloves and then produced a set of shears from her pocket as they approached the barren tree where the vine clung, using the trunk as a support for its reach toward the sunlight above. Lia watched, one hand shading her eyes, as her sister tugged on the green vine dotted with red berries to loosen its grasp on the tree bark. Then she snipped and snipped until she filled the basket resting on the ground at her feet.

Aster turned to smile at Lia. "That should do for now. Let's find some pine cones, some pine boughs, and maybe some cedar too. Then we can head back and I'll play around with arrangements."

"There's a cedar grove another mile or so into the forest." Lia ushered her sister back toward the dogcart, Merrybell patiently standing in the harness. Lia smiled at how nicely she behaved. Her training definitely produced the results she'd aimed for, that of docile and intelligent horses. If she could establish a solid reputation for breeding such animals then she'd have a steady income to help with expenses at Hopewell. Doing so was her way of relieving the guilt surrounding her secret baby.

"Do you mind coming with me? Are you feeling up to it?"

Lia frowned at her sister in confusion. "I'm feeling well. Why?"

"Little Travis asked me if you were feeling yourself. He seemed to think you were sad or something." Aster turned knowing eyes to her sister. "I think there's more to it than that."

How odd. What had Travis picked up on in her demeanor to evince such a reaction? What did her sister suspect as a result? Indeed, why did Lia have suspicions about each of her sisters? "Such as?"

"You've been different ever since your Mr. Day returned. I think you still have feelings for him."

Her sisters were ganging up on her. They shouldn't expect she retained warm feelings for the man after what he'd done. Even if she did. Lia shook her head slowly at her sister. "And if I do?"

"Then good. I like him. More than that other man you've been doing business with. He strikes me as an angry sort, not the kind of man for you." Aster placed her basket into the wagon and then clambered back onto the seat. "I want to gather some fresh magnolia leaves as well, so I can play with appropriate garlands and containers for centerpieces."

The irony wasn't lost on Lia that leaves of the tree she was named for would be featured at the charity ball. Which, given the magnolia was indigenous to Alabama, made perfect sense, of course. She quickly took her seat and soon they were rattling along the forest path again. Her thoughts spun back to Dylan, to the intensity of his gaze, the strength apparent in his frame, and the burgeoning awareness of his interest which sparked a nervous twinge in her gut.

"I am so torn about what is best for…me." She'd almost blurted out Travis's name instead. She didn't want to raise that specter. But she sensed the time was coming whether she wanted it to or not.

"You must think of your future which surely will include a husband and children." Aster slowed Merrybell as they approached a curve in the path. Eyes sparkling in the shadowy woods, Aster smiled at Lia. "Bryce's babies would be handsome and smart just like him. You could do worse."

If only her sister knew the evident truth of her claim. Travis was indeed much like his father. Cute, smart, and fond of working with his hands. Even his obsession with whittling. She recalled the piece of cedar she'd blessed and given to Bryce before he left, a talisman in hopes of bringing him safely back to her. Then he'd ended her hopes of a future together. Ultimately, he had come back for her.

"Rose thinks Mr. Blackwater has his own intentions toward me. He seems like a nice enough man, but I do not know exactly how I should handle his attentions. Bryce feels I should not have any dealings with him."

Aster shot a surprised look at her. "Why? Is he jealous, perhaps?"

"Possibly." She smirked at her sister as she thought about Bryce's reaction to the idea of Dylan courting her also. "Bryce was upset at the suggestion that Dylan might wait upon me. Not that I would entertain such a thing. Because, I do have feelings for Bryce and always will."

"Then you've made your decision. Will you tell Bryce the truth of your feelings?"

Her heart stuttered then resumed its rhythmical beating. The direct question deserved an honest answer. She should tell Bryce the whole truth before he made any final decisions about their future together. Perhaps she could see how her sister reacted and that would lend itself to showing her the way to tell the others. Hope flared in her soul that she might be able to navigate her way through the dangerous terrain ahead. "If I tell you the truth, you must keep it to yourself for now and try not to judge me too harshly."

"That sounds serious. Very well." Aster reined the horse to a halt so she could address her sister with all of her attention. "I'm listening."

She drew in a deep breath and let it out slowly as she laid a hand on her sister's forearm. "The truth is that Bryce is Travis's real father and I am his mother."

"You and Bryce?" Aster cried. "Oh my. I thought… Never mind. Why, that's wonderful. I knew you two loved each other once." Then a frown settled onto her sister's brow. "But that means…"

Lia's admission meant that everything was about to change. Bryce surely would be upset and shocked. Travis would be confused and hurt. Laura and Samuel would lose a son. Her parents' reaction didn't bear contemplation. She couldn't think about how others might react to the damning revelations she'd just shared with her sister.

"Please keep this to yourself for now, Aster. I will tell him. I will tell everyone in my own time. I have to, I know. It's just…"

"Hard?" Aster nodded. "It's up to you to let him know he has a son. He needs to know."

Swallowing the rising emotion, Lia worried her lips. "Yes, he does."

✳ ✳ ✳

THE LATE AFTERNOON sun shone down from a clear blue winter sky, illuminating the plans for the replacement trestle in Bryce's hands. He frowned at the page, some small detail niggling uncomfortably in his subconscious. He'd overlooked something but what? After spending days thinking of little else but the design—and Lia—he had told the men to begin. The supplies had arrived and were piled about waiting for the destruction to complete before they started the

rebuild. He studied the page, trying to put his finger on what both-
ered him.

Hoofbeats sounded behind him, growing louder with each beat,
but he ignored them for the moment, concentrating on attempting to
grasp the elusive error. Scanning the various angles and measure-
ments, he finally saw the problem. He'd angled the eastern support
truss a fraction more than desired for a staunch and lasting structure.
He pulled his pencil out and made a note on the plans about the
necessary correction. Satisfied with the easy fix, he rolled the sheet
into a tube and then slowly pivoted to greet the new arrival.

Charlie halted his horse and rested his wrists on the pommel. "You
look like you're finally content with the plans."

Bryce tapped the tube on his other palm. "I had to make one small
adjustment, but it won't change the numbers I already gave you.
Nothing should delay the crew's good progress."

"I'm relieved to hear that. I just came to verify everything arrived
as I ordered. So I'll see you back at the depot." Charlie saluted and
then without waiting for a reply reined his horse around to trot off
toward town.

Bryce let his gaze drift around the juncture of trail and river. The
wide creek chattered over rocks as it hurried past. The surrounding
hills stood coated with pines intermixed with hardwood trees still
dropping their multi-colored leaves onto the forest floor. The only
other sound he heard was the sound of men pulling apart the bridge
in the distance. He could well envision the effort it had taken to build
the trestle the first time. The fighting over it. He'd witnessed the
cycles of building and demolition. During the war, the bridge may
have been blown up or dismantled more than once, and thrown back
together in-between. Each iteration would have weakened the
supports and thus the overall structure, which explained its deterio-
rated condition.

Now that he was on the job, he'd make sure the replacement lasted
a long time. After all, they couldn't risk the safety and wellbeing of the
passengers or the cargo trains. His job, as engineer and designer, was
to ensure the best possible way of seeing to that requirement. The

crew busily pulled apart the wooden structure as ordered, setting aside any boards that could be reused elsewhere. He didn't need to stay at the site to supervise them. They'd be more comfortable without him hovering about.

Bryce moved toward where Jet stood tied to a wagonload of tools and equipment. He slipped the tube into a case strapped to the saddle as more hoofbeats sounded behind him. Many hoofbeats. He wasn't expecting anyone else to come out to the distant work site. He tensed, his instincts alerting him to potential danger.

The trio of men glared at him as they reined to a halt, kicking up a cloud of dust as their horses shifted violently in the dirt. Bryce recognized Blackwater but not the other two scowling men. Their slouch hats shaded their features into obscurity. Intentionally? Bryce kept his hands on his saddle for a moment and then stepped away to confront the men. Figured Dylan realized he couldn't defeat Bryce alone so brought help.

Dylan swung out of the saddle and strode toward him, dropping the reins so his horse could trot out of the way. Faced with his dark regard, Bryce swallowed back anything he might have said. Better to see what the man had in mind. And prepare to defend himself.

"I've been hearing talk about you, mister." Dylan sauntered aggressively closer until he stood a few feet away. He glanced at the work crew and then back at Bryce. "I don't like what I'm hearing, either."

"I'm sorry?" Bryce splayed his hands in confusion. "I have no understanding of what rumors you may have heard about me. Care to enlighten me?"

"I hear you're a unionist." Dylan flexed his big hands at his sides, his shoulders bunching under his dark gray overcoat.

He'd been warned about his military service coming back to haunt him with the rebels in these parts. Their previous altercation stoked Blackwater's ire all the more. Bryce kept quiet, not wanting to make the situation worse by admitting or denying anything. He'd regretted the previous conversation with the men and had hoped it would end there. But no. He crossed his arms over his chest and waited.

"And I hear..." Dylan smacked one fist into his other open hand. "I hear you rode with the First Alabama Cavalry along with that dastardly Sherman. Burning and destroying as you went." Another fist smack into the other hand. "Do you deny it?"

The belligerent threat in Dylan's eyes evoked a heart-felt desire for Bryce's gun. A gun which nestled in its holster affixed to the other side of the saddle, way out of reach. Still, he served honorably for his country and he would not be made to feel otherwise. Especially not by this ape of a man who only knew threats and belligerence as a means of obtaining his aims. He squared his shoulders, flexing his hands to warm up the muscles in preparation for the fight ahead.

"What of it?" Bryce widened his stance to brace for whatever came next.

The other two men dismounted and joined Dylan. His henchmen. They'd come prepared to fight, dressed in work clothes, overcoats and battered hats. Each was a daunting opponent but the three together? He cast an assessing gaze over their physiques. Bryce's heart sank at the realization that he was vastly outnumbered. Alone and unarmed, he'd do his best to defend himself with his fists. As long as the crew didn't join in the fun, he had a chance. A slim one, but still.

"You're not welcome around here." Dylan chuckled menacingly. "We have a lesson for the likes of you." He smacked his fist into his hand again as he closed the small distance between them.

Bryce ducked the first swing, landing a punch on the other man's stomach. Then the henchmen got around behind him and grappled him to a standstill while Dylan pummeled him with both fists. Ribs. Stomach. Jaw.

The world spun around him, the sound of the three men's laughter loud in the quiet countryside. They let him drop to the ground and he lay there in a daze.

"Let that teach you to fight on the right side and to stay away from a certain lady you have no business seeing. Do you comprehend me?" Dylan kicked Bryce in the ribs with his heavy booted foot.

Bryce moaned and curled into a fetal position to protect himself from further abuse to what he felt was certainly broken ribs. His jaw throbbed. But he didn't agree to the man's edict. He closed his eyes and feigned he'd passed out. After several long moments, he heard the creak of leather as they remounted and then the pounding of hooves as they fled the scene of the attack. Breathing shallowly to avoid the stabbing pain of his ribs, he finally felt able to try to move. He couldn't stay there. He needed help. Silence from the men witnessing his beating told him he wouldn't find help from them.

Pushing slowly and cautiously to his feet, he gasped with pain each step he took to his horse. He pulled a wool scarf out of his saddlebag and wound it around his chest, tying it as tightly as he could manage to support his ribs. Then he struggled into the saddle, Jet standing stock still as though he understood his rider was in vast pain. With a cluck, he urged the stallion into a walk, and headed slowly home.

Some unknown time later he realized Jet had indeed taken him back to Samuel's, stopping at the front hitching post. He roused himself and stared at the small house where Samuel worked, the door so very far away. The ground so far below him. The mere thought of landing on the dirt beside Jet made his ribs throb in anticipation of the pain at the jolt of boots meeting the ground. He waited, hoping someone would notice him and come to help him but no movement greeted his squinting glance. He'd have to do it by himself.

Steeling himself, he gripped the pommel and stood in the stirrups to ease his leg over the saddle. Not letting himself think about what he was about to do, he pushed away and let himself drop to the ground. He crumpled at the pain, crying out as he lay splayed on his back.

"Bryce!" Samuel appeared at his side, reaching out to help him. "What happened to you? Never mind. Let's get you inside so I can examine you."

In a daze from the tortuous process of moving him inside, Bryce did whatever his friend commanded. After a quick inspection of the damage, Samuel wrapped a proper supportive bandage around his ribs, applied a cold compress to his throbbing jaw, and then made sure he was comfortably propped on his bed in the ward. Before Bryce could thank him, Lia scurried into the room with shock on her face.

"Aster said she saw you practically carried in here. Bryce, what happened? Are you alright?" She scanned his entire person to assess the injuries for herself. "Whoever did this should be arrested and put in jail."

Bryce appreciated her defense and abhorrence of his attack but he couldn't let her rail against unknown men. How could he tell her it was Blackwater who'd beaten him? She wouldn't believe him. She'd think he was trying to smear the other man's supposed good name. "Don't worry about it, Lia. It's nothing."

She blinked at him as astonishment flooded her face. "Nothing? You've got broken ribs and a split lip and it's nothing? I'm going to ride to town and tell the sheriff what has happened."

"No, you're not, Sister." Samuel shook his head at her and then pointed to a nearby chair. "Sit down and stop fuming. Bryce is right in that it's not worth getting the law involved in this dustup. The law would likely side with the rebels anyway." He crossed the room to a small table holding a basin and ewer of water, pouring some into the basin and picking up a bar of soap.

"You're unbelievable. A dustup, hm? That's ridiculous." She folded her arms tightly across her breasts. "Boys will be boys? Is that what you think?"

Bryce waved Lia's protest into silence. "No, but it's still very soon after the war and emotions are running high as a result. He has a right to his opinion, after all, even if I strenuously disagree with him. With them."

Samuel narrowed his eyes as he dried his newly washed hands on a towel. "How many?"

"Three." Bryce didn't want to relive the beating. But he did plan to do something about Dylan Blackwater. "They outnumbered me. I won't let that happen again."

"You think they'll attack you again?" Lia widened her eyes as the horror she felt seeped into them. "I can't bear it."

"You do not have any role in this." Bryce held out his hand until she laid hers on his fingers. Closing his long fingers around hers, he squeezed once. "Do not worry so, sweetheart. I will address the situation in due course."

He would not let his woman be upset by the hurtful shenanigans of his former enemy, now a fellow countryman. Making that transition on an emotional level would take some time and compromise. But if Dylan Blackwater thought he could dictate who Bryce could court, then he had another level of emotional adjustment to make. One which may include more fists.

But first he had to heal. Lia squeezed his fingers in return, worry plain in her eyes. He couldn't stand seeing her in such distress. Once he could move without wincing, then he'd make sure she never had to worry about him again.

CHAPTER 14

The kitchen smelled of fresh pine, cedar, and magnolia combined with the tantalizing aromas of a buttery pound cake and a savory chicken pot pie baking in the oven. Lia paused in her flower arrangement task Aster had given her to drink in the love and joy filling the room just as much as the scents. Piles of fragrant pine boughs stacked on a side table while a large basket held a quantity of large magnolia leaves, glistening dark green on one side and a subtler nut brown on the other. Spools of red, gold, and silver ribbon waited at one side of the large table where the sisters worked. Rose studiously stripped leaves from the bottom of a cedar bough before wiring it to the growing garland snaking across the center of the work table. Aster swooped back into the room carrying an apronful of red apples and orange clementines to use in the garlands and vases of boughs.

Aster carefully rolled the fruit onto the table and Lia quickly corralled them to prevent them falling off the edge. Rose snagged a ceramic bowl and placed it nearby for all hands to transfer the fruit into a safe place. Lia smiled to herself at the teamwork they automatically fell back on. She loved her sisters and couldn't imagine ever doing anything to break them up. Except perhaps lying to them for so long. Her smile wilted as she pressed her lips into a hard line.

"I forgot to bring in the pine cones." Aster frowned at the table's contents for a moment and then sighed. "But we don't need them quite yet."

"I think Sam might still have some silver and gold paints we could use to make them festive, too." Rose leaned on the table, her hands braced apart as she looked at each of her sisters. "Want me to go see?"

"As long as you don't disturb Bryce. Doctor's orders." Lia sorely wanted to cross the yard and inquire as to Bryce's wellbeing but she'd promised to let him rest.

How she longed to be with him. Being in the ward again with him, where they'd spent so much loving time together, had reawakened every memory they'd made there. Although she'd resisted it, her attraction to him continued to grow. She wanted to feel his lips on hers again, to hold his hand, walk together and talk about anything and everything like they'd done before. She recalled the feel of his five o'clock shadow under her fingers as she'd caressed his jaw before placing her lips on his. The sensation of connection between them as they'd kissed for several glorious minutes under the shading branches of the magnolias.

"What happened to him?" Aster asked, a puzzled frown on her face. "I mean I know he was attacked, but why? And by whom?"

The image of Bryce's face, scraped and battered, floated before Lia's mind's eye. He'd likely develop some dark bruising over the next day or so. In addition to the broken ribs. He hadn't revealed who had beaten him, at least not in her presence. Did she know the man responsible? Is that why Bryce refused to say? If she knew the culprit, she'd not condone his actions and would avoid having any further discourse with the person. No matter who it was or why he'd attacked her man.

"He didn't say much about the why or the who only the fact that he was attacked." Lia shrugged away the deep-seated worry about a repeat attack by the unnamed men. "Sam said he's got a couple broken ribs to complement his swollen jaw and split lip. Why do you think anyone would have beaten him up? I don't understand."

"I'd venture he tangled with some former rebels who didn't appreciate his union sentiments and service during the late war." Rose straightened up to fold her arms across her chest. "Father and Samuel have both cautioned us against disclosing our unionist leanings for fear of this very reaction."

Even so, that was no excuse for behaving so basely. Gentlemen should have higher standards of conduct for themselves, to her mind. Ladies didn't resort to such violence over a difference of opinion, even one which loomed so large in their minds. The war had settled the debate in favor of the United States of America, not the blasted treasonous Confederacy. Those who had sided with secession now had to realize the error of their ways and come together for the benefit of the country as a whole.

"The war is over. They need to put that bloody disagreement behind them." Lia's face warmed as anger simmered inside. "They need to stop being so immature."

"Give them a little time and perhaps they will, but it's only been a few months really." Aster lifted a pine bough and a small knife to strip a couple of outgrowths from the bottom. She curved it around to form a circle and wired it together as the foundation for a wreath. "I can imagine they haven't let go yet of their belief in the Confederacy."

"If they ever do." Rose heaved a sigh and shook her head. "I merely want peace."

"And safety." Lia chewed on her lower lip as she returned to arranging boughs in vases. The ribbons would come last, after she finished the couple of dozen containers to place on the tables at the ball. "We can't have our menfolk being beaten. I won't tolerate that."

She never wanted to see Bryce in pain such as he displayed earlier that afternoon. His injuries would take a long time to heal and for the bruising to fade. She'd make a point of helping to care for him if her brother permitted her assistance. Hell and furies, even if he objected she would find a way to make sure Bryce had everything he needed to recover fully.

"Agreed but we can't do anything about what other men resort to." Rose dropped her hands to rest her fingertips on the table. "What do you want me to do, Aster?"

"Here, put some decoration on this wreath and I'll make some more of them." Aster slid the freshly created wreath toward Rose. "We don't have to finish all of this tonight. We still have a week until they need to be done. And several of Mother's friends will also provide decorations."

"I'm glad of their contributions." Rose positioned the wreath in front of her and reached for an apple. She poked a wire into its core and then began wrapping the end of the wire around the bough until the apple nestled among the green branches. "It's nearly time for supper and I'm hungry."

"Mother said she'd be back when it's time to take out the chicken pot pie."

"Don't forget her pound cake that's making my mouth water." Lia grinned at Aster. "I know it's your favorite, too."

"You're not lying, sister mine." Aster chuckled as she wired another wreath together. "I wish we could skip the pot pie and go straight to dessert."

Lia opened her mouth to chastise Aster about her reference to lying. What could she say in front of Rose that wouldn't raise her suspicions about Lia's carefully guarded secret? The secret she knew must be revealed and soon, just not yet. She needed to find the right time and in the right words first. She settled on sending a stern look at Aster with a quick shake of her head. Aster blinked and then mouthed "I'm sorry" before bending over to study the bough in her hands.

"If only Mother would allow such a transgression to tradition." Lia forced a laugh to lighten the mood in the suddenly tense kitchen.

"What transgression?" Natalie asked as she hurried into the room and across to the iron cookstove to open the hefty door and pull the cake out of the oven, using her folded apron to protect her hands from the hot pan.

"Oh, Mother, that smells heavenly." Aster moaned in anticipation.

"Aster would like to have dessert before supper." Lia grinned at her mother as she reached inside the oven again and withdrew the bubbling, golden-brown pot pie.

"Well, I hate to disappoint but the cake needs to cool a bit before we can remove it from the pan and then eat it. So let's set the table and enjoy our supper together. Father has just arrived and will be ready to eat after his long day at the office."

"Yes, Mother." Lia glanced at her sisters, sharing a rueful grimace as they went to do as their mother requested.

Stewing in her heart was the awful, inevitable truth that she would have to fess up to sooner rather than later.

* * *

THE HOUSE WAS QUIET. Bryce relaxed on a padded chair in the front parlor with an after-dinner glass of scotch. Out the window only darkness met his eyes. The sun had set while they'd shared dinner in the dining room a little while ago. He could hear Samuel speaking somewhere in the house but not what he was saying. A fire crackled and popped in the small brick fireplace nearby, keeping the chill out of the room. He returned to the history book in his hands, trying to focus on the words rather than listening for Lia's voice. A silly thing considering she wasn't even in the same house. No, she was across the yard in her own home with her sisters and parents doing whatever she did on a Friday evening. While he was alone and lonely for her. In a few minutes, he'd say goodnight and head back to his single bed. By himself. He sighed.

If he felt better he'd go see her, talk to her, hold her hands, perhaps kiss her. If only. But Samuel had been adamant he stay put and give his bones a chance to mend. His jaw was better after Samuel had applied a cold compress to it so at least he could comfortably read for a while. While away the time even though he longed to be with Lia. Stare into her beautiful eyes and run his fingers through her silky hair if she'd let him. Like before. Like he hoped she would again.

Pounding footsteps alerted him to the boys playing a game

through the house, chasing each other from the sound of it. Those boys were so good together. He could tell they had a very strong brotherly bond, much like the one he had with his own brothers once. Since Bryce had moved from the central part of the state to Huntsville years ago, that bond had weakened due to distance and infrequent communication. He should write to them, let them know how he was doing and where he was living. *That* he was living. He'd purchase some stationery the next time he was in town so he could write a few letters to them and his parents.

"I'm gonna get you!" Ian yelled as the herd of boys raced into the front parlor where Bryce sat reading.

"Whoa, now, boys." Bryce held up a hand as they barreled toward him. "That seems like an outside game not one for inside."

The five boys skidded to a halt, jostling and pushing until everyone had quieted down.

"Sorry, Mr. Day." Michael, the oldest, shrugged off their miscreant behavior. "We got carried away, I guess."

"I understand. Now how about finding something quieter to do with your energy." Bryce tilted his head to one side and then straightened up again. "Like read a book?"

"Ah, that's no fun." Travis shook his head at him. "That's just sitting."

"Because you can't read yet." Ian punched Travis on the shoulder, making him wince and step away.

"You'll learn before too much longer, I'm sure." Bryce studied the youngest for a long moment. "When I was in the service, I carried a book with me to read when I had a few minutes between missions."

Theo moved to sit on the footstool in front of a side chair, leaning forward to peer at Bryce. "What did you do during the war?"

Bryce flashed his eyebrows up and down in surprise. How to answer such a question from a young boy? "Mainly followed orders."

"But what kind of orders?" Adam asked as he plopped down on the carpet beside the chaise. "Pa said you were in the cavalry and even rode with Sherman. Is that right?"

Bryce suddenly had an attentive and curious audience of five boys, eager to learn more about his service in the cavalry. Some of that service involved details which their parents surely wouldn't want him sharing with them. Killing and destroying might be necessary at times but these young, impressionable minds were not ready for that reality.

"Yes, I did."

"What was he like?" Michael asked from his spot by the fireplace.

"What kind of horse did you ride?" Ian asked on the heels of his brother's question.

"Did you shoot anyone?" Theo's eyes widened as he stared at Bryce's startled reaction. "You did, didn't you? How many?"

He couldn't tell them the number because he'd stopped counting after a dozen or so. Tried very hard to forget the awful acts in the heated battles he'd fought in with gun and saber both. Yes, he'd been under orders and he had to fight for his own life on more than one occasion but that didn't mean he found any pleasure in taking another man's life. Even one who was declared as his enemy. He kept thinking about their families futilely waiting for them to come home. Well, they might have had their bodies return home but even that was doubtful. Most were buried on the battlefield where they'd fallen. He focused on the alight faces surrounding him instead of the horrific memories swarming in his brain.

"Now, boys, it wasn't like it was a fun adventure. War is not something any of you want to fight in." He speared each of them with his serious gaze. "You must listen to me. Be very glad the war is over and you can stay safe and whole here in your home. Trust me, I dreamed of the war ending and returning home every day."

Samuel eased into the room through the open doorway to join the group around Bryce. His slight frown indicated his concern as to what Bryce might say next but he didn't interrupt. Merely stood with his hands in his front pockets while waiting for the story to continue.

"I think it sounds exciting to be slaying your enemies." Michael waved an imaginary saber through the air from side to side as though attacking invisible men.

Samuel raised his brows at his oldest son. "Michael."

"What? Isn't that how you handle a sword?" Michael cocked his head to one side to blink at his father before turning his gaze to Bryce. "Isn't it?"

"Well, yes, to a point but I think your father is commenting on the fact that you shouldn't be playing at killing anyone. It's not something any of us should want to do. We should be looking out for each other, not killing each other. Understand?" Samuel nodded at Bryce's explanation.

"Then why did you kill men?" Ian asked.

Bryce drew in a deep breath to give himself time to formulate an appropriate response to the boy's question. Why indeed? So many reasons floated through his mind. Letting it out slowly, he settled his eyes on Ian. "Because sometimes men have such a strong disagreement that only through physical confrontation can they resolve it. It took far too many lives for this most recent one to be settled. I hope we never have another conflict like it ever again."

Samuel nodded as he took a step forward to get his sons' attention. "On that note, your mother says it's time for you to go to bed." He made a shooing motion toward the door. "Off you go."

"Ah, do we have to?" Travis slowly got to his feet but paused to shake Bryce's hand. "Thank you, sir, for sharing but I have to go bed now."

"Anytime, Travis. I'll be around for a while yet." Bryce grinned at the boy, fond of his manners and ways. "Sleep well."

The boys trailed out of the room, glancing back at him as they passed through the doorway. He heard their footsteps fade away up the back steps as Samuel lingered for another minute.

"Thanks for not encouraging any violent tendencies those boys might have hidden away." Samuel looked through the open door where his sons had traipsed away. "And for not telling them more about what you actually did."

"Some things are best left unsaid." Bryce stood up to walk carefully toward his friend. "And unremembered if possible."

"Indeed. Keeping your service to yourself is better, and safer, for everyone including those boys. I wouldn't want them to inadvertently say too much to the neighbors."

"Yes, I agree." He reached out with his right hand to shake hands with Samuel. "You have my word I'll not do anything which would put the boys in harm's way."

"See that you don't. I don't want to have to take you to task over such a lapse." Samuel grinned at him as he released his hand.

Despite the pleasant expression on his friend's face, Bryce understood his stern underlying warning. Keep his family safe or else.

CHAPTER 15

"Hark! The herald angels sing…" Lia sang along as Rose played the familiar traditional carol on the beloved piano in the formal front parlor.

A four-foot pine graced the center of a sideboard, its trunk swaddled with a worn-out, dark-green skirt donated by Aster. The festive fir was surrounded by several wrapped packages waiting for the big day. Small gifts of candy and fruit nestled among the branches between the ribbons and bows and carved birds decorating the tree. A fire provided warmth and atmosphere to the room as the sisters finished the song. Aster sashayed into the parlor carrying a tray of greenery, lemons, and red ribbon creatively tied to make a beautiful centerpiece.

"You should perform at the ball." Aster placed the silver tray on top of the piano, shifted it once and then again, and smiled at Rose, then Lia. "What?"

"Are you insane?" Lia gaped at her sister. The very thought of singing in front of such a large audience sent chills down her spine. No. She couldn't possibly make such an exhibition of herself.

"Surely you are joking." Rose rested her hands in her lap as she regarded her younger sister. "I can't imagine playing in such a venue."

Aster waggled a hand in the air with a chuckle. "Of course. I know neither of you would savor such attention."

Rose lifted her hands to play a few notes of another song. Finally settling on Jingle Bells, she glanced at her sisters. "Sing with me?"

"Oh, Jingle Bells! One of my new favorites." Aster fairly hopped in place with enthusiasm.

"One of mine, as well," Lia agreed. Even if the composer was a rebel, the song still proved enjoyable to sing. After all, it was time to put the past dispute behind and move on.

The Christmastide seemed as good a time as any to do just that, too. Focusing on the happy memories created in previous years and on creating new ones should be everyone's aim. Her mind drifted back to the pre-war Christmases filled with shiny wrapped packages, candies, and fresh fruits and nuts as gifts. She glanced down to her faded and mended dress, recalling when Rose had made it for her before the war. Finding material during the war years had been hit or miss, with more misses than scores. Now that the railroad was returning to a more regular service, more products and staples flowed into town. Even with one trestle out of service, the dry goods had managed to trickle into town. Thus selecting fabric and notions for new gowns for the ball had finally felt like old times.

Rose pressed the ivories to play the introduction to the carol. She peered up at Lia for a moment until Lia nodded she was ready. Aster joined in as Rose played and sang.

"Dashing through the snow
In a one-horse open sleigh..."

The lyrics resurrected the delightful memory of Lia and Bryce out in a two-horse sleigh five years ago when she'd first met him. The surprising snowfall created the opportunity for an impromptu training session of her matched pair of geldings to learn how to pull a sleigh. They'd quickly taken to the new concept of runners instead of wheels, smart boys that they were, pulling the heavy sleigh easily through the several inches of snow. Sitting close to Bryce's heat on the front bench of the two-bench sleigh kept her from freezing. She'd worn her heaviest cloak and gloves but her feet turned to ice in her boots.

"Over the fields we go
Laughing all the way…"

And they had, too. Despite the cold, the joy she felt from both pride in her horses and the love she'd found in the man beside her filled her up. Granted her feet remained cold, but the rest of her seemed warmed by her happiness. She'd even let Bryce handle the traces on the return to Hopewell. Naturally, as a skilled horseman he had a gentle touch on the reins and the horses' mouths as a result. His gentleness had spoken to his overall personality and bolstered her confidence in pursuing a relationship, a future with him.

Natalie and Richard sauntered into the room, side by side but not touching. They approached the girls, stopping beside Lia and the piano as the sisters continued to sing. Something was on her mother's mind. What though?

"Now the ground is white,
Go it while you're young,
Take the girls tonight
And sing this sleighing song."

Her father's brows rose slightly at the rather risqué lyrics but Lia merely smiled as she finished the final chorus in a strong voice.

"Jingle bells, jingle bells
Jingle all the way,
Oh what fun it is to ride
In a one-horse open sleigh."

They held the final note for several beats as Rose ended on a flourish, her fingers flying over the keys. Her parents started clapping and smiling as Lia took a bow, followed by Aster. Laughter followed at their playful antics. My, how Lia loved her sisters and parents. The love and support, the commiseration and understanding they shared all melded into a close-knit family. That belief in each other, the trust that the others had the best interest of everyone at heart, had sustained them through the hardships and horrors of the war. Trust she'd relied upon all of her life.

"Very nicely done, girls." Richard crossed his arms over his chest and smiled at them. "We have a question for you."

"Yes, Father?" Rose asked, placing her hands in her lap.

"What would you like for Christmas this year?"

Lia's first thought was the expense. They were already spending so much on the ball gowns and decorations and such. She didn't really need anything, truth be told. She'd get by without her parents putting out more money on her behalf. Their shared love would suffice.

"I don't wish for anything this year, Father." Lia shrugged lightly at her parents. "I have what I need."

Aster snapped her mouth shut then opened it again to say, "Me too. I am content."

"Oh come now, girls." Richard frowned at them each in turn. "Surely there is some bauble or thingummy you'd like."

Rose shook her head slowly as she shrugged. "I can't think of a thing worth worrying over."

Natalie arched her brows at the three sisters. "What is this about?"

As the oldest, Lia felt obligated to take the lead yet again. "With the inflated prices…"

Richard held up a hand to stop her speech. "The cost is not your concern, my dear. I appreciate your thoughtfulness but it is unnecessary for you to sacrifice receiving a small gift out of some sense that money is short. I can assure you that I wouldn't be asking if it were."

His stern gaze spoke volumes. She'd hurt his pride by suggesting he couldn't afford it. Which was not her intention. She must ease the hurt she'd caused. She suppressed a sigh and merely bobbed her head a few times. "Very well, then I would appreciate a small, lined pocket book to carry with me to keep track of my breeding and training schedule and such."

"That's more like it." Richard pursed his lips as he slid his eyes to look at Rose. "What about you, my dear?"

Rose pressed her lips together in thought and then her eyes brightened. "Perhaps some new sheet music from some of the latest songs?"

"More music in the house sounds wonderful to me." Natalie moved to wrap one arm around Rose's shoulders. "I do enjoy hearing you play."

Richard contemplated his wife and daughter for a long moment and then turned to Aster. "And you, dear?"

Aster sidled around to take her father's elbow. "I'd like a new book to read, something tantalizing and interesting. Perhaps some of Emily Dickinson's poems?"

"I'd love to read her work, too, if you don't mind." Lia smiled at Aster, glad they shared yet another aspect, that of a love of reading. "Her poems are moving and evocative."

"We will see what we can do." Richard nodded once. "Now, if you'll excuse us, we have some shopping to do."

Lia watched her parents, arm in arm, walk out of the parlor with a lingering look between them. The love they shared seemed to create a golden aura surrounding them. She wanted the same kind of marriage, the same kind of strong love and trust her parents enjoyed.

There was that word again: trust.

Could she trust Bryce to stay this time? Could she confess her secret but retain her family's trust? Or at least rebuild it once she brought her dark secret into the light? Would they ever trust her again, especially Bryce who had already stated he didn't condone deceit of any kind? It might take a miracle.

But Christmas was the time for miracles so perhaps she could hope.

* * *

He was utterly and completely bored. Another quiet afternoon without any visitors other than Samuel to check on him and Laura to bring him sustenance. He sat in a chair by the window in the ward, relieved that the pain had eased though not vanished. Only a few days had passed since Blackwater and his thugs beat him up. Nonetheless, he couldn't sit around on his butt doing nothing when he had work to supervise on the railroad trestle. Indeed, he needed to carry the revised plans out to the crew boss as soon as possible. He needed to work because he needed the money, which he wouldn't earn looking out the window at a pastoral scene. He needed to inform Charlie of his situation and condition and reassure him as to his ability to complete the task assigned.

What should he do to counter Blackwater's attack on him? Anger seethed in his chest at the thought of the other man, especially his actions toward him and his interest in Lia. Blackwater tended to resort to violence, to the physical threat in order to seize power and control. Exactly what Bryce disdained. He'd seen enough blood and destruction and now looked for peace and safety to dominate his mind and attention. If Blackwater would let him.

First, he needed to send word to Charlie about his intentions and plans. Damn it, he still hadn't gotten into town to purchase stationery. Hell, he hadn't gone anywhere. Frustration simmered inside as he drummed his fingers on the arm of the chair. How could he send a note without anything to write it on?

"Bryce, can I come in?" Laura's melodic voice called through the closed door.

"Yes, please." Perfect timing. Perhaps she could lend him some paper and pen.

After a beat the door swung open to allow her to enter, juggling a small tray on one arm. "I have your afternoon tea with your favorite almond cakes."

"Wonderful." He smiled up at her as she placed the silver tray on the small table beside his chair. "The aroma is divine. What kind of tea is that?"

She lifted the tea pot to pour some steaming amber liquid into a cup. "A blend of mint and chamomile, something to bolster your mood. I can only imagine how bored you must be after sitting here for days."

He chuckled. "You know me well."

"Do you need anything?"

"Yes, I need paper and pen so I can send word to Charlie about what has happened."

"That is easy to remedy." She strode to a small casual table along one wall and pulled open the drawer.

She lifted out several sheets of paper and pulled a steel dip pen from a narrow container on top along with an inkwell. He blinked and shook his head, embarrassed by his lack of awareness. He'd not even considered looking around to see if what he needed might be in the room. His brain must really be mush after the beating. Perhaps the forced rest Samuel had demanded would actually help clear his brain so that when he did return to work it was functioning as sharply as possible.

"Here you are." She set the pages and writing implements on the table. "Anything else?"

"If you'll give me just a moment, I'll dash off a few lines to Charlie and then I'd appreciate it if you'd have one of the boys take it to him immediately." He waited for her swift nod and then lifted the pen to write his missive.

Mr. Smythe,
Unfortunately, I have been injured and thus under doctor's orders to
rest for a few days. However, I understand the importance of
completing the trestle and so will be back on the job come Monday
morning. You can trust me to ensure a timely completion of the
project.
Your obedient servant, etc.
Bryce Day

He folded the paper quickly and thrust it into the air toward Laura. "Thank you for your help."

Laura arched a brow. "Let me see what you're planning." She opened the page and skimmed its contents before refolding it and sliding it into her apron pocket. "You're planning to return to work tomorrow? As in, get on a horse and ride with broken ribs?"

He clenched his jaw, anticipating the pain and discomfort of his plan. What choice did he have? The plans were in his possession and must be shared with the crew. Plus, he didn't get paid if he didn't go to work and he desperately needed the money in order to make his other plans come to fruition. Besides, he didn't want Blackwater to think he'd succeeded in whatever his nefarious intent might have been. So he nodded grimly at her.

"Exactly."

"I doubt Samuel will approve." She arched her brow at him again. "But that's between you two. I'll send Michael immediately with this."

Laura huffed as she spun about and marched out of the room. Bryce sighed. His intent would upset his friend. It had already upset the good doctor's wife. No matter what else, come the morning he would get dressed and ride into town to report for work before heading out to the jobsite at the trestle.

He stared out the window, the floral draperies hanging sedately to either side. The sun shone brightly on the brown grassy expanse but he could tell from the cold seeping through the glass panes that the sunshine was deceptive of the wintery day beyond. His knee ached, indicating approaching precipitation. As long as it warmed up a tad, that would stay rain but it had been cold for days so he held out little hope of not seeing snow. Snow which could delay completion of the project he desperately needed to finish.

Michael rode down the lane stretching away in front of the house, heading toward town and the housing community for the railroad workers where Charlie had a nice home. One day Bryce had every intention of building his own quality house where he could ensconce his bride and begin a family. One step at a time, though. The first step being to keep his good-paying job long enough to save up the money needed to purchase the property. Or perhaps he should court Lia first while he worked to save the money. Yes, he liked that concept much better. He didn't want to wait to resume their relationship. She might even have ideas as to the kind of dwelling he should look for. He smiled at the thought, certain he'd struck on a fine path toward the future he craved.

A future featuring the woman he'd dreamed of for years no matter what conditions or what atrocities he'd witnessed. Indeed, keeping her in his thoughts and carrying the cedar talisman all that time probably saved his body and soul. Hope springs eternal, after all. He still held hope close that she'd permit him back in her life. He wanted and needed to be with her, to touch her strong and graceful hand, her lovely face, her silky hair. To kiss her sweet lips and hold her close, as close as the hope he held deep inside of him.

One possible obstacle to his dreams and plans was Blackwater, but he wouldn't be an impediment for long.

* * *

LIA COULDN'T STAND NOT KNOWING. Three days had passed since Bryce was beaten up and she hadn't had a good excuse for going across the yard to see for herself how he fared. She'd promised her brother to leave him alone and she had, reluctantly, throughout the weekend. But now that a new week had begun, she had to know. Early Monday morning, she donned her cloak and pulled on her mittens before hurrying across the frosty way to her brother's home. In her heart, she carried the hope of having a long, satisfying conversation with Bryce if he felt up to it. In her hands, she carried a plate of freshly baked sugar cookies, primarily for the family but also for Bryce.

"Hello?" She closed the kitchen door behind her, scanning the empty kitchen for a good place to set down her offering.

Footfalls sounded in the hallway announcing Laura scurrying toward her. "Oh, hi, Lia. What have you there?"

Lia held out the chipped porcelain plate stacked with two dozen sparkling cookies. "Sugar cookies, warm out of the oven."

"They smell wonderful." Laura accepted the plate and turned to set it on the work table in the center of the room. Then she winked at Lia before opening her mouth to call out, "Samuel! Boys! Sugar cookies!"

Lia laughed out loud as the house rocked with the pounding of footsteps converging on the kitchen. In a flash, the boys raced into the room, following their noses to the plate on the table. Sam came more slowly but still in a rush to get hold of one of the delicate goodies before they were devoured by the always-hungry boys.

"What do you say to your Aunt Lia, boys?" Laura chided.

Mumbled "thank-yous" came from their full mouths. Lia grinned. "You're welcome. Save some for Mr. Day."

Sam reached for another cookie then darted a glance at her. "He's heading out to work, so he just might miss out on them entirely."

She frowned at her brother's statement. "Is he well so soon?"

Sam shook his head with a grimace on his face. "That's not going to stop him."

Lia lifted her brows in alarm. "Something should. Where is he?"

"In his room."

"Alright." If Samuel didn't feel up to the challenge, then she'd have to see about the stubborn man's intent to leave the property before he'd healed sufficiently. She brushed past the crowd devouring the cookies to march down the hallway to the front of the house and out the front door. Without pausing to reconsider, she swept through the front door of the small house and marched into his room. Then came to an abrupt halt at the determined yet hard expression on Bryce's face when he espied who had barged into his room. No matter. She couldn't let him leave. "You're going to work? You should not."

He continued dressing, slipping on his suit coat and tugging it in place. "I have much work to do, so yes, I should."

"Samuel said you're not healed enough to return to work. You need to rest." Her heart clamored inside, battling with her crushed hope of sitting and conversing pleasantly with him and her horror at his intention.

"My boss demands my presence so we can reopen the trestle as soon as possible. I need to ensure the crew is on schedule and doing a quality job. I can't sit around doing nothing when that is so vital."

"But what if those beastly men come back? They might kill you."

"They've said their piece. I don't think you need fret over such an unlikely occurrence." He frowned as he scanned the room for a moment and then met her astonished gaze. "Besides, I have no intention of resorting to or permitting further violence to occur in my presence. I've had enough and won't condone it further."

Stunned by his stubbornness, Lia wrapped her arms around her waist. The man was going to get himself injured or worse, certainly if he had no desire to defend himself, and she simply couldn't stand by and say nothing. The mere thought of his being hurt upset her to her core. "I cannot allow you to put yourself at risk. Please, Bryce, stay home another few days."

"You need not worry about me, sweetheart. I am tougher than you're giving me credit for." He crossed the room to lift a hat from the standing coat rack. As he pivoted around to face her again, the boys chased each other into the room. The jostling of five young boys as they played tag between the two adults pushed Lia closer to Bryce as she hurried to avoid being run into by the reckless youth. He steadied her with both hands as Travis tucked behind him to avoid being tagged by Ian's outstretched hand.

"Boys, take your game outside." Bryce's deep voice halted the fun, the boys freezing in midstride to swallow sudden apprehension at the umbrage resonating in his tone. "You should know better than to rough house in here like that."

"Yes, sir." The older boys hung their heads as they left the ward, glancing back to gesture to the younger boys. "Come on, we gotta go." Once in the front office, they all perked up and ran to the front door to continue their game.

Only the youngest, Travis, remained behind, his little hands gripping Bryce's pant legs. She couldn't help the swell of love in her heart as she saw the two of them together. Not that they were aware of the reality of their relationship. Father and son looked only somewhat alike despite sharing certain traits and interests. If only they knew, how would they feel about being related? She cringed at the thought of saying something. Failed to do so yet again. Soon though she'd have to tell Bryce at least. Lia freed herself from Bryce's grasp and sidled around him to peer down at Travis. He bit his lip as he stared up at her, fear of punishment glittering in his eyes.

"You too, Travis." Lia laid a gentle hand on the boy's shoulder to pull him out from behind Bryce's legs. She smiled reassuringly at him as she urged him to follow his brothers. Slowly he made his way to the door, glancing back at her as if seeking her permission to go. She nodded at him and shooed him out the door. After he'd gone outside, she turned back to meet Bryce's curious expression. Something in his eyes gave her pause. Did he guess? "What?"

He shook his head as a frown briefly dimmed his eyes. "It's nothing, I'm sure. But I must go. If you'll excuse me." He tapped his hat onto his head and then picked up the portfolio from the writing desk nearby, sliding it into the saddle bag waiting on the chair before starting for the door.

"I wish you wouldn't."

"Please don't start again." He continued out the door and across the front room.

Lia trailed after him, wishing she had more influence over his actions. But if he insisted on going, then perhaps she should ride along and make sure he arrived at the depot safely. She could do that much.

In the barn, he quickly saddled his horse while Lia went to do the same with her favorite mare, Gem. She could use some light exercise to keep her fit. Lia hadn't ridden her the last few days, but it was high time she did so. As she slipped on the bridle, Bryce led Jet down the aisle and stopped at the stall where she was fastening the leather straps with gentle care.

"What do you think you're doing?" A touch of steel threaded through his tone as he frowned at her.

"Going with you. Somebody has to make sure you're safe." She patted Gem's neck and then gathered the reins in her hand. "So, go on so I can bring her out."

"I do not need you to protect me. Do not proceed with your attempt to coddle me, sweetheart. I will not tolerate that." He gazed at her for a long moment until she relented with a pursing of her lips. "Thank you. I will see you later."

He very slowly mounted, direct evidence of the pain he tried to hide, and rode away. "Oh, Gem, should I go after him anyway?" She worried her lower lip as she debated with herself. But the firm tone he'd used finally convinced her to refrain from her desire to protect him. This time.

* * *

THE NERVE OF THE WOMAN. Bryce rode slowly toward town, giving his temper time to cool. How could she insinuate he wasn't man enough to take care of his own business without some female playing nursemaid to him? Granted, he hadn't healed yet and his ribs ached with each step of the horse. Still he had work to do and he aimed to see it through. After an interminable hour, he finally reached the depot and tied Jet to the hitching rail out front. He planned to check in with Charlie and then ride out—ribs be damned—to the trestle to deliver the revised plans and assess the men's progress. And prove to them, and to himself, that the beating hadn't left him beaten.

He climbed the stairs to the second floor and Charlie's office. He didn't hesitate at the door but strode in briskly to stand by his boss's desk until the man paused in his scribblings in the ledger before him.

"Good day to you, Bryce. What did you mean by you were injured?"

After returning the greeting, Bryce shrugged away the discomfort and unease recalling the attack left inside of him. "Oh, a few men took exception to my presence apparently."

Charlie's brows dropped over dark eyes. "Which men? Some of yours?"

Shaking his head, Bryce sat on the chair in front of the desk, needing to rest after the strain of riding. "No, but my men didn't stop them either."

"Who was it then? Do you know?"

"The leader was Dylan Blackwater, a former rebel apparently who objects to my service." He held back the personal slant of that man's interest in Bryce's woman, not wanting to say too much. What could Charlie do about any of it anyway?

Charlie tapped his pencil on the lined pages of the ledger for a few seconds. "And? What are you leaving out?"

Damn. The man's instincts were just as sharp as ever. Probably why he survived the war with only a lingering limp after all the precarious and dangerous situations he'd faced. More so than what Bryce had even seen.

Reluctantly, he filled Charlie in on Blackwater's interest in Lia. "I don't think she returns it though."

"You said this is the same woman you left behind during the war, right?" At Bryce's shrug, Charlie nodded slowly and dropped the pencil onto the desk. "I can tell you're angry. Is it about Blackwater or something else?"

"Crimey, Charlie, does nothing get by you?" Bryce clawed through his hair with one hand and then gripped his nape. "How can a woman be the answer to all of my dreams one minute and then turn around and make me so angry the next?"

Charlie burst out laughing. "Oh, brother, you've got it bad. What did she do?"

"She wanted to escort me to work to keep me safe." He clenched his nape again and then forced his hand to relax and drop into his lap. "Of all the silly, embarrassing things she could venture."

"I think that's her way of showing you she loves you right back." Charlie fingered the pencil, wiggling it between thumb and forefinger. "What are you going to do about that?"

Bryce stilled and regarded his boss for a long moment. "What I've wanted to do for a long time."

CHAPTER 16

 After a very long day in the saddle and supervising the men's satisfactory progress on the trestle, Bryce finally turned his horse toward home. He kept one arm snugged against his ribs as he rode up the lane and to the barn at Hopewell. Bracing himself, he swung one leg over the saddle and hesitated before dropping the short distance to the ground. He bit back the exclamation and settled for a grunt as pain swept through him. Drawing a breath, he stopped halfway due to the increase in discomfort from expanding his ribcage. He longed to undress and lay down in bed, to stop moving and hurting. First, he had to take care of Jet, then he'd slip into his room and rest. Tomorrow would be another long day.

He moved slowly, carefully, to lead Jet into the barn and untack him. Lugging the saddle and bridle into the tack room hurt as much as dismounting but he kept his complaining to a minimum in case anyone else appeared. He didn't want anyone to think he wasn't up to doing his job, getting on with his business and his life. With a final pat on the neck, he left Jet to eat his mash and hay and strolled to the house. He let himself into the kitchen with its savory aromas and was immediately surrounded by young eager faces.

"Mr. Day! Mr. Day! Tell us a story b'fore dinner!" Travis tugged on Bryce's coat sleeve. "Please!"

"Yes, please." The older boys echoed their youngest brother with bright, hopeful smiles on their faces.

"I don't know if…" Bryce began and then stopped as Laura shook her head.

"Leave him be, boys." She stirred a kettle of something steaming hot and smelling delicious. "I'm sure Mr. Day is tired after working all day and ready for some hot chicken stew."

Bryce's stomach rumbled in response to the invitation and the mouth-watering aroma. Still, he didn't feel much like eating, more like sleeping. "It smells really good, Laura."

"Samuel is already in the dining room. Go on in and I'll bring in supper in a moment." She studied him for a few seconds and then shooed him toward the hallway door. "Pour yourself something to drink on your way in. You look like you could use it."

He could use a nap more. But he couldn't deny his hostess anything after all of her care and concern in nursing him back to health. Relenting, Bryce unbuttoned his overcoat with one hand. "Thank you for the compliment, my lady." He grinned at her, letting her know he was joshing with her.

"You're welcome, my liege." She huffed a laugh as she turned back to the pot and began ladling its contents into porcelain floral bowls arrayed on a large silver tray resting on the table beside the cookstove. She called over her shoulder, "Boys, you go along with Mr. Day."

So now he was the boys' shepherd, too. He smiled to himself at the thought. One day he hoped to have his own flock of children. Hopefully with Lia if he could fix things between them. He envisioned a house as large or larger than the one he stood in, with several bedrooms for the kids. And a large dining room table in order to seat not only his family but the guests he expected to visit frequently. Hmm. So he wanted a lifestyle similar to Samuel and Laura's. Why not? They seemed perfectly content and happy with their lot in life. His smile grew as he began leading the boys down the hall and into the dining room.

The room welcomed him with its family-size table covered with a cheery red-and-green plaid tablecloth, evoking the hopeful theme of the upcoming holiday. A festive vase of greenery and citrus sat in the center of the table, flanked by matching silver candelabras alight with flickering flames. The paneled walls reflected both the candlelight and the light from oil lamps mounted on the walls around the room. A cozy and welcoming space for everyone. The atmosphere his friend had created made his weary soul feel lighter, welcomed. It made coming home something to look forward to while working.

Samuel sat at the head of the table, a newspaper in his hands. He appeared relaxed and at peace with the world as he turned the page and glanced up at Bryce. "Oh, there you are. How did it go?"

"I'm still in one piece." Bryce chuckled as he stationed himself at the drink cart to pour two fingers of whiskey into a rock glass.

"Glad to hear it. Boys, take your seats and I'll read this Letter from Santa to you."

"Santa? Yay!"

"What's he say?"

"Is he coming this year after all?"

Bryce pivoted away from the cart and carried his glass to his place at the foot of the table. Samuel insisted he take up that place as a nod to his importance in the family. The foot was second in hierarchy only to Laura's place at Samuel's right hand. The five boys sat on either side of the shortened table. Since the entire family wasn't eating at one time, a couple of leaves had been removed and stored in the hall closet. Thus the distance between the head and foot of the table had shrunk to only six feet instead of the ten it was for the holiday meal a few weeks back.

"Now, quiet, boys, and let me read." He cleared his throat and then scanned the eager faces watching him. "Here goes. Ahem.

"To the Little Folks of Huntsville. Well, my dear little friends, how have you all been, and what have you been doing all this long time since I saw you last? And which of you have said the oftenest, 'dear old Santa Claus, bless his heart! How I wish he'd come to see us once more?' And so I will my dear, this very Chris'mas though your old

Santa isn't quite as rich as he used to be; having lost his two best mules, Childs friend, and Good gift, besides a great deal of other property. So you mustn't expect as many pretty and good things as I used to give you…"

Bryce snickered at the comical tone of the letter, listening more to the sound of Samuel's voice than the words. Samuel did a fine job of acting the part of Santa as he read, emphasizing certain comments more than others. He probably read to his boys frequently so had plenty of practice. Something Bryce would copy when he had his own children to read to. He merely needed to make amends with Lia, find a way to convince her to give him another chance.

"So there you have it, boys. Santa is coming to town this year." Samuel folded the paper and laid it aside. "Be sure to write him a letter now, you hear?"

Laura came in carrying the large tray of steaming bowls of stew. She set the tray on a small round table in the corner and then began doling out the bowls. When she finished, she took her place to Samuel's right and nodded to her husband.

Samuel lifted his spoon and took a bite, the signal to the rest of the family to begin eating. After a few bites, he paused. "Bryce, how are you feeling? You look rather pale to me."

"I'm fine." Bryce glanced at the boys as they scooped stew quickly into their mouths, hoping they wouldn't chime in with more negative commentary on his appearance. "Have you spoken with Lia today? I think I should go talk with her."

"She's been busy helping her sisters with ball preparations from what I understand." Laura held a spoonful of stew over her bowl to allow it to cool. "I'm sure she'd welcome your attention after so many years of not seeing you. She missed you."

"She did?" Bryce searched Laura's peaceful expression for clues as to how much Lia might have missed him. Maybe enough to forgive him? "She said so?"

"No, but I could tell. Especially at first…" Laura shifted her gaze from Bryce to Samuel and then slipped the spoon into her mouth.

Bryce waited for her to swallow, expecting her to complete her thought. She continued to spoon stew into her mouth, averting her gaze from his. Finally, he couldn't wait any longer. "You were saying, Laura?"

"May we be excused?" Michael asked into the ensuing silence. "We want to go play catch before it gets too dark outside."

"Yes, go ahead." Samuel swallowed hard, his Adam's apple sliding harshly up and down.

Laura smiled at her sons until they'd left the room, then slid a guilty look toward Bryce. "I didn't want to say in front of them. Lia had some trying times after you left, but she wouldn't talk about her feelings."

"I know she was heartbroken but what else did she have to confront?" Curiosity raced through him, chased by concern as Laura shook her head slowly at him.

"You'll need to ask her if you want to know more." Laura pressed her lips together as she glanced to Samuel. "Right, dear?"

"Indeed. It's up to her whether she wants to share with you or not."

Unease swept through his gut. Something lurked in the shadows at Hopewell. Lia hid something from him, but what? "What is this all about? Give me a clue so I know whether it's worth pursuing."

Samuel drew a breath and let it out slowly. "I can only say that her relationship with one of her nephews has a complicated beginning. She'll have to tell you more, if she so chooses."

Secrets. He hated secrets. They often led to lies and he couldn't tolerate such deceit. In fact, his father had beaten that lesson into him whenever Bryce had ever so much as didn't tell the whole truth, let alone a white lie or a fib. But to have a lie based on secrets, that proved untenable for his comfort and trust in others. He pondered what his friend had said about the boys. After a moment, he nodded to himself. Samuel must be referring to Travis since the other boys were already in the picture when Bryce first met Lia. He stared at his friend and then Laura but refrained from pressing them further. He'd have to ask Lia about her complicated relationship and see what she said. Would she tell him her secrets? Would she tell him the truth?

Only one way to find out.

* * *

THE NEXT AFTERNOON Lia relaxed on her front porch, a blanket about her shoulders while she read her book. She hadn't spoken to Bryce since the tense conversation about his going to work the day before but she'd seen him come and go since. She supposed he'd gone to work at the railroad again that morning since his horse was gone. Her impulse to protect him had come upon her suddenly. Why exactly? She couldn't decipher the motivation for her actions other than to say she cared for him in ways stronger and deeper than she'd allowed herself to admit. By sitting out on the porch, despite the chill in the air, she hoped he'd come to speak to her instead of her having to seek him out.

A little while later she heard a horse approaching and looked up from the fascinating novel in her hands. Bryce returning home. She'd recognize his silhouette as he rode anywhere. Sitting tall, his wide-brimmed hat shading his eyes, hands lightly holding the reins. And of course, she would know his horse from its beautiful coloring and fine lines. Gladness eased through her at having him on the property again. She pressed her lips together and addressed the page in front of her. She didn't want to appear too eager for his company. Despite her racing heart and tension in her shoulders as she tried to be patient. Would he stop and talk to her? Or ride on by without a word?

The hoofbeats stopped at the foot of the porch steps. "Lia, we need to talk."

She raised her eyes to see his serious countenance from where he sat on his horse. Why hadn't he dismounted? Apprehension washed through her. "Come join me?"

He hesitated for a moment and then dismounted, tying the reins to the hitching post. With one stride, he traversed the steps and then crossed to sit in the chair opposite the small table in-between. He didn't relax into the seat but remained sitting upright. He pulled the small piece of wood from his pocket. "The talisman you gave me worked to bring me back to you, safe and sound as you had hoped."

He fingered the beautiful carved keepsake. "I shaped it into a magnolia blossom to remind me of you."

"Yes, it did and it's lovely. But is something wrong?" Lia asked, bracing for a lecture of some sort. "You seem tense."

"I think you've been keeping something from me. Samuel mentioned to me last night that your relationship to Travis is complicated but didn't say exactly what he meant." He slid the talisman back into his pocket.

Lia's heart skipped a beat before setting off at a gallop. What did he know? What did he suspect? What had Samuel told him? Oh dear Lord, what should she do? Her mother's cautionary words echoed in her mind. "It is."

"Would you care to elaborate?" Bryce gripped the front edge of his chair with both hands. "How is being the boy's aunt complicated? You've been an aunt for years."

"The truth?"

"Always." Bryce shifted in his seat, clasping his hands together as he leveled his assessing gaze on her. "I cannot abide anyone who doesn't speak the truth. My father beat that into me as a boy so I will not tolerate deceit from those I care about."

She nodded slowly as she swallowed the fear in her mouth. Would he claim Travis as his and take him away from his lying mother? If she told the truth, would he not want to be with her because she had deceived him? Either way, she'd never see either of them again if so. Bryce wouldn't allow her to be with her son even as his supposed aunt. If she fessed up, would it ruin everything? She'd forgotten about his father's strong-armed way of ensuring his sons always spoke the truth. Nonetheless, he deserved to know. She had to set the record straight. She knew that but did it have to be so soon? The steady gaze of her interrogator left her no doubt as to his sincerity when he said he wanted the truth.

She braced for his reaction and then shrugged once. "The truth is that Travis is my son."

Bryce's eyes widened as he leaned forward. "Your son? Then why is Samuel raising him?"

"To quell any adverse effect to my reputation and my future happiness. Travis' future as well. I couldn't raise him. I couldn't give him what Sam can. And he has brothers to play with. It's for the best." She should have told him the whole truth, but fear contorted the words into a half-truth. Lord, forgive her.

"I can't believe you're his mother." He drew in a long breath. "So you didn't wait for me after all."

Of course he'd assume she'd slept with someone else after he'd left. Why wouldn't he? Still his opinion of her lack of commitment stung. But that assumption gave her a little more time to eke out the truth in bits and pieces instead of all at once. Ease the impact of what the truth would change for everyone. What it would change would be everything and not necessarily for the better.

"Like I said, it's for the best that he is treated as one of Samuel's children."

"Does Travis know?"

"No. We decided we'd wait until he's older, if ever, to tell him."

"He needs to know someday. He needs to know who his parents are. All of them, apparently." Bryce continued to stare at her. "No wonder you tried to mother me yesterday." He let out a sigh. "I don't need you to mother me, Lia."

"I'm sorry I tried." Lia pressed her lips together as she glanced away to scan the area. Slowly, she'd come to see how hurt and upset he must have been by her attempt to coddle him the previous morning. "I was worried for you."

"I appreciate your concern if not your actions." He fell silent for a long moment as he fidgeted in his seat. Then he met her gaze with raised brows. "I get the feeling you're not telling me everything. Which makes me wonder if I can trust you like I thought I could. Are you telling me the whole truth?"

She hesitated, considering how to respond. She wanted, really wanted to tell him everything but abject fear kept her silent. Fear of his reaction to the truth of Travis' parentage. Fear of how Travis might react to it. But mostly fear of how it would change absolutely everything for Travis's future. Still, one day, she'd have to confess all and deal with the consequences.

"Your hesitation tells me everything I need to know about you." Bryce stood up and looked down at her with glistening eyes. "I thought we'd raise a family together and grow old together but I see now that can't be. Not if I can't trust you. Goodbye, Magnolia."

He marched down the steps and swung into the saddle, riding toward the barn to stable his horse.

She stared after him, shocked into silence. The talisman brought him home to her and yet. Tears coursed unheeded down her cheeks as he left her in every sense. They'd grown closer over the last weeks but now everything she'd dreamed of had been rent asunder. Keeping the whole truth from him had caused the very pain she'd hoped to avoid, that of losing him all over again. What had she done? She gasped as the pain of his words crashed through her core. Wrapping her arms around her waist she rocked in her seat, anguish and heartbreak consuming her. After several minutes, she dashed away the tears when she saw Bryce emerge from the barn to stride to Samuel's house. He disappeared inside, leaving her alone and lonely.

Lia grappled with her composure, finally calming enough to gather her things in preparation for going inside to fix the evening meal alongside her mother and sisters. From a distance, she heard the steady thudding of someone chopping wood behind Samuel's house. Ignoring the urge to investigate who, she hurried inside.

CHAPTER 17

*D*isappointment melded with a simmering anger with each swing of the axe. Wood chips spurted upward as the blade sank into the hardwood log propped on a stump. He winced at the ache in his mending ribs but kept going. A little physical discomfort might distract him from the raw emotional pain his own principles created. Bryce had just ended his future. It was that simple. He hefted the blade and then swung it behind, up and over, to finish splitting the log. Everything he'd been working toward lay at his feet like the wood chips, in bits and pieces scattered about. He'd walked away from the love of his life. She represented everything he wanted: a loving, intelligent wife, a heap of healthy and happy children they'd raise together, a home to build and fill with their loving family. All now broken dreams. How could he ever trust her though, when she was obviously hiding something from him? Their break-up left him feeling empty yet filled with misery and grief.

Propping the axe handle on the stump, he snatched up the pieces of wood and carried them to the wood pile nestled up to the backside of the house. He plopped the sticks of wood onto the pile and then strode back to continue chopping wood. His hands vibrated from the concussion of the axe on wood. He'd chop more, vent the frustrated anger through action. Despite the large pile already stacked near the back door for easy access from the kitchen and its cookstove and fireplace. He had to do something to burn off the grief filling his soul. She'd disappointed him, thwarted his plans and hopes for their life together. But he'd seen the hurt in her eyes at his words, his severing of their budding courtship. He could kick himself. He never thought he'd ever have reason to hurt her. He blew out a breath as he grabbed the axe and got back to work.

"So what's wrong, my friend?" Samuel halted a few strides from where Bryce swung the axe in a wide arc. "You only chop wood when something is amiss."

Bryce glanced at his friend and lowered the axe. "It's over."

"You'll need to clarify. What is over?"

Bryce sighed as he hefted the heavy tool. "I've ended my courtship of Magnolia."

Samuel crossed his arms. "Why?"

"I cannot trust her like I thought I could." Bryce played with the axe handle, rocking the heavy blade back and forth like a pendulum where it rested on the ground. "She's hiding something from me. I cannot tolerate deception. Especially from someone I love."

"Everyone has private thoughts and feelings they don't want to share." Samuel moved closer to Bryce, a protective brother defending his sister. "I'm sure you have not revealed everything in your past to her, right? Like what exactly you did during the war."

"You've told me not to share that." Bryce shrugged. "I agree it's probably best to leave the past behind me."

"Which is your right. Lia also has the right to choose how much she shares with you."

"I agree to a point, but lying is not acceptable behavior."

"Of course not, but is she actually lying or just being circumspect in how much she reveals to you?"

"Is there a difference?" Bryce pondered the fine line his friend was drawing.

Bryce had been raised to always tell the truth. He'd been punished by his father when he suspected that he'd prevaricated on the story he told. Especially when something was broken or someone was injured. Like the time he'd gotten into an argument with his youngest brother and they ended up in a punching and hitting spree. He'd come away with a split lower lip but his brother, being younger and smaller, had bruises and a loose tooth. When asked, he'd lied about what had happened and whose fault it was. Father had beaten him with a green switch until he'd cried real sincere tears. His authoritarian father held no tolerance for any form of deceit. A lesson Bryce had learned well.

"Just because you don't reveal every single detail about a situation or feeling does not mean you're hiding something. It means you're keeping some things private to protect yourself or others."

"Why do I get the feeling then that she's keeping something from me about what happened to her?"

"I will tell you what I know so that you'll have more faith in her, and will better understand her reluctance to share it with you. I'm sure she's concerned knowing what happened to her might change how you see her, how you'd treat her as a result."

Chagrin flooded Bryce's heart. He'd not considered such a situation. What would Samuel share with him and could it change his view of Lia? "I'm listening."

"I will only tell you that when she found out she was pregnant, Laura and I agreed that we would raise the child, Travis, as our own."

"To protect her reputation." Understanding settled on his shoulders like a heavy blanket. "I can understand why she doesn't want to talk about it. Giving up her child must have been difficult even with him living nearby."

Understanding what happened to her in the past furthered the amount of dismay simmering inside at how he'd hurt her. The anger he'd felt toward her now redirected to himself. He'd made everything worse by making assumptions based on a dearth of information. He had accused her of deceiving him when she was merely protecting her and her child's reputations, perhaps protecting him too. In fact, knowing the sacrifice she'd made for Travis' benefit did indeed change how he saw her. She'd relinquished her son to be raised by others more capable to provide him a decent life. She was far more loving and possessed a strength of character greater than he'd realized.

"We don't talk about any of that, and Travis doesn't know yet that Lia is his true mother. We'll tell him when he's old enough to understand."

"That is for the best." Bryce stared at Samuel for a long moment, his mind racing with ideas on how to apologize to Lia for his harsh words. While Samuel hadn't offered any new information about Lia's past, he had shone a light on a different perspective. He must clean up the mess he'd created by jumping to conclusions and acting too impulsively. Nothing suitable popped into his mind. The task of persuading her to give him another chance would have to be the perfect moment. But when? "I need to make things right between us. To get her to give me another chance. But how?"

He needed enough time to make her listen to him. He feared he'd become tongue-tied under the pressure of saying the right thing at the right time to convince her to let him back into her life, to let him court her. He must make her understand how sorry he was for jumping to wrong conclusions about her intentions and actions. Which meant he should have a plan in place, one that included a sincere apology before he asked her to marry him. He'd also need that ring. A unique one to match the unique qualities she possessed. He'd ride into town the next day and purchase a beautiful ring she'd adore. Then he'd go straight to her and fix the mess he'd made.

"Christmas is a time of miracles." Samuel winked at him as they started walking toward the back door. "You'll need a miracle to get her to listen to you."

"Yes, you're right. But I shall make my own miracle tomorrow." He smiled at Samuel as he imagined how he'd arrange to talk with her. Imagined holding her hands as he sincerely professed both an apology for hurting her and a promise to strive to never do so again. Hope sprung into his heart the more he contemplated what he'd say and do. "I feel better now that I have a plan in mind."

"Who is that coming around the house?" Samuel pointed to a burly man driving a carriage toward them.

"That's Charlie Smythe." Alarm and surprise rushed through Bryce as he recognized his friend and boss. "I wonder what's wrong."

Charlie stopped the carriage and motioned to Bryce to come closer. "I'm sorry to interrupt your evening, Bryce, but an important shipment is waiting up the line. You need to go out to the work site and get that trestle open. I've already ordered them to work round the clock until it's open and that they'll be paid more per hour to ensure the work is done as fast as possible."

"Fine. I'll ride out there tomorrow morning." Bryce quickly recalculated his plans for the morrow. "I can be there at first light and see what's happening."

"No, I need you to go tonight. Plan to stay on site until it's done so we don't have any missteps or delays."

Bryce's heart sank at the demand from his employer. He couldn't very well say no without risking his job and the money flowing into his pockets that represented. Besides, his professional reputation was at stake. He'd designed the replacement trestle and he'd make sure it was built to his specifications so it did the intended job of safely carrying cargo and passengers. And completed as soon as humanly possible to boot.

"I'll grab my bedroll and stuff and head out in a few minutes, then." Bryce glanced to Samuel. "If you'll let the others know where I've gone?"

Samuel nodded as he glanced between Bryce and Charlie. "Of course."

Charlie gathered the traces in one hand, preparing to drive away. "Thank you, Bryce. I know it's a sacrifice but it's necessary. Keep me updated on progress."

"I will." Bryce saluted his boss. "You can count on me."

"Right." Charlie nodded and then urged his horse into a trot.

Bryce watched him drive away, thinking about what he'd need to gather quickly. Evening approached and he'd rather not ride in the dark out to the site. Still, the timing couldn't be worse. He'd go, and he'd urge the men to work as fast as they could. Then he'd execute the other plans he'd made. Only… Would she wait for him until he could return? Again?

* * *

WHEN BRYCE ARRIVED at the trestle later that evening the other men had already set up a makeshift camp beside the river. A campfire burned in the center of a ring of beige canvas tents with men perched on folding chairs around it. The smell of roasting meat and coffee permeated the air, evoking memories of life during the war. How many endless nights had he spent camping out? Too many to count.

After seeing to Jet's needs, Bryce strode to the campfire gathering. "Good evening, men."

Muttered greetings blended together as they continued with their eating and drinking.

Clearly, they weren't very happy to see him. Well, he hadn't forgotten nor forgiven them for not helping him when Blackwater beat him up. He couldn't let them off so easily. Without another word, Bryce set up his own puptent at the outer edge of the ring of others. It seemed surreal to be surrounded by men in work clothes versus the blue uniforms with a gold stripe down the pant leg he'd worn during the recent war. Thank goodness all that fighting and death was behind him. After a short interval, he returned to the fire and stood with his fists on his hips as he addressed the men.

"I know you don't much like me, but we have a job to do. Not only the corporate bosses but our friends and neighbors are counting on us to reopen this railroad line and soon." He slid his gaze around the circle of faces staring back at him. "Now that you've had a rest, let's get to work. Bring those lanterns and let's get this done. Are you with me?"

A few moments passed before anyone moved. Moments during

which he feared mutiny floated in the men's minds. Finally, they settled down as one man cleared his throat.

"Yes, sir, we are." Stephen Brenner, the leader of the crew, stood up and wiped his hands on his jeans. "We signed on to do the work, so let's get to it."

"Very good." One battle won at least. Relief eased the tightness in Bryce's chest.

The men worked in four-hour shifts through the night, taking turns securing the heavy beams into place. A man broke out into song, singing carols one after another with other men joining in from time to time. The deep bass leading a chorus of tenors helped speed the work along, setting a pace and blurring the passage of hours. The men worked well together, teamwork born of many days applying their skills to the task at hand.

The next morning dawned clear and cold with a hint of snow in the air. Bryce emerged from his tent and paused to stretch, yawning after only a handful of hours of sleep. His back ached from the hard ground beneath his bedroll. He hadn't seen any rocks but his muscles as well as his achy ribs felt them. Pounding and singing continued apace in the distance. A few men sat around the campfire, sipping coffee from metal cups. He grabbed his mug from the table by the tent and strode over to join them, pouring strong, hot coffee into his mug from the porcelain pot suspended over the flames.

He took a cautious sip but still burned his tongue on the scalding liquid. "Damnation, that's hot."

"What did you expect?" A bearded man shook his head and chuckled. "Course it's hot."

Bryce craved the jolt of energy he anticipated from the hot brew but common sense made him wait a minute to allow it to cool. He scanned the crew's faces until he found that of the crew boss. "How are we doing on finishing up this project?"

"Another day and a half and I think we'll be done," Stephen offered. "Friday night should find us sleeping in our own beds again."

Bryce chose a vacant chair and sat down to sip his coffee. "My back thanks you. I'll go see what I can do to help after I grab some-thing to eat. I want to help wherever I am needed."

Stephen spat into the dirt. "Not sure having an outsider will help the crew be more efficient."

"I've worked on railroad tracks and bridges. I know what I'm about." Bryce straightened his spine as he contemplated the other man. What would it take to be accepted? "Surely there's something I can do."

"We don't need no unionist elitism slowing our work. You just sit back and watch and we'll get it done." Stephen spat again, then poured more coffee into his mug. Standing, he loomed over Bryce. "Does that work for you?"

"Not really." Bryce set his mug down and pushed to his feet. "I have many years experience in addition to my training. The more hands the faster we'll accomplish this work. So I'll pitch in wherever I can as I see fit."

Stephen spat once more, aiming close to Bryce's feet but not hitting his boots. "You're the boss. But don't get in the way or I'll teach you a lesson you won't forget. I know about your past, about what all you did in the war, and I don't cotton to no unionist crap on my job. Got it?"

The man carried a huge grudge toward Bryce, or unionists in general, that was certain. He needed to cut that animosity off at the knees. "I'm not playing the unionist against the rebels game you seem to want to play. That argument has been settled, for good or bad. The war is over and we need as American citizens to find a way to move forward together. We cannot continue to have one country with two such disparate ideologies. Therefore, I ask that you give me a chance to prove to you that despite our previous differences, we can find common ground and common goals. Such as getting this trestle open for the benefit of all of our people and our commerce so we can restore prosperity to our community. Can we agree on that?"

Several of the other men around the fire had risen to their feet and now nodded in response to Bryce's question. Stephen continued to stare at him for a couple of seconds before slowly nodding.

"Aye. But that don't mean I can trust you completely just yet." Stephen poked a finger into Bryce's chest. "You'll have to earn that."

A flash of anger shot through Bryce at the poke but he quelled it with a pasted on grin. "I'll do my best to do so. Now, let's get this job done so we can all enjoy the upcoming holidays. Shall we?"

CHAPTER 18

"You're so patient with her," Aster said from where she leaned on the corral fence.

Lia smiled at her sister as she worked with teaching Merrybell how to longe in a circle using voice commands in the corral. "She is a good girl. I have high hopes for her."

The young horse was not only a good saddle horse but beautiful, which would make her a good brood mare as well. Passing on both her chestnut coloring as well as the white markings would produce pretty offspring. Her personality and conformation would also throw intelligent and willing fillies and colts. As a result, Merrybell represented the future expansion of the breeding program at Hopewell.

"Whoa, now." Lia repeated the command as she pulled on the longe line to slow the mare to a stop. She gathered the braided cotton rope into her hands as she walked toward the horse standing at one side of the circular pen, her long tail swishing side to side. "That's enough for today."

Leading the horse to the gate, pride welled inside Lia. She smiled at Aster, who had opened the gate to let Lia and the horse through. Then she spotted a pair of riders cantering up the lane between the houses and toward the corral at the rear of the property. She recognized one of the horses as Rowdy with his distinctive chestnut coloring and white blaze on his face. His rider must be Dylan Blackwater. She didn't recognize Dylan's companion nor the horse. The two men halted in front of the corral and dismounted with easy grace.

"Good morning, Mr. Blackwater. How may I help you today?" His handsome face was a welcome distraction to her wayward thoughts drifting toward self recriminations and grief over hurting Bryce and dashing any possibilities of them getting back together. He'd made it abundantly clear it was over between them. She'd have to try to move on yet again. Somehow.

"Good day to you both, ladies." Dylan removed his hat and bowed his head briefly. "Please allow me to introduce my good friend Mr. James Kincaid. Jim this is Magnolia Merryweather and…"

"Aster Merryweather, my sister," Lia supplied. "Nice to make your acquaintance, Mr. Kincaid. You have a fine horse. Might I ask his pedigree?"

The man beside Dylan removed his black bowler from his head, glanced at Aster, and then peered at Lia. "His pedigree? I believe his sire was Crimson Thunder, a thoroughbred in racing and his dam was Gingerbread Dreams, also a thoroughbred."

"I see. I can tell he's got some fine legs which would support your claim to his lineage connected to horse racing." Lia smiled at the handsome young man, noted his luxurious brown hair and gentle blue eyes. Eyes which kept straying to peruse Aster. Interesting. She returned her own gaze to Dylan once again. "How may I be of service to you today?"

"By simply bestowing your beautiful smile upon me you have brought sunshine to my otherwise gloomy day." Dylan replaced his hat on his head with a tap of his palm on top. "We were out for a ride to take some fresh air and as we were passing I suggested we stop to inquire as to your health and to let you know I have been spreading the good word about the quality of your horseflesh. You should be receiving some additional inquiries as to suitable mounts in the near future."

"Why, thank you on both counts, Mr. Blackwater." Surprise and gratitude mixed inside Lia's core. "I very much appreciate your endorsement."

And his attention. Since Bryce had disappeared Tuesday evening after he'd ended any hope of a relationship, she had fluctuated between hurt and blaming herself. What happened to the man? Samuel had merely said he had to go to work, but for days on end? Well, she might have caused him to not trust her, but that didn't warrant his absence without any by-your-leave. Surely he needed to come home to refresh his clothing and his person. But she'd not seen any hint of his presence for days. Would he even return for the ball in three days, on Christmas Eve Eve? What about Christmas Day in just five days? She had a little gift for him but she might not even be able to give it to him. That thought sobered her smile.

Aster shifted closer to Lia as she nodded. "That was very generous of you, sir."

"You're welcome." Dylan stepped toward Lia, closing the distance between them until only a couple of feet remained. "As payment..."

Something in his eyes forewarned her of his next words. "Payment for what exactly?"

He chortled at her abrupt interruption. "As payment for my enthusiastic endorsement, I'd like to claim your first dance at the upcoming charity ball. Assuming of course that you will be attending."

She'd be there whether she really wanted to be or not. She wanted to support the fundraiser but must it all be so dramatic? Rose had completed her dress and they planned to have a conference the morning of the ball as to what jewelry would work best with each of the three sisters' gowns. They only possessed a limited assortment of pendants and earbobs between them so they needed to make careful choices for best effect with the various styles and colors of gowns they'd chosen. She'd longed to dance with Bryce, but sure as sunrise that wouldn't occur.

"I am the hostess, so yes, I shall be attending." Lia smiled at him, encouraging his continued regard. "I'd be delighted to put your name down on my dance card for the first spin around the floor that evening, sir."

"Wonderful. Will your lovely sister be there as well?" Dylan asked.

Lia noted the increased interest from James as she formed her reply. "Yes, she will."

"Very good." Dylan bowed to each of the sisters, followed by James doing the same. "Then we will look forward to dancing with you both this Saturday evening. Until then." He bowed again and then they smoothly remounted. "Good day, ladies."

After they'd ridden away, Lia smiled at Aster. "I think this charity ball may be more fun than we'd thought."

"James was handsome, wasn't he?" Aster grinned at Lia and looked down the lane where the dust from the horses hooves slowly drifted away.

"And interested in you." Lia patted Aster's arm and then clucked to Merrybell. "I'm going to put her out now and then I'll see you inside."

"Don't be long. Luncheon will be on the table soon."

Lia waved her sister away and then put Merrybell into the back pasture with the other mares. As the horse trotted off to join her herd, Lia couldn't help but wonder about what might transpire at the ball and with whom. Would Bryce even show up? How much did she want to get to know Dylan better? Could Aster have a new beau? Only time would tell.

* * *

OH, the joy of a job well done. Bryce grinned as Stephen made a production out of pounding the very last spike into place on the new trestle. When he finished, a cheer went up from every one of the workmen who had striven to perform their own Christmas miracle. Lots of shaking of hands and patting of backs followed. Their payoff was more than dollars and cents but also a sense of accomplishment and relief to return to a normal work schedule.

For Bryce, the end of the daunting work in a shortened time frame meant also that he could finally do a little shopping. They'd finished in time that they could attend the ball the next evening as well. Dance with his lovely Magnolia, too. He reached into his left pants pocket to finger the cedar magnolia blossom he always carried with him. His lucky talisman.

Stephen grabbed hold of Bryce's other hand before he even realized what was happening. "You done well, sir."

"You as well. I never doubted your expertise." Bryce smiled at the man, sensing a change, a softening of attitude toward him. "Now we can enjoy the holidays."

"Without worrying about working or losing our jobs, eh?" Stephen chuckled as he watched the other men's antics as they celebrated. After a second, he sobered and pointed with his chin to something behind Bryce. "Wonder what my good friend is doing way out here again?"

A chill wiggled down Bryce's back as he pivoted to face the new arrival. Blackwater. Striding toward him as if he owned the place. As if he belonged on the M&C Railroad work site. As if he were wanted. Bryce turned to address Stephen again before the intruder could interrupt them.

"Once the cavorting is done, feel free to order the men to break camp and pack up. Let's go home."

"Yes, sir!" Stephen mock saluted him.

"Don't be taking orders from that traitor." Blackwater halted beside Stephen, a scowl etched on his face. "He doesn't have any real standing in this community."

"Mr. Blackwater, is there something you need? What brings you so far out of town?" Bryce didn't want to deal with the man's animosity. He wanted to end whatever business the man had with him. He had other tasks to take care of and he was running out of time to do them.

Blackwater stood with feet apart, hands in his front pockets as he smirked. "I thought I'd let you know that Miss Magnolia Merryweather is looking forward to dancing with me first tomorrow evening. She knows it's best to stick with those who supported the right side during the war." His hard eyes perused Bryce from head to toe and back. "Seems pretty obvious she's wised up."

"Why do you say that?" Lia didn't hold such sentiments so the man was lying to him. Ire rose in his gut but the bastard wasn't worth the effort. Bryce should let it go. Not rise to the thug's bait. Walk away and hope ignoring the matter would make it all go away.

"Why, she practically panted at me when I asked to claim the first dance." Blackwater's eyes glittered as he sneered. "I think she wants a real man to pay her attention, so that's what I aim to do."

White-hot anger seethed inside Bryce at the challenge flaring in Blackwater's eyes. His demeaning depiction of Lia as some kind of animal desiring the braggart set his jaw. His fist formed without conscious effort. Bryce had determined that fighting the man would do no good to putting the past behind them. Reason and diplomacy must rule the day, must rule his anger, must win in the long run. He inhaled slowly and eased out the breath, forcing his hands to relax.

"Miss Merryweather will do as she likes, true. She has promised to dance with me as well. So I guess her card will be busy. If that is all?" Go away, man. He didn't want to get into it with Blackwater, not there and then if ever. But, damnation, if push came to shove, he'd not back down.

"I think you're chicken. You're scared to defend yourself, aren't you?" Blackwater smirked at him as he shook his head in mock disappointment. "You chicken shit."

"Fisticuffs will not solve anything. Now if that is all, I have some other business to attend." Bryce tipped his hat to Blackwater and then spun away, walking briskly to deter any further conversation and to put distance between his fist and that man's face.

* * *

THE MORNING OF THE BALL, Lia joined her sisters in their bedroom. The lone bed they shared stood across the room from the door, covered by the beautifully stitched quilt their grandmother had made for them before she'd passed years before. Two wardrobes flanked the lone window in the room. The wood floor was covered with a soft wool carpet. They'd shared this bedroom above their parents' bedchamber all of their lives. Aster had performed her usual miracle with plants and gathered together a beautiful arrangement of winter

181

stems which graced the writing desk by the door. A comfortable room most of the time.

However, Lia would much rather be out with her horses, or even merely cleaning her tack. She felt awful about the whole affair. Not only had she ruined everything with Bryce, but he'd disappeared for the last several days. Sam claimed it was work related but she wondered at the length of time he'd stayed away. Their fight probably inspired him to put distance between them both emotionally and physically. The scarf she'd crocheted for him would have to go to someone else, she supposed. No point wasting a warm bit of clothing. She glanced longingly out the window, wishing she could avoid the fashion show they were about to have in preparation for the dance that evening. Wishing she'd had the opportunity to try to make things right all the way around.

"Lia, you're not listening," Aster chided.

Her tone made Lia feel even worse. She turned away from the window and faced her sisters as they inspected their gowns. "What did I miss?"

"Rose said your dress is waiting for you to try on." Aster motioned to the emerald green dress draped over the chair by the desk. "I'll help you if you'd like."

"She should be able to fasten everything herself." Rose slipped her navy blue gown on, then made a show of buttoning up the front of the bodice. "I designed them to be easy to put on since the women who will eventually receive the dresses will likely not want to need help."

Lia crossed the room with measured strides. "That's a fine idea." She took up the satiny cotton dress and held it up to appreciate the details. The ribbons edging the bodice and the hem. The row of bone buttons decorating the front of the bodice. The fine stitching which was nearly invisible. The shimmer of the brushed fabric with a pattern of faint lines radiating from the waistband to the bottom of the skirt. She glanced at Rose with a smile. "This is absolutely beautiful. Thank you."

"Try it on and let me see how the gown makes you feel." Rose nodded at her as she smoothed her own skirts into place. "It should hopefully make you feel happy and confident. Let me help you with those buttons."

Lia turned so her sister could begin unbuttoning the long row of buttons. She could only wish for happiness. She removed her day dress and stepped into the fine material, pulling it up and onto her shoulders. Then she buttoned up the front of the bodice before spinning slowly. "How does it look?"

Aster tilted her head to one side as she studied the dress from every angle. "Bryce will love you in that gown. I'll fix up your hair real pretty, too."

Lia stiffened and shook her head slowly as she came to a halt. They simply didn't understand. She needed to change the subject away from the man. She had to find something else to think about. But what would distract her sisters? "What kind of baubles should I wear with it?"

"We can try a few things in a minute." Rose lifted one brow as she briefly pursed her lips. "But do you feel happy wearing the gown?"

She could tell her sister really hoped she'd say yes, but Lia still felt sad. How could she phrase her response to be encouraging? The next woman who wore it would more likely find joy from having a new dress. For Lia, the dress represented a dance she didn't want to go to, not when she couldn't dance with the man she loved. And she did love him even if she'd angered him. If he'd come home, she'd find a way to tell him how she felt and see if they could try again.

Pasting a smile on her lips, she shrugged. "Perhaps a little."

"What's wrong?" Aster asked, moving closer to Lia to lay a hand on her forearm.

"I had a fight with Bryce and now he's gone and I can't do anything about it," Lia said in a rush. "I don't know what to do."

Rose laid a hand on Lia's other arm as her smile faded. "I'm sure he'll return soon and then you can have a conversation with him."

Aster squeezed Lia's arm. "He will forgive you, I'm sure. He cares deeply for you, after all."

"I don't think so. He said he couldn't trust me and so couldn't be with me." Lia shook her head for a long moment. "I doubt he'll even speak to me again."

"He said he's going to the ball, so you'll see him there." Rose wrapped an arm about Lia's shoulders and gave her a brief squeeze. "Then you can apologize or explain."

"I shouldn't go. I'll just dampen everyone's good time." She laid her head on her sister's shoulder as tears smarted her eyes.

"I will not allow you to miss the results of all of our planning and efforts." Rose squeezed her shoulders again before pulling away to peer at her. "You shall not sit at home and mope. It's Christmas Eve Eve and we're going to go and have a wonderful time."

"I don't feel much like dancing." Not without Bryce. Not even the knowledge that she'd promised the first dance to Dylan boosted her mood. She had hoped it would, but that hope had faded away.

Aster lifted her chin as she gave Lia a stern look. "Mother would be sorely disappointed if you don't go. I can't allow you to hurt her feelings that way. So you're going with a smile."

Lia glanced at her two determined sisters and realized she was outnumbered. They'd made very good arguments as well. She really didn't want to see disappointment in her mother's expression after she'd worked so hard to orchestrate the charity ball. She suppressed a sigh and shrugged lightly. "Very well. I will try. Now what kind of earbobs or combs or other accessories would go with this gown?"

CHAPTER 19

$\mathcal{B}$ryce hurried inside the Easley Hotel, intent on finding Lia and apologizing for his unexplained and unplanned absence. In his pocket, he carried a ring box with a one-carat blue sapphire. He hoped to give it to her very soon. He feared she'd think the worst and he hadn't had the time to get back until now. But the work was completed and the trestle reopened in time to permit any last minute guests and goods to arrive in town safely. He had the next few days off to enjoy the Christmas holiday as a result of all of his extra hours. Time he hoped to spend with his woman.

The ballroom at the Easley Hotel glittered with candlelight and shiny ribbons tied to the swaths of garland decorating the columns and mantels. The yellow of lemons, orange of clementines, and the red of apples provided a burst of color against the dark green garland. On each of the many round tables an elegant arrangement occupied the center of the white cloth-covered surface. He knew that most of the decorations were Aster's inspired handiwork and silently applauded her talent. A banquet table stretched down the side of the room, the aromas of roasted meats mingling with the scent of pine, cedar, and magnolia boughs. Off to his left, a chamber orchestra of five played festive carols for the dancers in the center of the room.

He spotted Aster dancing with an unfamiliar gentleman, her radiant smile telling of her pleasure. Natalie and Richard danced past him as he hesitated at the edge of the dance floor. Rose came up to him with a pleased expression on her face.

"Bryce, I'm so glad you made it. Lia was upset at your absence."

"I'm sorry but it couldn't be helped." He gestured to the crowded ballroom. "Looks like the whole town has come out to support the charity event."

"Seems so but what else would you expect when my mother is involved?" Rose chuckled as she scanned the roomful of dancing and dining couples.

Bryce looked around the elegantly decorated space. He nodded a greeting to Charlie and his lady companion seated off to one side with some other people, apparently enjoying the delicious refreshments catered by Dentler. So many people had turned out to help rebuild the school.

But where was Lia? He scanned the crowd searching for her distinctive auburn hair until he finally spotted her. With Dylan Blackwater. The first dance she'd promised the arrogant man. Unacceptable. Anger surged in his gut at the sight of the two of them together. That man had no business horning his way in. Lia didn't understand who Dylan was and what he wanted from her. He'd end their dance in short order. He made his way through the crowd bordering the dance floor until he'd reached where Lia and Dylan danced toward him. When Dylan saw him standing there, he reared back his head as if in preparation to fight him again. Not now. Not ever. But his waiting upon Lia had come to an end.

"Miss Merryweather, I believe the next dance is mine?" He aimed a bold smile at her, keeping his eye on the other man. "If you're still willing."

She blinked at him for a second and then nodded, glancing nervously at Dylan's affronted countenance. "Of course."

Dylan held fast to her hand. "We aren't finished our dance. You can wait your turn." He tried to pull her back toward him but she resisted.

"Unhand her. She has decided to switch dance partners." Bryce stepped closer to her and used his bulk to force the other man to relent. "You have no right to intrude upon her time and attentions when she wouldn't want them if she knew your true nature. I know she would object even more knowing you and your thugs attacked me."

"It was you?" Lia snatched her hand away from Dylan with an exclamation. "You beat Bryce up? I cannot have anything more to do with someone who would hurt my friends or my family. You should go. Now."

"But…" Dylan stared at her for a moment before emitting a low growl of disgust. "You promised me a dance and I will have it."

"No, you won't." Bryce stepped in front of the other man and raised his fist in his face. "I will not permit you to strongarm anyone into anything they don't want to do. Now, you've been asked to leave but if you decide to resist, then we will take this outside to settle the matter. Either way, you will not be dancing with Miss Merryweather. Understood?"

Dylan bristled at the threat but the other dancers had stopped and were peering intently at the trio. He grunted out a sigh and stepped back, away from Bryce and Lia.

He mockingly bowed to them. "Never mind. It's not worth the effort. You two deserve each other."

Bryce wanted to grab the man by his lapels and bodily remove him from the premises. With Lia standing so close to him, doing so put her at risk. He couldn't indulge his desire at her peril. "I suggest you depart immediately before I cannot restrain myself from returning the favor of a sound beating."

Dylan shook his head as he muttered, "As you wish." Then he turned and stalked out of the ballroom without a backward glance.

After he'd departed, Bryce held out his hand to Lia. "I'd like to claim my dance with you if you'll permit me."

The orchestra started playing Silent Night as Lia smiled up at him. "I would enjoy dancing with you."

He loved having her in his arms as they danced to the slow song, her gentle expression filling his heart with happiness. She'd moved easily into his embrace as they sedately danced with many others around the floor. "How are you enjoying the ball?"

She glanced away and then back to him as he steered them around another couple. "Much more now."

Her admission made his heart soar. "Miss Merryweather...Lia." He drew in a fortifying breath and let it out in a rush. "I want to apologize for overreacting during our last conversation. I've come to realize you were probably trying to protect yourself from my prying. I am sorry. I will never do so again. Can you forgive me?"

She tightened her grip on his hands. "If you can forgive me for being unforthcoming. I am sorry I upset you."

She peered at him until he nodded twice. Then she looked away again. "Is something amiss?" he asked her, drawing her attention back to him.

"No, everything is fine." She smiled softly at him. "I'm glad you came back. I had wanted to tell you how sorry I am about our disagreement."

"I came back because I wanted to tell you..." He swallowed, suddenly nervous to say what he'd been rehearsing for days. In her vibrant green eyes, he detected her patient curiosity as to his next words. "I love you, Lia. I have since those weeks we spent together five years ago."

"I love you, too." Her smile grew as she held onto his hands.

He pulled her closer and she came willingly. "Sweetheart, I will always care for you and we can make a grand life together." He recalled her previous hesitance to talk to him. He didn't want her to fear doing so. "You can tell me anything without worrying it will somehow create a rift between us. Nothing can do that."

She stiffened in his arms as she swallowed hard. "What are you saying?"

"If there's something you've held close but wish to talk about, I'm here listening." He held onto her, guiding her around the crowded dance floor while also trying to understand her sudden resistance. "I know about what happened after I left. Samuel told me everything so I'd comprehend your reluctance to tell me. I don't blame you for what happened. You can trust me with however much you want to tell me. I'll love you forever."

"Samuel told you about..." Panic swept into her eyes as she stopped dancing to stare up at him. "Oh my. I do need to talk to you, but not here and now. Tomorrow morning I will come to your room and tell you everything. But not now..."

She spun around and raced out of the ballroom. Shocked, he stood still as she fled, confusion and dismay ricocheting in his chest. What was she hiding and why? Whatever her truth might be had her fearful to reveal it to him even as she promised to do so. Somehow he must convince her to tell him before they could begin a life together, one built on mutual love and trust.

* * *

SHE WAS A COWARD. She stared into the mirror in the ladies' wash room as she struggled to catch her breath. To compose herself after her mindless escape. She'd nearly blurted out the entire awful secret right there on the dancefloor. Where everyone would witness her terrible truth. The one that would upset everything and everyone. Her son's life would irrevocably change through no fault of his own. Rather, all the angst and shock was her fault. Trembling, she pressed her hands to her cheeks.

"Lia, darling, are you alright?" Her mother hurried up behind her to peer at her.

She turned to face her mother directly instead of via the reflection. "No."

Natalie clasped her shoulders and studied her worried expression. "What did Mr. Day say to upset you so?"

"Oh, Mother, I just couldn't tell him..." She covered her eyes with her hands, tears flowing down her cheeks. "Not after he said he loves me and I admitted as much to him."

"That's wonderful, but tell him what?" Natalie squeezed Lia's shoulders until she looked at her. "Why the tears?"

Lia had exhausted all of her excuses, her weak reasons, for keeping her secret. The look in her mother's eyes told her she'd need to confess the truth. No matter what the consequences might be. And she knew there'd be consequences. The time had finally arrived.

"Mother, I need to tell you the truth. I've told a terrible lie." She worried her lower lip as her mother's tender smile sobered into a flat line. "I thought it would be for the best but I know now I shouldn't have lied. I should have told the truth from the very start."

"I thought I raised you to know better than to lie." Natalie dropped her hands to grip them together. "What did you lie about?"

"Travis is my son, not Samuel and Laura's." She saw understanding light in her mother's eyes as she studied her.

"How exactly did you manage to get with child?" Her mother stared at her, her expression hard. "And why didn't you tell me?"

Chagrin and guilt consumed Lia as she searched her mother's face. "I slep...had intimate relations with Bryce Day." More than once, but she wouldn't share such personal details of the relationship she and Bryce once shared so many years ago. One she hoped she could find a way to restore and continue until the end of their days. If only...

Her mother's brows rose. "Travis is Bryce's son. You've kept that from us? Oh, honey, I'm so disappointed you didn't feel you could tell us that truth. We admire Bryce and would welcome him into our family. He's a much better man to father children than that Mr. Blackwater, in my opinion. So there's that comfort."

"Bryce wrote me that he had changed his mind about wanting us to be together at about the same time I realized I was carrying his child." Lia willed her mother to understand. "I feared how folks would talk if they knew I'd had relations with him and he abandoned me."

"I see. Rightly so. But you cannot continue to deny that man his son. You have to tell him."

"Yes, but I couldn't tell him in there. It was too public for such a private exchange."

"If you want to have a good marriage with Bryce, then you must tell him soon." Natalie gave her a long hug and then stepped away. "If you don't, I will. He deserves the truth. Then we will figure out how to move forward."

Lia nodded slowly, distinctly aware that her mother was perfectly capable of spilling the beans if she didn't do as she demanded. "Tomorrow. I'll tell Bryce then see how things fall."

* * *

THE NEXT MORNING, Lia wrapped her cloak around her shoulders with shaking hands, tugged her mittens on, and walked resolutely to the small house where Bryce waited for her confession. She hadn't slept much, fretting about what she'd say, how he'd likely react to her revelation, and musing over how everything would change as a result. She had skipped breakfast, her stomach roiling with tension and dread. But she held to her resolve to see through her promise to tell him the truth. No matter what the consequences might end up actually being.

She entered the office and crossed to knock on the door to the hospital ward. The door opened on her second rap to Bryce standing there in his shirt sleeves, collar open and his hair damp. How temptingly sexy he looked, evoking memories of their time together. A distraction she could ill afford when she had such news to share with him. With luck and his understanding, she hoped to make new loving memories with him. But first, she must confess all.

"May I come in?" She steeled her spine to quell the inner turmoil. Her mission was to tell him everything and then see what they'd do together. If anything.

"Of course. I have a pot of coffee and some rolls, if you'd like some."

She shook her head as she slipped her mittens from her hands and opened her cloak. He lifted the heavy garment from her shoulders and draped it on one of the beds. Then he led her to where two chairs were positioned to either side of the light breakfast he'd mentioned. She sat down slowly, clenching her mittens on her lap, and crossed her ankles in front of her. Cleared her throat. Swallowed. The time had arrived.

Bryce plunked down on the other chair and leaned forward. "You wanted to tell me something. I want you to know that no matter what it is, I will still love you. Please, tell me what you were afraid to tell me last evening while we danced."

She nodded once. She could do this. "The whole truth that you need to know…is that Travis is *our* son. I found I was with child a few days before your letter ending our courtship arrived. I didn't know what to do, but Laura and Samuel decided it would be best if we pretended that Travis was their son. So I went with Laura to her sister's place in Tennessee until the baby was born, then we came back and she claimed him as her offspring. I am sorry I didn't tell you, but I didn't tell anyone other than them."

"I have a son?" Bryce clasped her cold hands in his, the warmth thawing the dread inside of Lia. "We have a son. Oh, Lia, thank you for telling me."

"You're not angry at me?"

"Not at all." He shook his head as he squeezed her hands. "I'm upset with myself for putting you in such a predicament without even considering that our lovemaking might have gotten you with child. I'm sorry for that. But now we have all the more reason to marry and start that family we talked about."

"Marry?" Relief at his ready acceptance rapidly morphed into hope for their future together.

"We need to make some plans, of course." Bryce smiled at her. "We'll need a place to live and to raise our son after all."

"But Travis… He is happy as is. Can we disrupt his future like that?" A whirl of emotions at the pace of considerations coming at her had her head spinning.

"He needs to know who his parents actually are, Lia. Samuel has said he would one day tell the boy that he was adopted, so we should talk to them about having that conversation together. We'll decide all together what's best for the boy. I promise. What do you think?"

A swarm of thoughts and feelings cascaded through Lia as she held hands with the man she loved with all of her heart. His understanding and compassion made her love him all the more. He was such a fine, decent person. She wanted to spend the rest of her life getting to know him more, to see just how much she could love him. And have his children. More of his children.

"Yes, I think we need to talk to them next and then bring Travis in for a talk. He needs to know how loved he is by all of us, including you."

"Fine." Bryce rose and pulled her to her feet. "I think there is no time like this moment to go seek out your brother and sister-in-law."

"Right." She squeezed his hand once, glad of his strength. "Let's go."

* * *

THEY FOUND Samuel and Laura and the boys in the dining room, finishing breakfast while Sam read the weekly paper. The bickering and teasing stopped as Bryce stopped beside his friend's chair. The boys—and his son—looked at them with curiosity in their eyes. His son. His heart nearly burst with love and pride at the thought.

"Samuel, we need to talk to you and Laura." He had no patience to wait to claim his son, but he couldn't jump the gun either. One step at a time. "Do you have a minute in private?"

"Something serious?" Sam hesitated, searching first Bryce's eyes, then Lia's. He laid aside the paper and pushed back from the table. "Let's go in the parlor then. Laura? Can you come into the parlor, please?"

"Of course. Now, boys, you finish up then take your dishes into the kitchen. I'll be back in a few minutes." Laura rose gracefully and followed Sam and Lia into the parlor.

Bryce trailed after the threesome until they were ensconced in the small parlor with the door firmly closed. "We should sit down for this conversation."

"Sounds very serious." Samuel sat on a sofa and Laura settled beside him. "I think I know what this is about. Lia?"

"Probably." Lia took a chair across the low table from them and studied their tense expressions for a long moment. "I've told Bryce everything."

Bryce sank onto the flanking chair beside Lia as he nodded to his astonished friends. "She has. And we need to decide how we handle this with the boy."

"Handle what?" Laura glanced between them.

"Telling Travis we're his parents and that you adopted him, for one thing." Bryce stated the obvious but realized as he did so how harshly that news might be received by the young lad. "Or at least we need a plan for how we want to continue with raising the boy. With you and your sons or have him come live with us."

"But you're not married and have just managed to find work. You don't have the wherewithal to provide for him." Samuel's concern flowed from him in waves. "He's our son in everyway except biology. How can you want to take him away from the home he knows?"

Laura gripped Samuel's hand but remained silent, her gaze shifting from Bryce to Lia and back again.

"We've always known we'd have to tell him. It's just come sooner than I thought." Lia grimaced as she lightly shrugged. "I hadn't planned any of this, but with Bryce coming home the true story inevitably came out. You know how grateful I am that you adopted Travis and have done such a wonderful job of raising him."

"Yes, that much is vastly apparent, my friend." Bryce smiled at him, trying to assuage any concerns but knowing how fraught the conversation had become. He sensed the tension and hint of fear at the disclosures. "But I feel he needs to know that I am his actual father. He is my son and I want to claim him as such."

Samuel's jaw couldn't be more clenched. Bryce tried to comprehend how the couple must be feeling at the sudden news and their questions as to the boy's future. But knowing Travis was his son made it impossible for Bryce to let the boy go on believing the lie of who his parents really were. Painful though it might be, they'd find a way to tell him with all the love and compassion he possessed.

"Perhaps we should start slowly by telling Travis we're his parents but that doesn't mean anything has to change as to where he lives for now." Lia laid a hand on Bryce's forearm to draw his attention to the worried look she aimed at him. "I mean, Sam is right that we're not married, nor do we have a home of our own even if we were. Not yet. We can take this gently and see how things play out for Travis so we don't upset him too greatly."

"I can agree to that approach." Bryce put his hand on top of Lia's, glad to have a workable solution to the dilemma of how to broach the subject with a four-year-old boy. His son. Pride swamped his heart but he stemmed the tide with a sense of caution as to not want to traumatize the lad.

"Very well. I will call him in but let me tell my son. Give me that boon." Samuel firmed his lips as he stood and walked to the closed door to drag it open. "Travis? Come here, please."

His friend's words reminded Bryce of the close relationship between Travis and the only parents he'd known. Nervous energy had him springing to his feet to pace across the floor to the snapping fireplace and back again to grip the back of the chair he'd vacated. How would the boy take the shocking news?

"Yes, Papa?" Travis came into the room with a hint of uncertainty in his eyes. "You wanted me?"

"Come have a seat with me and your mother." Samuel resumed his seat on the sofa, and drew the boy gently onto his lap. Laura smoothed the child's hair back from his face with gentle swipes of her loving fingers. "We have something we'd like to share with you but first we all want you to know how much you are loved. You're in a safe place and will always be, understand?"

The boy nodded, doubt mingling with the uncertainty in his expression.

"Travis, I want you to know that as much as we love you, we are not your true parents. We adopted you when you were born and have loved you like all of our sons and always will."

"What's 'dopted?" The child frowned at his father.

Bryce wanted to smooth the creases from his brow. So hard to stand there and not say or do anything to comfort the boy. Bryce gripped the chairback all the harder to keep from moving or interfering.

"It means," Laura quietly interjected, "that two other people who also love you very much were your real parents but they were not able to care for you at that time."

"So we agreed to do so." Samuel lightly touched the boy's nose as he bestowed a father's loving smile on him. "And we've never, ever regretted our choice to have you in our home, in our lives."

"Who are my real parents then? And do I have to go live with them now?" Travis's frown deepened and then morphed into a sad expression as tears glittered in his eyes. "I don't want to leave you." He turned to hug Laura, nearly falling out of Samuel's grasp but the man managed to keep ahold until the boy was safely in his mother's arms.

Bryce stiffened, understanding the transition would not be an easy one for any of them. As much as he rejoiced at learning he was a father, he also needed to be patient and understanding of giving his son time to adjust. They needed time to make plans in the best interest of all concerned. Not rush into changes that would only cause hard feelings.

Laura looked over Travis' head at Bryce and then Lia. "Travis, listen to me. Your real parents are right here in the room with you. Aunt Lia is your mother, and Bryce is your father."

Travis sat up to peer at Bryce and Lia with tear-streaked cheeks glistening in the firelight. "You?"

Bryce merely nodded, stunned into silence at the half-smile on his son's face.

"And you don't have to move or leave your brothers at all. We're still going to live at Hopewell, Travis. We'd never take you away from your family." Lia stood and went to lay a hand on his head. "We all will live here together."

"So now what?" Samuel asked into the lengthening silence. "We'll need to tell the entire family in order for all of this to work."

Lia glanced to Bryce with a gentle smile on her face. "I have the perfect time to tell them if you can wait another day without letting all of this slip out."

CHAPTER 20

Christmas morning dawned cold and gray, the cold bite of snow in the air. Lia dressed with care, preparing for her big reveal after something hot to break their fast. And to delay just a few minutes longer until she had to face the surprise and shock she expected. Lia fastened the last button, ran a comb through her hair, and joined her sisters going down the stairs to join the boisterous group in the dining room. Everyone would gather in her parents' house for breakfast. The table would barely seat them all and only if they squeezed in together on the benches on either side. Her father always sat at the head of the table and her mother at the foot on ladder-back chairs.

"Merry Christmas, everyone." Laura smiled as the three sisters came to a halt. Samuel stood beside her and nodded to them.

"Merry Christmas to you as well." The sisters answered together and then everyone chuckled.

Bryce nodded to Lia in greeting, his kind eyes inviting her closer, but remained mute. She returned his silent greeting, drawing courage from the steady gaze aimed her way. She'd promised to be the one to share the truth of Travis' parentage but as the time approached her nerve threatened to fail her. Would everyone despise her for lying to them? Could she make them fathom her reasons for keeping the truth from them? A chasm of fear opened inside of her the more she considered how her admission had and would change everything.

"Come on, girls. Help me put the food on the table and we'll eat." Natalie smiled at her daughters as they followed her into the kitchen to retrieve the various bowls and plates. Lia chose the basket of warm rolls and plate of butter and carried them back to the table. Rose added a platter of poached eggs, and Aster the plate of sausages. Natalie carried a large bowl of steaming roasted potatoes and placed it on the corner as she sat down.

"Find a seat and let's enjoy our fine meal." Richard pulled out his chair and sat, snatching his napkin to drape on his lap. "I'm famished."

"I doubt that, but let's eat." Natalie laughed from her place at the table as she cast a matronly eye over the brood surrounding her. "Merry Christmas, everyone."

"Thank you for inviting me to join your family this morning." Bryce smiled around the table, his gaze lingering on Lia for several seconds.

"You're most welcome, especially after that wonderfully successful charity ball the other evening. We'll have a new school before too much longer," Richard said. "We are happy to include you in our family celebration and look forward to many more."

Lia pressed her lips together as the impact of her selfishness careened through her soul. She'd deprived the man she loved of family, of being part of her family and of the family they had started together. All because she didn't want the knowing looks and snide comments from others. Her mother was absolutely right to demand she tell everyone the truth. What did it ultimately matter what the neighbors thought as long as the family was content?

She stared at the meal her mother had cooked. Her stomach turned uncomfortably. Poached eggs, sausage links, and roasted potatoes lay on her plate, her stomach in knots so that she moved a bite around and around. Finally she laid down her fork and dabbed her mouth with her napkin. What she was about to do would change the world for all of them. A momentous and monumental concept.

"Are you not hungry?" her mother asked, a slight frown on her face.

"I'm sorry." She laid the napkin on the table. She glanced at her sisters and parents in turn. Then skimmed over the boys to meet Bryce's encouraging grin. On each of the adult faces she saw concern reflected back at her. The boys continued eating, unaware of the tension simmering in Lia's chest, but Travis kept his eyes on her. Travis took a bite of egg, chewing slowly as he waited for her to speak. His life was about to be upended in ways she could only guess. She swallowed the unease and drew in a breath. "I need to tell you all something."

Natalie's frown transformed into an encouraging smile and nod of her head. "Go on, dear."

"I have a confession to make. About Travis' real parents." She inhaled a steadying breath and then met Bryce's curious gaze. "I'm deeply sorry we lied to you all. I was afraid of how you'd all react if I told you the truth. So we pretended his parents were Samuel and Laura to cover my shame."

"Are you saying you're Travis' mother?" Rose speared her with a hard look. "Not Laura. And who then, if not Sam, is the father?"

"I am." Bryce swept his gaze around the table, landing on Travis. "I've just learned that Travis is my son, a child of the love shared between me and his mother. I can't be happier at knowing the truth now."

"But, Lia, why didn't you tell us, your own parents?" Richard tapped the table with a fist. "You know you can tell us anything. We love you."

"I do know that, Father. The child needed a good home, parents who could provide for him. I couldn't do that on my own. So Samuel and Laura agreed to raise my child. They've given him a solid foundation to build his life upon and I'll be forever grateful for that. I'm sorry, maybe..." But she had to confess. She simply couldn't go on with the lie.

"Lia, I have a question to ask you." Bryce rose from his chair to move to stand by Lia's place at the table. "I need you to trust me and come outside with me for a little walk. Will you do that?"

Her mother shooed her with a wave of one hand and an encouraging grin. Lia nodded and Bryce helped her push her chair away from the table. He took hold of her elbow and escorted her to retrieve her cloak before heading outside. She glanced at his sober countenance and wondered what he was up to at such a critical junction in the conversation.

* * *

As he opened the door to usher her outside, he blinked in delight as he looped the crocheted silver-and-gold wool scarf around his neck, Lia's lovely gift to him. Snow fell thickly from the leaden skies to powder the landscape. He hadn't seen such snow in ages and rarely in the Deep South. The fresh snowfall wouldn't last long but the timing couldn't have been better for what he had in mind.

"Careful going down the steps," he cautioned, holding her elbow firmly in his grasp. He guided her slowly toward the magnolia trees, hoping she'd remember how they'd first kissed standing near the tall, sheltering trees. He turned her to face him, clasping both her mittened hands in his. "Lia, my love, I recognize how difficult the situation became after I left and didn't hold up my end of the promise. I must apologize to you again for that. I don't blame you for making the choices you had to make." He tugged her closer so he could press his lips to hers for a moment.

The front door opened in the distance and the boys tumbled out of the house to cavort in the snow. He glanced over to see them playing together, the five boys, one his son. The joy filling his heart with that knowledge couldn't be dimmed by also understanding the time he'd missed with Travis. It was his own fault. He'd have to do whatever he could to make it up to the boy and to his woman. As the rest of the family leaked out of the house, he turned back to Lia.

"Lia, do you forgive me for abandoning you as I did?" He searched her eyes and saw her willingness to do so in the small smile twinkling in the depths of her emerald eyes. "Even with the best of intentions."

"Of course, Bryce. I am thankful that you are not mad at me about Travis." She smiled up at him. "You're not, are you?"

"I'm mad at myself, not you. But I need to know one thing, sweetheart." He gazed down at her upturned face with hope filling him as he pulled the small ring box from his pocket and opened it. Her gasp of delight made him smile and encouraged him to continue. "Magnolia Merryweather, would you do me the honor of becoming my wife, the mother of my children, my soulmate and life companion?"

"Say yes!" Rose called from where she stood with the rest of the entire family in a cluster. "We're cold."

Lia chuckled and then met Bryce's expectant gaze with a big smile on her lovely face. "Yes. I will marry you."

Bryce slipped the round sapphire onto her left ring finger, then with a whoop of joy he lifted her up and spun her in a circle. As he set her on her feet again, the family cheering, he kissed her until she broke away laughing.

"Mr. Day, you must control yourself in front of the children." Her eyes sparkled with suppressed laughter.

"They will need to become accustomed to seeing me kiss you, sweetheart, because I intend to do so often."

She winked at him. "How often? As often as snow blankets the magnolias?" She gestured to the white snow coating the broad, dark green leaves of the trees around them.

"No, my dear, every hour of every day we're together. Your beauty may be as rare as snow on magnolias, but our love will be constant from now until the day I die."

"Then, Mr. Day, kiss me again. I love you."

"And I you." He lowered his head and pressed another kiss onto her delicious lips. When he ended the kiss, he smiled down at her. "Let's go begin our life together."

She tucked her hand onto his proffered arm. "I cannot wait to become your wife."

Rose fell in beside them as they strolled toward the house. "I have some wonderful ideas for the perfect gown for your wedding."

"And so it begins." Lia chuckled up at Bryce. "You may regret becoming part of my family."

Bryce glanced around at the large group of people making their way back inside. Each of them had become dear to him in their own ways. Now he understood why he'd had a special fondness for Travis and his desire to whittle, just like him. Why hadn't he noticed that detail? He shrugged away any remorse. "I'm delighted to be part of your family and you part of mine."

EPILOGUE

Christmas Day 1866

"Merry Christmas, Travis dear!" Lia called out to her son. Out the window she could see the sun shining down on the horses in their pastures. She'd already fed them all and now it was time to walk from their new single-story house at the edge of the forest to her parents' home. "We must hurry to join the rest of the family for our traditional breakfast together."

"Christmas!" Travis flung the blankets off and rolled out of bed. "I hope Santa Claus came. Did he come, Mama?" Grabbing his pants he pulled them on and quickly fastened the buttons of the front panel. Lia held out a freshly laundered and ironed shirt for him to don.

"I believe so." She smiled down at her son, joy at celebrating the special day with him filling her heart and soul. "Your father is waiting for us, so we must hurry."

"Yes, Mama." Travis tugged the shirt down, shoving the tails into his pants, before running a hand through his hair. "Ready."

"Try a comb, please." She handed him the toothed bone comb so he could swipe it through his hair. "Now, you're ready. Let's go."

She shooed him out of his bedroom at the back of the cozy bungalow Bryce had built with the help of Samuel and her father, and even some from the boys. She watched Travis race to the parlor at the front of the building, where a decorated tree stood upon a small table by the window. Much had changed but in a good way instead of the fears she once harbored. She rested a hand on her expanding waistline, a kick rewarding her gesture. A new house. A loving son who had adjusted to the idea of her being his mother, as if he'd always suspected. And he had adjusted to accepting Bryce as his father much the same. Now they were expecting another child, perhaps a little girl, just to be different. She grinned at the idea of having a little girl to dress and teach. Bryce's job at the railroad led him to start his own consulting firm for building all kinds of things: homes, stores, bridges. Whatever anyone needed, either he designed it or he had one of his employees do so. Her horse breeding efforts had paid off grandly, with a waiting list for foals from her mares and stallions a mile long.

She grabbed her cloak and hat to put on, then tugged her mittens onto her hands. Bryce entered the parlor, already dressed and wearing his top coat and hat. She loved him more each day. He crossed the room to kiss her several times while Travis stared at the toys under the tree with his mouth hanging open. But then he squealed and jumped up and down when he espied the small whittling knife in its box. He turned to stare at them. "Can I? Really?"

"Yes, but remember to be careful so you don't hurt yourself or anyone else. Understood?" Bryce asked with a firm voice. "You don't want me to take it away, right?"

"Right." Travis ran to hug his father. "Thank you!"

Bryce hugged Travis as he looked at Lia with a look of amazed joy on his face. "I love you both."

"I love you." Lia went to him then and gave him a peck on his lips over their son's head. "I always will. I am so very happy."

"We have a good life."

"The best, I think." Lia made a motion with her hand to indicate they should head out. "Let's go share some Christmas joy with everyone."

ABOUT THE AUTHOR

Award-winning author Betty Bolté is known for authentic and accurately researched historical fiction with heart and supernatural romance novels. A lifetime reader and writer, she's worked as a secretary, freelance word processor, technical writer/editor, and author. She's been published in essays, newspaper articles/columns, magazine articles, and nonfiction books but now enjoys crafting entertaining and informative fiction, especially stories that bring American history to life. She earned a Master's Degree in English in 2008, emphasizing the study of literature and storytelling, and has judged numerous writing contests for both fiction and nonfiction. She lives in northern Alabama with her loving husband of more than 30 years. Get to know her at www.bettybolte.com. Be sure to check out materials for book club discussions at https://www.bettybolte.com/bookclub.